Every House Needs a Balcony

Every House Needs a Balcony

A NOVEL

RINA FRANK

TRANSLATED FROM THE HEBREW BY
ORA CUMMINGS

HARPER

An Imprint of HarperCollins*Publishers*
www.harpercollins.com

HarperCollins books may be purchased for educational, business, or sales promotional use. For information, please write: Special Markets Department, HarperCollins Publishers, 10 East 53rd Street, New York, NY 10022.

First published in Israel in 2006 by Miskal-Yedioth Ahronoth Books and Chemed Books.

FIRST EDITION

Designed by Pat Flanagan

Library of Congress Cataloging-in-Publication Data has been applied for.

ISBN: 978-0-06-171423-8

10 11 12 13 14   OV/RRD   10 9 8 7 6 5 4 3 2 1

To Sefi
I can see you
Laughing or crying
Reading the book —
If you were alive

Every
House
Needs a
Balcony

The Day My Sister Saw God

I was born on the second day of the Jewish New Year. When I discovered that Yaffa, the third daughter of our Syrian neighbors, was born during Hanukkah, I assumed that children were born on holy days—as a special gift from God. When I realized that my sister, who is older than me by one year and eight months, was born in January and I could find no holy day in her vicinity, I became very worried and afraid that she was damaged. I shared my deep concern with her. My sister laughed and, with all the wisdom of a seven-and-a-half-year-old, explained to me that children are indeed born only on holy days; she, on the other hand, while still an embryo in our mother's belly, had decided that she wanted to be special and different from everyone else, and so she persuaded God to arrange for her to be born on a regular weekday. And God agreed.

Because my sister Yosefa knew God.

Two families and Tante Marie lived in our three-room apartment and kitchenette. The apartment belonged to my father's oldest sister, Aunt Lutzi, and her husband Lazer.

They were lucky. They had emigrated from Romania in 1948, right after the War of Independence, and were already regarded as "veterans" because they had managed to take over apartments abandoned by Arabs who had previously occupied Stanton Street, which made them instant property owners. Actually, their son the policeman, Phuyo, who had immigrated to the Land of Israel at the age of fourteen, had set aside an apartment at 40 Stanton Street for his parents. When members of the local police force were allocated the best apartment block on Stanton Street, Phuyo immediately commandeered the first floor, and three of his colleagues took over the remaining floors; for several months thereafter they took turns guarding the empty apartments, to prevent any undesirable Jewish invaders from entering and occupying them before their parents and the rest of their families arrived in Israel.

Vida, Father's second sister, and her husband, Herry, also made a beeline to Wadi Salib in search of an apartment in which to set up home. At 47 Stanton, they found a two-story building abandoned by its Arab inhabitants. They didn't fancy the furniture on the first floor; in the second-floor apartment, however, not only was the furniture relatively new but there was an indoor toilet, rather than one in the yard, as was normal in Arab houses. They settled unanimously for the apartment on the second floor. Herry, who was multitalented and very resourceful, installed a tin water tank on the roof, and a solar collector. The result was a supply of free hot water almost all year.

My parents, who lingered for a further two years in Romania in order to do it for the first time in their lives and produce Yosefa, my only sister, did not have this good fortune. And thus the Franco family, comprising Moscu, Bianca, and their eight-month-old baby girl, arrived in Israel and were given the kitchenette. It was an inner room with no window, and no access to the high-status balcony that overlooked Stanton Street.

Moscu and Bianca did it for the second time in their lives in Tante Lutzi's small kitchen, because they were depressed at having to live in a tiny, windowless room and because Father really wanted a son. When I was born, one year after they immigrated to Israel from Romania, Father was so disappointed with "that one who doesn't know how to produce a son" that his sister Lutzi, who loved her attractive younger brother with all her heart, gave us the third room that faced the stylish balcony and connected between all the other rooms. The room had been reserved for Phuyo the policeman, who was responsible for our having the house in the first place. But Phuyo had married a Frenchwoman, Dora, who flatly refused to share a house with her mother-in-law, Lutzi, and that is how our occupation of the room with the elegant balcony became a fait accompli.

From the balcony, you could overlook the entire Haifa port with its fleet of ships, as far as the yogurt-bottle-shaped oil refineries, and when you closed one eye you could even see Acre on your outstretched hand. There was no need even for binoculars; no boat or ship could infiltrate our little country via the port of Haifa without us noticing it from our balcony. Except, perhaps, a submarine.

The houses on Stanton Street were built of good-quality local stone, not the usual crumbling gray plaster, but stone blocks that gave the buildings a special elegance and made them stand out in the surrounding landscape. And all the buildings had balconies, one balcony facing the other, with no difference between the outside and the inside. The stone walls had been designed as a buffer only against the cold or the heat, not between the people and the neighborhood and the families who lived there. There were no curtains in the windows, and everyone was able to see everyone else, as if on a conveyor belt. Your entire life was laid out there on the balcony, illustrated in the piles of bedclothes hung out daily on the banister for airing. All the neighbors knew how often, if at all, every family changed its sheets. And if it wasn't enough that everything was visible to all eyes, there was also the laundry, pegged out to dry on ropes stretched along the length of the balcony, revealing the patched clothes and the underwear and nightgowns worn and faded from too much washing. It was as if all your belongings were displayed there each day for public auction.

During the long summer nights, people sat out on their

balconies. Father ran out an extension cord from inside our apartment to plug in a lamp, brought out a small table, and they played rummy every evening on the balcony. The game didn't prevent my parents from engaging in conversation with the neighbors across the road, but even if they didn't talk, we already knew everything that was going on, because every word shouted in every apartment could be heard all over the street, especially by anyone sitting on the balcony. Our street was very vociferous; it was as if the neighbors all knew that Mother was hard of hearing and did their best not to make her feel left out. Conversations from one balcony to another were a matter of routine. Sitting on the balcony was practically the same as sitting in an armchair and watching television. For us, the balcony was our television, and what we saw was real life, played out with authentic actors in real time.

Stanton Street is the place where reality TV was first invented.

Thursdays were the days on which bedclothes were not put out to air; instead, the carpets were brought out and laid over the balustrade. After being left alone to soak up a few hours of dry, hot, and dusty *hamsin* air, the carpets were beaten with the cruelty they deserved, so as to be clean for Shabbat. As if by mutual signal, in unison, with a rhythm that sounded like the beat of tom-toms, all the ladies of Wadi Salib thrashed the living daylights out of the carpets as they hung over the balconies of their homes.

All the ladies and my father.

There they all stood on the balcony railing, straining downward to reach the very edge of their carpet, potential *shahids* to cleanliness, until they caught sight of my father. As soon as Father stepped out with his carpet beater, all the ladies in the street started flirting with him.

"Hey, Moscu, when are you coming over to bang my carpet with me?"

"Hey, Moscu, is Bianca so worn out after last night that you're out here banging in her place?"

When the ladies laughed at him, Father smiled back kindly and said that they were clearly dying to swap their husbands for him—and none of them ever denied it.

The main room in Lutzi's apartment in Wadi Salib's Stanton Street belonged, of course, to Tante Lutzi and her husband, Lazer. Lazer was a barber. He owned a barbershop downtown, next to the only decent café in the area. To tell the truth, the barbershop was more a hole in the wall, with two chairs and a single shared mirror. Since he was always appropriately dressed in a barber's coat, the local gentlemen stepped in for a haircut, although he never failed to botch up their appearance with a phenomenal lack of talent.

We girls had our hair cut at home. We refused to go to his shop, claiming that it wasn't fit for ladies. Lazer would place a kind of round plate on our heads, which served as a template around which to snip off the ends, and we'd finish up with a haircut that was a perfect circle. Until we revolted and no longer allowed him to touch us, my sister and I looked like a pair of round satellite dishes with bangs.

In fact, with our Uncle Lazer, "touch" was the operative word. He used to sit me on his lap and say that, as an uncle who loved his nieces, he was responsible for checking my growth, to make sure that everything about me was in order. His examination focused mainly on the glands on my chest, rather than on my height, which was measured against an inch tape and markings on the wall.

My sister, apparently, wasn't fooled by Uncle Lazer's honeyed words and told him to go measure the growth process of his own children, because only our mother and father and the school nurse had the right to check ours.

It was obvious that black-haired Yosefa, with her brown slanting eyes, was the smartest child in the neighborhood, and I was just pretty. There was an ongoing debate in our home over what would best suit my sister, who was destined for greatness, a future as a physician or a career in law; as for me, they just prayed that someone wealthy would marry me.

One day I was playing jacks downstairs when my sister called me from the balcony to come up immediately because Grandmother Vavika had died.

"So what?" I shouted back, even though I was almost six and had only one grandmother. I threw the ball vigorously and knocked over all the stones.

When I saw the ambulance parked at the entrance to the

building, I stopped throwing the ball at the stones for a moment and watched as two white-uniformed male nurses got out, carrying a wooden stretcher. They entered the building, carrying the stretcher in an upright position as if it were a ladder; I lost interest and went back to my game.

I went up to our apartment only when I had beaten all the others as usual.

My sister was very agitated and said I had missed something important.

"What was there to miss at home, where everyone is miserable, whereas downstairs I squashed seven jacks single-handed?" I asked indifferently.

"You missed God," she said reproachfully. Yosefa was proud of the fact that she was the only one who had seen God, because she was standing alone on the balcony when the entire family was indoors beside our dead grandmother and I was stupidly playing jacks downstairs. And it's a well-known fact that God reveals Himself on balconies.

My sister told me that she was standing on the balcony when suddenly a ladder descended from the skies; it was very, very long, like Jacob's ladder, and two angels dressed in white went up to Grandmother and grasped her on both sides, and together, the three climbed up the ladder that reached up to the skies, not forgetting to wave good-bye to the lone girl standing on the balcony and watching their every move.

When they had reached very edge of the sky, my sister,

who was older than I by two years minus four months, told me that the heavens had opened, and God's kindly face peeked down to welcome them home.

"So what does he look like?" I asked my sister grudgingly, piqued that she had seen God and I hadn't.

"Very handsome," answered my all-seeing sister. "He's got black hair and green eyes. Looks a bit like our dad."

Ever since, I have lived with the knowledge that I missed seeing God and His angels, and only my sister had the good fortune to see them. And she had even called me home, but I wasn't listening.

It wasn't love at first sight with the man, even though he was tall and handsome and she had always been attracted to tall, handsome men.

"I thought all the men in Spain were short," she challenged him in English, in the kitchen, two weeks after he'd joined the staff of the Jerusalem engineer Ackerstein, where she too was employed. At first she had little faith in the amount of height taken up by a six-foot space—he gave the impression of being out of reach and exuded a cultured European scent. Over those two weeks when their eyes met, she had made do with a light nod of the head that instantly ruled out all options.

"I'm the proof," he replied in English and shook her hand firmly. She didn't know that it was possible to shake hands quite like that; she was used to handshakes that were more limp and involuntary. She wondered if he was

Jewish and delved into the depths of her memory to try to discover if any Jews had remained in Spain after the Inquisition over five hundred years ago. She remembered that none had.

"Perhaps it's because I'm a Barcelona-born Jew," the man said, as if reading her thoughts.

"First time in Israel?" she asked him with uncharacteristic courtesy.

"Seventh time in the last three years," he replied.

Man of the world, she thought to herself. She herself was twenty-two and didn't even own a passport; at that time the Sinai Peninsula was still under Israeli control, and that was the most "abroad" she had ever visited.

"What's there to love about Israel?" she asked enviously. He had flown so many times, and she had never seen the inside of a plane, not even on the ground.

"The women," the guy answered, "they are all so beautiful and so tall." He dropped his glance from his six feet down to her five-foot-nothing. "And I haven't been to Haifa yet. I'm told that Haifa women are the most beautiful of all."

"Whoever told you must know," she replied, expecting him to ask her if she was from Haifa, but he didn't.

"So, what is about Israel that you love so much and makes you fly here every couple of days?" she asked, and he replied, "The fact that they are all Jews. I find it very exciting to think that everyone you see in the street is Jewish—even the street cleaners."

"The street cleaners are more likely to be Arabs," she said, trying to put a damper on his enthusiasm.

"Still," he said, "everyone speaks Hebrew, and that makes me very proud. The bus drivers are Jewish, the owner of my local grocer's shop is Jewish, all the staff in this office are Jewish. You are Jewish."

She gazed at him in amazement. It was during those days of euphoria following Israel's huge victory in the Six-Day War and before the humiliation of the 1973 Yom Kippur War; and here before her stood a Jew, a Zionist heartthrob emanating a scent of Europe, and perfect English. To her, he appeared absolutely unobtainable.

Later, in the kitchen, Maya the secretary told her that he was an engineering student who came to work in Israel for the summer so he could immigrate formally after completing his degree, and he was staying in Jerusalem with his sister, who was also a student.

When she returned to the rented room in the apartment she shared with two young women who always patronized her because she wasn't a student like them, she asked one of them if she had any reading material on Barcelona.

"My subject is China," the student replied in a faintly condescending tone.

"Is it far from there?" she asked her arrogant roommate, who didn't bother to reply.

The following morning she spent a long time in front of

her open wardrobe before choosing a red miniskirt and a knit top that emphasized her figure.

She walked into the office with joy in her heart and was soon called to Ackerstein's room, where the boss explained that she couldn't come to work dressed in a red miniskirt. He said nothing about the top but studied her firm breasts as he said nonchalantly, "You've got to dress modestly." She ignored his impertinent glance and walked out of the room.

"Where does he get off telling me to dress modestly?" she complained later in the kitchen to Maya the secretary. "It's a democratic country, and I'll dress however I want."

"Anything wrong?" asked the man as he walked into the kitchen to make himself coffee.

"Jewish wars, that's what's wrong," she explained, her face flushed with anger, to the man in whose honor she had dressed that morning. This is not the way she wanted him to see her, red-faced and eyes spewing fire. "I was asked not to turn up at work in a miniskirt."

"With legs like yours it's nothing short of injustice," he said immediately, agreeing with her. "But why?" he still wanted to know.

"Because it might cause the pious to commit a crime." She tried unsuccessfully to explain what she meant by "crime," using a mixture of English and Spanish.

"You know Spanish," he said, pleased.

"I learned from my father; he speaks Ladino. But I only

know a few words," she added in English, before he got the impression that she really could speak Spanish.

"What do you expect? He has several religious clients, and David is only asking you to consider their feelings. You can't very well show a devout Jew a blueprint of his new home when you're sitting opposite him dressed in your miniskirt," Maya the secretary explained to her with the logic of a forty-year-old.

"Then he should keep his eyes on the blueprint and not on my legs," she retorted with the stubbornness of a twenty-two-year-old.

"You know, it's his office and it's his right to make the rules," Maya explained, still patiently. "If you don't like it, you can always pick up and go." She said this in a tone that made it clear that her boss could also tell her to pick up and go.

She got the message, and told Maya that she'd wear a miniskirt whenever she liked, after work hours.

"Would you like the chance to wear a miniskirt?" the man asked her. "Let's take in a movie this evening. I've heard that there's one worth seeing, not far from here."

That evening, as they sat in the movie house, she felt she recognized the lead actress, but couldn't remember which movie she'd seen her in.

"She looks a lot like you," the man told her when they were standing beside the bar during the intermission.

"Who does?" she asked, offended, noticing a girl standing by his side, holding a cola can in her hand and wearing a minute miniskirt and a lace blouse that showed off her generous cleavage, her long hair spread artlessly over her back. The girl appeared so self-conscious as to provoke her instant aversion. Despite her promise, or maybe because of it, she herself was wearing jeans, a pale blue button-up shirt, and high heels—in an attempt to slightly reduce the difference in height between them, and so he wouldn't think she was tempting him to commit a crime by dressing immodestly. She had always been contrary. At home they called her "Little Miss Contrary."

"The actress," the guy replied, "you are very much alike. You both have small faces and very short hair and laughing green eyes, with a sad look about them."

"Thanks," she said, flattered, and thought that he might not be all that unobtainable, if he'd managed to notice the sadness in her face.

After the movie they went to a restaurant, and she busied herself with the drinks and dessert menu.

"They do a very good schnitzel," the man told her. "I've eaten here a few times in the past."

He, the stranger, had already been here several times, while she, who had lived in the town for eight months, didn't know any restaurant except Meshulam, because whenever she did have any money to spare, she preferred to spend it on a skirt or a new pair of jeans that were hers alone and didn't have to be shared with anyone else, or some dress for her mother or some underwear for her dad. She didn't buy things for her sister, who had a boyfriend who took care of all of her needs. It seemed to her excessive to waste money on a single meal in a restaurant.

Still, when he mentioned the tasty schnitzels, she remembered that she had been too excited all day to eat anything.

"No, thanks," she said. "I'm not hungry. I'd just like a cup of coffee."

"Why?" he asked, surprised. "They do an excellent schnitzel, and they'll stuff it with cheese and ham if you ask them quietly. You're not kosher, are you?" He seemed alarmed for a moment.

"No, no. Don't you go worrying about whether I'm kosher or not. It doesn't worry me at all."

He smiled, and she felt her mouth filling with saliva. Her mother and the Romanian food she cooked; schnitzel wasn't exactly a part of her repertoire, so to her, Wiener schnitzel was high-class gourmet food; moreover, she was hungry.

"I'm not really hungry," she said.

"You must order something, I won't enjoy my own food if I have to eat alone," he said coaxingly. "Did you know that there's a restaurant in Vienna that serves only schnitzel? Well, this restaurant doesn't fall short of that one."

But she was embarrassed; after all, her mother had told her often enough that people were usually just being polite when they offered things, and perhaps he didn't have enough money and was just being courteous, and she went on insisting that she wasn't hungry because she'd had a big lunch. And maybe her real reason for refusing was that she felt uncomfortable about Leon, her boyfriend, who cooked schnitzels for her every weekend, and she didn't want to feel she was betraying Leon's schnitzels by eating Wiener schnitzel in a fancy Jerusalem restaurant.

The man ordered Wiener schnitzel with mashed potato, and she sat facing him with a cup of coffee and an apple strudel that he'd ordered without asking her.

She started playing her daily game of signs. If he eats a piece of schnitzel together with some mashed potato, she thought, that's a sign that he's broad-minded and there might be a chance here. If he eats his schnitzel first and his mashed potato at the end, or the other way round but still one thing after the other, he's boring and a waste of time, and if he cuts off a piece of schnitzel and piles a lump of mashed potato on top, there's no chance of even a quickie with such a glutton.

He held his knife expertly between his long fingers, cut off a piece of schnitzel and popped it in his mouth, followed by a forkful of mashed potato. He cut off another piece and offered it to her: "Why don't you try some after all? We can still order one for you if you like it."

She scrutinized his plate enviously, remembering the sandwiches she used to take to school. Most of her friends bought a roll and cheese from Menashe's grocery store, and she would watch them, her heart sinking. She had never asked her father for money. He always wanted to give her some, even though he had none to give and she insisted that she didn't need any. She accepted only enough for her Carmelit tram fare to school on Hillel Street, and that was to avoid having to climb up those steep Haifa streets. On the way home she would leap down the stairs at a gallop, her schoolbag on her back. She remembered how she had wanted to buy a roll from Menashe; only in retrospect did she understand that it was with envy that the others had looked at her homemade sandwiches, those sandwiches that her dad had prepared with so much love out of Bulgarian cheese and thin slices of tomato that absorbed some of the cheese's saltiness and added moisture; or that excellent *kashkaval* cheese that the Romanians love, not just any old dry yellow cheese.

Years later, when they were already married, she told the man about the rolls with yellow cheese that she had remembered with such longing on their first date, and he wanted to take her to Menashe's grocery store and buy her all the rolls with yellow cheese in the world, to prove to her that she hadn't missed out on anything, but Menashe was dead and the grocery store was now occupied by an upholsterer. Once the school had been transferred to the French Carmel, there was no longer any need for it—neither for Menashe, nor for his rolls.

"How did the Jews end up in Barcelona?" she asked on their first date. And he told her that some Jews had escaped there from a burning Europe during World War II. His parents, he said, had lived in France, and when war broke out, his father had stolen across the border to Spain and lived there for three years until his wife joined him. "With their blond hair and blue eyes," he explained, "my mother and her twin sister looked like Aryans. So they remained in France with their parents, until my mother crossed the border on her own and joined my father and his brother."

"So, all your family lives in Barcelona?" she asked.

"My sister moved to Israel three years ago, when she was twenty. My parents have just bought her an apartment here in Jerusalem, and I've been given the job of fixing it up."

"And what about you," he asked, "have you ever been to Barcelona?"

"I've never been out of Israel," she said.

"I'm not surprised," he said. "With the kind of salaries they pay you here, I don't see how anyone can even finish the month. Life in Barcelona is much cheaper, and salaries are much higher. Do you know that the nine-hundred-square-foot apartment they bought here cost more than the twenty-seven-hundred-square-foot one we bought in Barcelona?"

"Do you have a girlfriend?" she asked him suddenly. She was more interested in his response to this question than in real estate prices in Israel. In any case there was no way she could ever afford to buy an apartment of her own, even if she saved everything she earned for the next twenty years.

"Yes," he replied, and she almost choked. Luckily she didn't have any schnitzel in her mouth. So much for the romance; still, he was obviously broad-minded.

"Steady?" she asked, disappointed.

"Five years," he replied. "We're engaged."

"So when's the wedding?" She was annoyed that he hadn't bothered to volunteer the information in the first place. Then she remembered that that she hadn't actually asked him until that moment.

"Eight months after I return to Barcelona," he replied, frugal with details, as if they were of no importance. She looked dolefully at the plate of excellent schnitzel that was emptying before her eyes.

"And when exactly are you going back to Barcelona?" She needed to put some order into her life.

"In two months' time, when I finish the renovations. But what does it matter? I'm here now, and you are here, and I enjoy looking into those laughing eyes of yours, and I'd love to know why they are enveloped in sadness." Maybe it's because of Menashe's rolls, she thought to herself, but she knew that he didn't know Menashe or anyone like him, and wondered why he didn't ask her if she had a boyfriend.

He held her hand, and a tremor passed through her body. A woman who gets turned on quickly gets turned off just as quickly, she thought.

"And I am thinking," the man went on, scrutinizing her

eyes, which had become even sadder, "about your lovely legs in a miniskirt and your angry face when you are asked not to come to work in a short skirt and your laughter—you make me laugh."

"I'm glad I make you laugh." She didn't take her hand away from his.

"So I've noticed," he said, and began suddenly to make trumpeting sounds with his mouth and playing the theme song from *Love Story*. She looked at him and started to laugh. He trumpeted the song so nicely, it sounded as if he really was playing a trumpet; he even blew out his cheeks like a real trumpeter.

Then he covered both her hands with his and brought them to his chest.

She had to escape this confusion. "Are there any other specialty restaurants you know of, in other parts of the world?" she asked, wishing for this moment, with him holding her hands in his, never to end.

"There's one in Zurich, and of course in Paris." He said "of course" as if it was as matter-of-fact to her as to himself. "There's a restaurant there that serves only entrecôte. There's no menu, and the only thing you get asked is how you'd like your steak, medium or medium rare."

"What about well done?" she asked

"No such thing." He grimaced in disgust at the very suggestion.

When he returned her to the apartment she shared with

the two revolting students, he floated a kiss on her cheek and went off with a "See you tomorrow."

"Where?" she asked enthusiastically.

"At work. Tomorrow morning," reminding her that they worked in the same office, which is actually how they met.

When Mother Met Father

My mother didn't speak Hebrew. When they arrived from Romania, Dad joined an *ulpan* to learn Hebrew and Mom went out to clean houses; for this you don't need Hebrew. In Wadi Salib you didn't need to speak Hebrew for people to understand you. During the 1950s, with the huge assortment of languages in common use—from Moroccan to Romanian, Ladino to Yiddish, Arabic to Polish—everyone understood everyone else.

But not only did Mom not know Hebrew, she was also hard of hearing, which made it impossible for her to pick up the language of the street.

In Romania, apparently, they'd wanted to correct her slight hearing impairment; a "simple little operation," they'd told her when she was thirty, "one hour under the anesthetic—you won't feel a thing, and you'll be able to hear." But Mom wasn't listening to them. She knew you couldn't trust the doctors in Romania.

When she was twenty, Mom had had an attack of appendicitis and was rushed to an operating theater in Bucharest, but not before the doctors had explained to her worried parents that it was a very simple surgical procedure, she wouldn't feel a thing under the anesthetic and she'd come out of the whole thing as good as new. Two hours later the grim-faced doctors emerged and explained to my grandfather and grandmother, whom I never met, that something had gone wrong with the anesthetic, and the chances of Bianca ever recovering were extremely slim. Grandfather Yosef stayed by Bianca's bedside, while her mother returned weeping to their home, where her ten-year-old younger daughter was waiting alone. She collapsed in the middle of the road, and a passing car drove over her.

And so my grandmother's dead body was returned to the same hospital where her beloved daughter Bianca lay recovering from a botched appendectomy—a recovery that had to be swift, because she was now left to care for her widowed father, her seventeen-year-old brother, Marco, and her ten-year-old sister, Aurika.

Bianca raised Aurika as if she were her own daughter, with love and devotion that knew no bounds and with an overwhelming feeling of guilt.

One day, when she was twenty-eight, Mom walked into David's photography studio and laboratory and summoned him to the cemetery to take a photograph of her mother's gravestone. David's parents had died and bequeathed the photography studio to him and his brother, Jacko. David scrutinized the very thin, very elegantly dressed woman in the long brown coat and red hat, set at a jaunty angle. Mom had very curly brown hair, deep, highly intelligent brown eyes above high cheekbones, and fair skin. In those days women took great care to avoid tanning their faces, and a pretty woman was one who was interestingly pale. When they arrived at the cemetery and David saw that Grandmother had been fifty when she died, he asked Bianca what had been the cause of her death, and Bianca, out of a profound sense of guilt, replied that it had been "an appendectomy that went wrong."

David sympathized, "Those doctors, you can never trust them."

"And what about photographers, can they be trusted?" Mom asked in rebuke.

"Of course," he replied, "the pictures will be developed by evening. I'll deliver them to you in person." David was instantly invited to dinner and told to bring his younger brother with him. Because at that very moment, Mom had made up her mind that David was the man she was going to marry.

What's more, Mom had already decided, even before she'd met David's younger brother, that this was going to be a double wedding, hers with David and his brother's with her sister, Aurika.

That evening David delivered the pictures, and everyone

was thrilled at how sharp they were and how clearly Grand-mother's name showed up on the headstone.

Mom laid a tasteful table for dinner and served a carefully prepared meal, since it's a well-known fact that there is no better way to a man's heart than through his stomach.

Mom told David and his younger brother that she wished to send the photographs to her two older siblings in Palestine. She spoke with great pride of her brother Niku and sister Lika, who lived in Hadera and were engaged in drying swamps.

David showed a lot of interest in the situation in British Mandate Palestine and the ways in which the inhabitants made a living, and even asked if he could correspond with Niku and Lika, since he had been raised on the Zionist ideal, and now that his parents were no longer alive, he wanted to follow in their footsteps by realizing their great love for the Land of Israel.

Mom's endeavor had succeeded. After that family dinner, David asked if he could meet her again. At their fourth meeting, he asked her to marry him, and Mom accepted happily, but made her acceptance conditional on waiting for Aurika to come of age so she could marry his younger brother, Jacko. David agreed to this very logical arrangement.

In 1941, David told Mom that he had made up his mind to leave Nazi Europe, to emigrate to Palestine, and to set up a photography studio in Hadera, since her brother Niku had written that Hadera was now dry of swamps, there was a dearth of professional people in the country, and there was a demand for practically everything—or so he wrote. Mom knew that he simply wanted them all to join him in Israel, and that things weren't quite as rosy there as he wanted them to think.

It was agreed that David and his brother would be the first to go, and after they had settled in, Mom would join them with the rest of her family—and that is how my mother's life was saved.

David and his brother boarded the ship *Struma* in the Black Sea port of Constanza, together with a cargo of Jews wishing to make their way to Palestine. With its engine inoperable, the *Struma* was towed from Istanbul through the Bosporus out to the Black Sea by Turkish authorities with its refugee passengers aboard. It was torpedoed and sunk by a Soviet submarine on February 24, 1942, and all but 1 of its 768 passengers perished.

Even after marrying Dad three years later, Mom refused to become pregnant—something that was virtually unheard of in those days—until Aurika found a husband to replace the one she had lost at sea.

Dad, who was head over heels in love with a non-Jewish Romanian woman, was persuaded by his sisters to marry Bianca because she was single and had a dowry and because his mother, Tante Vavika, the one who died when I was nearly six and my sister saw God and the angels when they came to carry her off to the heavens, would never, but never, have allowed him to marry his Romanian shiksa.

By the time Dad learned that Mom had no dowry and Mom found out that Dad didn't know how to take photographs, it was too late and they were already married.

When Yosefa was born in 1950 in the Romanian capital Bucharest, Dad swore at Mom and accused her of not even "being capable of giving me a son."

Still, when he looked at the baby girl who had been born with the same black hair and slanting eyes as his, his heart melted, and he decided to raise his family in the land of the Jews. Mom protested fiercely; she didn't believe that anything good could come out of a small country surrounded by hostile neighbors, especially since ships were being sunk on the way there, but Dad was adamant. He wanted his children to grow up in a Jewish state. My father, who was probably the only Jew in the whole of Romania never to have experienced anti-Semitism, because everyone loved him, didn't want his children to ever know the humiliation of persecution merely for being Jewish.

All his life Dad was loved by everyone, except by Mom. But he didn't really deserve my mom's love, because he loved everyone except her.

In Wadi Salib my parents and my eight-month-old sister, Yosefa, were given the small kitchen, which lacked windows, air, and an outside view.

Mom whined to Dad, What could they expect already

from his side of the family? And to shut her up, they had sex for the second time in their lives.

When I was born, and Father was annoyed with "that one who doesn't know how to produce sons," we were given the room that opened onto the balcony.

The room was a hundred and fifty square feet in size and had all the advantages of a studio apartment. It had a separate entrance from the yard that opened straight into the kitchen. There was a kitchenette that included a slab of marble worktop, with a length of fabric hanging from a wire spring down to the floor, behind which, next to the sink, the laundry basin used for boiling the baby's diapers was hidden from sight.

Nearby stood the tiny refrigerator. When there was enough money to buy a quarter block of ice, it even managed to cool the watermelon that took pride of place inside it.

There was no need to store food, since the flour, sugar, *mamaliga*, and coffee were kept on the worktop, and everything we ate, *chorba* soup or *mamaliga*, was cooked and eaten on the day. Thursday, the day of the big clean, we ate chicken soup. Mom made the chicken soup from the wings and feet, after Dad had first chopped off the chicken's toenails with an ax.

Yosefa and I ate the wings with our soup, Mother ate the feet, and Dad ate out. Mom saved the choice pieces of chicken, the breast and drumsticks, for Shabbat dinner.

A single stair, hinting that the kitchenette began two steps away, led into our front room. The room was chronically overcrowded, without a scrap of exposed wall. There were three beds in the room, a double for the girls and two singles for the adults; these were pushed up against a wall, for fear of not being stable enough to stand on their own. Dad refused to share a double bed with Mom because she snored. The brown wardrobe leaned against the third wall and contained clothes and various objects; among them, hidden carefully in a used and oily cardboard box, was the Turkish delight that Mom kept for special guests. Loosely scattered next to the Turkish delight were a number of pungent-smelling mothballs that even as candy-deprived children we never mistook for anything other than what they were, even though they were round and white and just the right size to fill a mouth yearning for something sweet.

In the middle of the room stood the brown wooden table with the elegant slab of glass on top, as if it was the glass that protected the table from scratches or fading. The table was the focus of the room and fulfilled all the household's needs—a space for dining, regular games of rummy, and three-monthly painting of the rummy cubes; our drawing board and Dad's poster graphics table; and a place to sieve rice or flour, shell peas, or trim spring beans—and all this was conducted on top of the glass, above the family's photograph album.

Mom and Dad, handsome and elegant on their wedding day, looked out from beneath the glass on the table.

Mom in Romania, striking various poses, always fashion-
ably dressed in a warm coat and a hat placed at a jaunty
angle on the side of her head. A picture of her in her white
summer dress showed off her very shapely, very slim figure,
which may not have been considered pretty in those days,
but Mom, like Dad, was ahead of her time by being thin at a
time when being thin was tantamount to being poor. Family
pictures from Romania showed Mom's extended family,
including her five brothers; we girls were provided with
an extensive description of the three who stayed behind
in Romania because the Communists refused to grant
them emigration permits, and the two who had come to
Israel in the 1930s and drained the swamps in Hedera. In
time, the Romanian pictures were joined by others taken
in Israel, especially of us in our Purim costumes. In the
corner of the room Mom's sewing machine stood under
a pile of sheets and blankets that had been aired on the
balcony earlier in the day before being folded neatly. At
night, when we went to sleep, the sewing machine was
freed of its burden of bedclothes and Mom was able to
repair whatever needed to be mended, reinforced, patched,
or turned.

The apartment's western wall faced the sea, with tall
windows to the ceiling, rounded arches over the windows
in keeping with modern Arab architecture, and a glass
door that opened onto the balcony and provided a view of
everything that was happening below or opposite; we could

thoroughly scrutinize every movement or sound made or uttered by the inhabitants of the street.

The third time they had sex was on the day that Grandmother Vavika died. The noise woke me up in the middle of the night, and I saw Dad naked, with his bum in the air, lying on top of Mom.

The following morning I asked him crossly if he was beating Mom, the way our Syrian neighbor upstairs, Nissim, spent his days beating up his wife.

Dad told me that he was massaging Mom's back, which ached from all the housework she had to do, and because we were selfish girls who didn't take care of our mother during the day, he was obliged, when he returned from a day's work, to rub spirit into Mom's sore behind.

I told Dad that it wasn't true that he came home late from work, and that Mom always comes in later than he does, and I went to play hide-and-seek downstairs.

They quarreled all day. Not a day went by without my parents quarreling at least once. Their quarrels were loud, and the whole of Stanton could hear them yelling and screaming at each other. But there was never any violence; not like in other families, where they didn't shout at each other, only beat each other up. And because they didn't beat each other, my sister and I believed that Mom and Dad were very happy.

For the next two months she and the man met every day at work and every evening in each other's arms in the apartment he was renovating for his sister, who was away in Barcelona. She spent the weekends with Leon and her parents and didn't bother to invite the man, although he showed some interest.

She didn't want to bring him to her modest little room in the apartment she shared with the arrogant students. The room was actually the living room, which opened onto the kitchen and was separated off by a one-inch-thick sheet of plywood that Leon had installed with considerable flair.

The man either trumpeted in her ear or sang to her in English, and she wept silent tears as she counted the days to their separation. No man before had ever trumpeted in her ear. She had been sung to in Hebrew, and some rhymes in Turkish repeated themselves occasionally, but there had been no trumpeting in English.

On the final weekend before he was due to leave, she promised to return from Haifa on Saturday night so they could spend his last night in Israel together, but Leon insisted on driving her all the way to Jerusalem, so she wouldn't have to take a bus. Throughout the journey, she was troubled by her promise to the man and the knowledge that she wouldn't be able to say good-bye to him before he returned to his fiancée in Barcelona.

"Would you like me to stay in Jerusalem so that we can go house-hunting together?" Leon asked her, knowing how much she hated her two roommates.

"I'm not sure," she replied, irritated with him for insisting on driving her.

"You're not sure you want us to live together, or that I should stay the night in Jerusalem?" asked Leon, hurt by her sharp tone.

"Both," she replied, "I think I'm fed up with Jerusalem. My sister has suggested I come and live with them in Tel Aviv, and I think I might just take up the offer."

"And that's how you thought you'd tell me? After I've already informed my work in Haifa that I'm leaving and moving to Jerusalem?" Leon was in shock.

"What do you want? I didn't plan it." The only reason she was being nasty to him was that he was preventing her from saying good-bye to the man from Barcelona.

"And when exactly were you planning to tell me?" he asked.

"I've only just thought that I might move to Tel Aviv." She squinted at his angry face. "Are you annoyed with me?"

"I am furious with you for not taking the trouble to include me in your plans," said Leon, who was making arrangements to join her in Jerusalem, at her request.

"Would you like me to get out of the car?" she asked.

"Why not?" he replied, and to her surprise, he pulled up sharply in the middle of the climb up the Kastel.

She alighted, vaguely insulted that he was allowing her to walk away, rather than fighting to keep her with him—even stopping for her to get out halfway up the Kastel in the middle of the night, knowing of the terrorists and rapists roaming the region. She got out of the car and started walking, not looking back. In the corner of her eye she saw him overtaking her. She tried to hitch a lift, and the second car stopped for her.

The driver asked if she wasn't afraid to be hitchhiking at that time of night, and she asked him if he was planning to rape her.

"No," said the kind driver.

"Then I'm not afraid," she said, and within twenty minutes he had pulled up at the entrance to her block.

Leon was waiting for her in the darkened stairway. She jumped when she saw him and said, "You frightened me."

"I'm sorry, I didn't mean to. I didn't think you'd get out of the car," he said.

"I didn't think you would leave me in the middle of the road," she replied.

"I love you," he said.

"I know. Would you like to come in?" She considered having sex with him, a final act of mercy.

She unplugged the phone in case the man from Barcelona decided to call her to say good-bye. They walked into her room with its thin plywood divide and undressed quietly, not uttering a word or a groan.

When he'd finished, he asked her if she'd slept with him out of pity, and she told him that she had met someone and was very confused.

Leon got dressed quietly and left without saying good-bye. She'd wanted to ask him to stay the night, not to drive all the way back to Haifa, but she said nothing.

She was at work the following day when the man called her from the airport, disappointed at missing her the previous evening; she lied and said she'd been obliged to spend the night in Haifa and had come straight to work from there.

She remained in Jerusalem, and two months after he returned to Barcelona, promising that he would write to her, the Yom Kippur War broke out. He wrote her letters and even phoned a few times, but she didn't feel like replying. He was sitting there nice and safe, locked in the arms of his fiancée, while here her chances of ever getting married were decreasing drastically as her friends were killed off daily. Once she even called Leon in Haifa, only to be told that he had moved away. She didn't have the nerve to call his mother and ask for his new number. She was ashamed and imagined that his mother was angry with her—and rightly so.

Every day she went to Nahlaot to visit the parents of Kushi, so as not to be alone with all this tension. They had two sons in the war—Kushi, who was with the paratroops and had been her best friend since way back, when he was a boarder at the military academy in Haifa, and his brother, who rescued wounded soldiers by helicopter.

Ten days into the war, Kushi's brother came home on a twelve-hour furlough.

He described a horrific war in which soldiers were falling like flies, and she wondered how it would feel to be a mother whose son was returning the next morning to take part in a battle, with no way of knowing if he'd come out of it alive or on a stretcher, like the wounded and the dead that he evacuated every day. She decided she had to make her own contribution to the war effort, and especially to this Yemenite family she was so fond of, and who made her feel she was one of theirs. She was still watching him and listening to his horrible war stories when she decided that he would go back to the battle for the motherland with a personal gift from her. She decided to sleep with him, so that he would at least go back to that foolish war with a good taste in his mouth. Or in his memory.

As soon as she had made her decision, she knew that Kushi, who was fighting at that very moment in the Chinese Farm, would not be overjoyed by the idea that she was seducing his little brother, but the little brother would be happy to receive a good screw as a farewell blessing. And indeed, he responded to her first overture.

"Shall I make you some coffee the way I like it?" she asked him.

"How do you like it?" he asked in return.

"Strong. Really strong; so strong it penetrates deep down into my bones."

"Sure," he replied. He wasn't interested in wasting his last night on sleep.

When his parents retired to their bed, they picked up their cups of strong coffee and went into his room, as if it was something they did every day.

He was very sensual, and she felt her contribution to the war effort giving her a great deal of pleasure.

Several days later she received a letter from the man in Barcelona, worried because he hadn't heard from her for a while and wanting to know what was happening in Israel; she replied that everyone was doing his or her best and went on to describe what she had been able to do, without stressing just how much she had enjoyed her efforts. The day after receiving her letter, he called to say that he had just that moment landed in Israel. She was on her way to hospital to donate blood because the mother of a friend of hers had to have surgery. He suggested going straight to the hospital and meeting her there.

For a full hour a nurse tried unsuccessfully to find a vein

in her arm from which to draw blood. And then the man appeared, engulfed in the scent of Spain, lacking the signs of the strain of war that were so evident on the faces of everyone in the hospital. He had lots of veins, he said, and volunteered to donate blood in her place.

For the next few days they met in the small bedroom with the plywood room divider that Leon had built, making no attempt to be quiet. Every evening the two students flirted and flattered and invited them to the kitchen for a meal, but they demurred in Spanish and stayed locked in her room.

He went back to Barcelona ten days later and called off his engagement; he wanted to make his own contribution to the war effort by raising her morale. In those days, everyone contributed to the war effort to the best of his ability.

Only after they were married did he tell her that for a long time he had been mulling over his engagement to that wealthy woman, who took herself far too seriously and was concerned mainly with how she looked and her designer clothes and with inane chatter with her girlfriends in Barcelona cafés. But although he had already fallen in love with her during those summer months they spent together in Israel, he didn't have the nerve to call off the wedding at the last moment. It was only when she wrote to him about her contribution to the war effort and he arrived in the country he loved so much and was suddenly in mortal danger and could actually feel for himself the awful tension of being in a war zone that he was able to muster the courage to face his family and inform them that, actually, he didn't want to marry his fiancée.

His parents breathed a sigh of relief. It turned out that they hadn't really liked his choice, but had never dared tell him so.

But even before he made a formal proposal of marriage, and even before she had gone to spend three months with him in Barcelona, he called her at her sister's apartment, where she was staying because her brother-in-law had been called up for a long term of service, and informed her that he was coming with his parents to spend Passover at his sister's new apartment in Jerusalem and was inviting himself to the seder at her parents' home because he wanted to get to know her family.

"Wouldn't you rather be with your own family for the seder?" she asked, and he assured her that after spending most of his time with them, it was more important for him now to meet her family.

After some intense consultations with her sister, it was decided that if they were to avoid frightening off the prospective bridegroom right at the beginning, it would be best not to invite him to their parents' apartment in Haifa, but to conduct the seder at the home of their aunt who lived in Bat-Yam, the excuse being that it is easier to get to Bat-Yam from Jerusalem than to Haifa.

She remembered that just a few months earlier, Leon had told her how shocked he had been the first time he entered her parents' apartment in Hapo'el Street in Haifa, by how stark, not to mention wretched, it had appeared; that same apartment that her parents had succeeded in purchasing after huge effort, mortgaging away their lives to move from downtown Haifa to the Hadar neighborhood on the Carmel.

Her sister had explained to their father that if they didn't move house, the little one was liable to turn into a *pushtakit*, or petty criminal, and there'd be no chance of her ever finding a wealthy husband. Alarmed, the parents hurried off in search of an apartment that would suit their means, and after much effort and crippling loans, they managed to find one in an excruciatingly ugly building on Hapo'el Street. And it was of this very apartment, which she and her sister saw as a significant step up the social ladder, that Leon, the bleeding heart, had spoken after a six-month relationship, telling her that he was shocked by its paucity when he visited it for the first time. Leon, together with his mother and sister, had immigrated to Israel straight from an opulent house in Istanbul, which they had left after their father abandoned his family and ran off with his young secretary; sensitive Leon persuaded his mother to move to Israel, in the belief that a change of location could well herald a change in fortune.

This time the sisters, not taking any chances, decided to hold the family seder with their distinguished guest at Aunt Aurika's in Bat-Yam.

Her parents took up residence at the home of Aurika, Bianca's sister, about a week before the seder in order to dust away every crumb of unwanted *chametz*, and Yosefa sewed them both new dresses. She didn't like the look of her own dress, and even though she didn't want to offend her sister, she went to a stall on Dizengoff Street where the prices were similar to those in the Carmel Market and bought herself a gray-green dress the same color as her eyes that flattered her figure, despite its below-the-knee length. Her sister was wise enough not to take offense, and they managed to persuade their mother to have a new dress made and to go to the hairdresser.

"But my hair is so sparse," Bianca said, trying to convince them that a professional haircut, which would last for three days at the most with her fine hair, was a waste of money, but they insisted, waiting at the entrance to the hairdressing salon in Bat Yam until she emerged with her hair stiff with spray. The whole family, including her uncles, invested an entire month's salary in making a good impression on the tall man from Barcelona and waited, squeaky-clean and dressed to the nines, beside the table that had been laid to the very best of their ability. At seven thirty, instead of the doorbell, the telephone rang, and he said that he was terribly embarrassed, but his sister was furious that he wasn't staying at her place for the seder, especially since she had been slaving the whole day so that they could all sit together around her table in Jerusalem.

"Didn't you tell them you'd be spending the seder with me?" She tried hard to understand.

"I didn't expect my sister to be so incensed about it," he admitted truthfully.

She told him that it didn't matter and glanced at her mother's elaborate coiffeur. Her sister's husband smiled and said that in Spain people apparently obey their parents, and that he'd grow out of it, but she was terribly upset because she had worked so hard for this holy day to be perfect, to make a good impression on him.

"You could tell your sister that my parents have made a special journey from Haifa in order to meet you," she said, still trying to persuade him, peeved at the dozens of phone calls he had made, insisting on meeting her parents. Over the phone, she could hear him talking to his sister in French, and her angry response in the same language.

"She says that my parents made a special journey from Barcelona for us all to be together," he told her in English, and she was obliged to explain to her parents in Romanian why the "intended" had canceled his participation in their seder.

"I can come over for coffee later on," he said, but she refused; she thought to herself that there was no point in everyone sitting around nervously until eleven o'clock at night in the hope that he might turn up. "We can meet tomorrow," she said, repressing the disappointment he had caused her family.

He arrived at her sister's home the next day with a huge bunch of flowers, and they set off for a tour of the country in the tiny car that belonged to her sister and brother-in-law. Needless to say, they had a puncture on the way, and no one protested at all when he offered to change the tire. They felt they deserved some kind of reparation for the disappointment of the night before and had no pity for him when his hands stayed black and sooty throughout the rest of the trip. They were cramped together in the backseat, but when he wanted to put his arm around her, she told him that his hands were dirty and she was wearing a white shirt.

For ten days he courted her with a European fervor that she found very flattering: he opened the door of her sister's car for her; he opened the door to their building; and he was on her right side when they walked in the street, so that if God forbid, a building should blow up nearby, he would take the main brunt of the explosion. When they visited a well-known fish restaurant, he cut the fish down the middle, pulled out the spine, and taught her how to cut into the sides of the fish to get rid of the small bones. Then he fed her fish from his own plate, so she should at least taste it.

On another occasion, he ordered shrimp for her—something she had never tasted before—and showed her how to pull off the heads and peel off the hard crusty outside, and when they were brought lemon-scented water in a small bowl and she asked how they were supposed to drink out of something so small, he explained that the lemon water was for dipping their fingers in after handling the shrimp. He poured wine for her—when she had ordered cola—pulled out the cork and poured it into her glass and her heart skipped a beat. He was a man of the world, thoroughly versed in all the niceties; at night, after devouring her body without bothering to first remove her bones, he sang her lullabies as she fell asleep happily in his strong arms. She felt protected and loved, and she loved him for it.

After a week of shrimp, sex, and lullabies, he returned to Barcelona with his parents, but not before making her promise that next time she would come to visit him. Almost every evening for the next three months he called to say how much he missed her, but she was too tired to miss him. Working at two jobs in order to save money for the airfare and a pair of contact lenses left her completely exhausted.

She lived with her sister and brother-in-law in Tel Aviv during the entire period; they too were working hard to save enough money for postgraduate studies in New York, and when they all returned home at night, tired and starving, the only thing they found in the fridge was some 9-percent-fat white cheese. Only when their mother came to visit and filled the fridge did they realize that they were putting away every penny they earned toward their trips abroad—she to her "intended," and they to further their education.

She paid the equivalent of a month's salary for a pair of contact lenses and loved the fact that people could see her eyes at long last. Over the phone she informed the man that he wouldn't recognize her without the glasses that had been stuck to her nose since she was fourteen. She was so strung

up on the night before her flight that she closed the cover
down on one of the lenses as she was replacing them in their
small plastic container, and tore it right in half. All through
the flight to Barcelona, her first ever flight, she cried her
heart out over the ruined contact lenses. She had so wanted
to impress the man who would be waiting for her with all
his family. A whole month of hard work had gone down the
drain, and now she would have to arrive in Barcelona looking
ugly and bespectacled; and she was especially upset because
she had promised him that he wouldn't recognize her.

He recognized her easily, with her ugly glasses and red-
rimmed eyes.

"Come on," he said, "let's go and buy you some new
glasses. But first you must promise that when we do, you'll
smile for me."

She chose frames that didn't appear too expensive, but he
picked out some black ones with tiny diamonds in the corners and asked her to try them on.

They suited her perfectly.

"We'll take these," he said to the saleswoman, and she
noticed that they cost three times as much the ones she had
chosen.

She smiled at him, feeling pretty again.

"The laughter's come back to your eyes, just as I remembered," he said and hugged her.

"Where are we going?" she asked as they climbed into his
small SEAT car.

"To the apartment you'll be staying in—just so that you can drop off your things—and then I'll take you to my home, where my parents are waiting."

"Aren't we going to be living together?" she asked, horrified; after all, he'd invited her to spend three months in Barcelona so they could get to know each other.

"That was what I had intended, but when I told my parents that I wanted to live with you, they objected strongly and said that it's not done here for a young man to leave home before his wedding.

"My father was furious with me," he told her naively, "for thinking that it wouldn't matter if you were to spend the nights in a room of your own. Anyway, we'll be spending all our days together."

A man of good intentions, she thought, doing her best to console herself.

"The room I've found for you is in the home of my secretary, who has been looking for someone to share her apartment," he said. "She's very nice; her name's Mercedes, and her boyfriend's called Jorge, and their neighborhood is also nice and not far from where I work."

"So how come Mercedes and Jorge are living together?" she couldn't help asking.

"Well, they're not Jews. It's more complicated for us." She didn't really understand why a twenty-eight-year-old man, who had been engaged to be married for five years and who supported himself financially, couldn't simply inform his parents that he wanted to move in with his Israeli bride-to-be, who had left her homeland for the sole reason of being with him in a foreign country.

"Your sister left home when she was twenty." She was finding it hard to understand the man she had fallen in love with.

"She immigrated to Israel in order to go to college. If I'd left Barcelona for the same reason, there would have been no problem. But my parents object to my leaving home to move into a rented apartment with you. It's just not done here. Spain is a very conservative Catholic country," he added.

"But you're a Jew," she said, so quietly that he didn't hear. Or perhaps he did.

When Father Met Mother

My father didn't have a regular job and was forever changing professions. Well, not really professions; jobs. He didn't
have a profession. That was the problem.

When he entered a real estate partnership with someone,
it was he who did all the work; he was familiar with all the
houses in Wadi Salib and downtown Haifa and was brilliant
at persuading people to buy; he ran around all over town,
but in the end, his partner screwed him and threw him out
of the business that Father himself had established.

Father then opened a restaurant, and he was once again
screwed over. He opened a garage that sold tires, and Mom
yelled that no one in the region owned a car.

He went into partnership with a Moroccan and opened
a café, brought in the whole neighborhood to play backgammon, brewed strong Romanian coffee as only he knew
how, poured his soul into that *finjan*, together with the best-

quality ground coffee; the café lost money and had to be liquidated at a loss.

Between jobs, Father was the neighborhood graphic artist, painting store signs in colorful stylized Hebrew letters on cardboard marked out with lines, so the letters shouldn't spill over. Whatever was asked of him—a barber here, a cobbler there, a café and a real estate office. Father was paid no money for this work but was rewarded in other ways, such as free movie tickets or ice cream for his girls.

Our dream was for Father to have permanency. To us, *permanency* was a word that held promise, and smelled of money; we loved our father so much, but knew that without permanency it was hard to rely on him—and the guy suffered from an excessively good heart. It just spilled out of him in all directions, and he was quite prepared to give away everything he owned—except his daughters—if it would help the human race. He was charming and charismatic and very, very funny. And everyone loved to spend time in his company.

With his black hair and slanting green eyes that dipped slightly at the corners in a kind of self-conscious sadness, my dad was an extremely good-looking man. It was no coincidence that my sister thought he resembled God. He bestowed his green eyes on me; Yosefa, whom I called Fila, got their slant. We both inherited the sadness.

In Romania they had owned a movie theater—Nissa—near the Cişmigiu Gardens. Back then Mom and Dad had been important people, especially since they got to see all the movies and were familiar with all the actors. At home they spoke about Greta Garbo, Judy Garland, and Frank Sinatra as if they'd been to school with them. In a way they felt some kind of patronage over the shining Hollywood stars, since without their movie theater, the people of Romania would have never been exposed to all that glamour.

Before the war that began in the late 1930s and came to an end in the mid-1940s, when he was twenty, Dad and his brother-in-law Herry did odd jobs in Bucharest.

They went from house to house and always found some broken gate or peeling plaster, crumbling paint or a wobbly table that needed fixing. Dad, with his honeyed voice, had no trouble persuading the Romanian housewife to prepare a surprise for her husband, who, on his return home, would find it stylishly renovated and revamped to the glory of the Romanian nation, and all in return for such and such a sum of Romanian lei and a cooked meal for two. The women were captivated by Father's smooth and charming tongue and Herry's skilled hands, and as the result of an aggressive marketing campaign of an intensity that was rare in those days in Romania, Father and Herry found themselves with a reputation for being efficient and reliable odd-job men.

One day they entered one of the more elegant buildings in Bucharest, and a very beautiful woman opened the door to them.

"We're in the odd-job business," Father said and looked at Mrs. Dorfman with his piercing green eyes.

"I have nothing in the house that is out of order except my husband," replied Mrs. Dorfman.

"I'd be happy to mend your husband," Father told her and smiled a smile that melted her heart. He entered the house, his brother-in-law Herry dragging behind, and she led them to a dark room, where her husband, who suffered from multiple sclerosis, sat in a chair, his head drooping on his chest.

"Since you are here already, you can help me take him to the lavatory. It's quite difficult to do on my own," Mrs. Dorfman said to my father and gave him a cheeky smile.

For two months, Father would drop by every evening after finishing all his odd jobs and help her take her sick husband to the lavatory.

After two months, Father persuaded Mrs. Dorfman to take him on as an active partner in her movie house, he being the only one who could save the business from bankruptcy, because her husband's illness had forced her to stay home to care for him.

Mrs. Dorfman, who was a very pretty woman, was a member of the Romanian aristocracy. She was a devout Catholic and came from a very well-connected family in Romania's high society, with close ties in high places. Mrs. Dorfman took on Dad as a business partner and as a lover. And indeed, Dad saved her business. He devised novel advertising methods, and their movie house was soon bursting at the seams with patrons. His advertising campaign, with the slogan "Get out of the box and come see a movie," promised two movies and a cabaret for the price of a single movie ticket. During the long intermissions, everyone ate at the bar, which his sister Vida, together with her husband, Herry, operated under franchise. It was in my father's movie house that all the young talent—stand-up comics, male and female dancers and singers—were discovered, performing during the intermission between one movie and another.

My father's friends included members of the Romanian Iron Guard, and he employed them as bouncers in his movie house. He paid them generously, as if knowing that one day he would need their services. And they in turn kept the place in immaculate order and made sure no drunks and hooligans found their way into the business.

When World War II broke out, all the men were sent away to forced labor camps except my father. His friends in the Iron Guard arranged for him to be issued the necessary documents recognizing his work in the movie house as vital to the war effort by maintaining Romania's morale and fighting spirit. This exemption did not prevent the Iron Guard from persecuting other Jews and handing them over to the Germans; they justified their sympathetic attitude toward my dad by saying, "Well, you're a different kind of Jew."

My father's sisters, Vida and Lutzi, worked mornings for

an Italian company checking reels of film for scratches or tears; when any were found, they cut and pasted the film with gentle efficiency. This work was also regarded by Father's friends as being important to the war effort. In the evenings his sisters worked in Dad's movie house.

Vida and Lutzi were both very active in the Zionist movement in Romania, and throughout the war years they harbored Zionist activists on the run from the Iron Guard, who wanted to hand them over to the Germans. Under the noses of his Iron Guard friends and with Dad's full knowledge, the sisters hid Zionist activists and, later, youngsters who had managed to escape the death camps and made it to Romania on their way to Palestine.

For several months Vida's home provided shelter to four young Jewish youths who had escaped from Poland and Russia. During the day they were locked in the house; in the evening they went out to breathe some fresh air on a bicycle belonging to young Lorie.

Lorie was eight and desperately wanted to be accepted by her peers. When she was invited to the birthday party of the most popular girl in her class, she wore her best dress and brought an especially expensive gift. It was a birthday party in the middle of the war, in the middle of Bucharest, and they'd put on a magic show with a real-life magician. When the excited children clapped their hands, Lorie stood up in the middle of the room and said that she had some magic tricks of her own.

"What do you know how to do?" Lorie was asked.

"I can swallow medium-sized buttons and hairpins with nothing happening to me," she replied, and promptly swallowed all the buttons and pins she was given. That night her temperature rose to 106 degrees Fahrenheit.

Her mother, Vida, was terrified of taking Lorie to the hospital; she was certain that, far from being cured, the Jewish child would be instantly put to death.

My father reassured his sister, told her not to worry, and informed her that one of the doctors at the hospital was a friend of his. He took Lorie straight to the doctor, his friends from the Iron Guard clearing the road for him with a motorcycle escort, horns hooting loudly all the way, as if the king himself was being rushed to hospital. Dad explained to his medical friend that this was his favorite niece and that he must operate on her immediately in order to remove the buttons from inside her abdomen. In any case, Dad promised the surgeon that he would "make it worth your while."

That same evening, Lorie was taken to the operating theater, and the buttons and pins that she had swallowed in order to be loved by her school friends were removed from her belly. Later that evening, the pretty young vocalist who had appeared earlier in Father's cabaret could be seen lying replete in the arms of the kindly surgeon.

Lorie was released from hospital three days later, and no sooner had she walked into her home than a powerful earthquake—nine on the Richter scale—destroyed half of Bucharest. As Lorie scrambled around on the staircase searching for somewhere to hide, all the stitches from her operation came apart. Father took her back to the hospital, and again she was rushed to the operating theater, where the incision was restitched.

Another earthquake shook Bucharest the next day, but this time Lorie stood, still as a statue, in the middle of the room, not daring to move. The fear of her stitches coming apart again was greater than her fear of any earthquake.

Dad's brother-in-law Lazer, Lutzi's husband, was sent to a forced labor camp, where he was put to work clearing away snow from the railway tracks outside Bucharest. He contracted a severe case of pneumonia and would have died were it not for Mom's younger brother, Marko, who was a dental technician and "served" in the same forced labor camp. Marko nursed Lazer with great devotion and fed him antibiotics from the supply he kept in the dental clinic. Lazer was saved, although he had very nearly crossed the line.

In return for saving Lazer's life, my mom's younger brother, Marko, wanted to find his big sister a respectable *shidduch*. My mother was thirty-two already and decidedly unmarried, when Lazer announced that he had a brother-in-law, albeit a disheveled one, who was a thirty-four-year-old bachelor and ran his own movie house. Needless to say, he neglected to mention Dad's non-Jewish mistress, Mrs. Dorfman.

Marko hinted to Lazer that a substantial dowry was on the books, and my father agreed to meet with the new prospect. He was annoyed at that time with Mrs. Dorfman for refusing to leave her sickly husband and marry him, even though he knew full well that his mother and sisters (and their husbands) would firmly oppose his marrying any woman who wasn't Jewish.

Mom was a trim and slender woman, elegantly dressed and well educated, who was employed as an accountant. And although Dad's family didn't really fall in love with her, she made a good impression on them.

"She's an Ashkenazi snob," they told him, "not a warm-blooded woman like us Sephardis, but she's obviously intelligent and well educated and you can tell by her clothes that she's well off." And so Dad agreed to step under the chuppah with Bianca.

They got married without too much enthusiasm for each other, and Mom began immediately to manage the movie house, putting the books in order. She imposed her kind of order and made sure none of Dad's many impoverished friends were allowed in without paying full price for a ticket. No free rides here, she would say.

Father employed his entire family and circle of friends in the movie house. He was used to making people feel good; when he came to live in Israel, he continued to help everyone. Except that he forgot that he no longer owned a movie house.

So he went into the coffee distribution business.

He would wander around in downtown Haifa with a three-tier conical tray, selling extra-strong Romanian coffee with an aroma that wafted all over Wadi Salib. He made a point of buying his coffee only from the Arab Nisnas brothers, who, while the coffee beans were being ground, would invite us in to taste their baklava and pistachio nuts before packaging the coffee in small brown paper bags.

The preparation of Romanian coffee was a very accurate and measured process. In a small *finjan* you measure the water and add two heaping teaspoons of sugar. To the carefully measured water, you add a heaping teaspoonful of coffee for each serving cup, and then you turn on the Primus stove. The coffee grounds take several minutes to sink into the water, and it is then that you have to stir carefully so as to prevent the viscous coffee that has been joyously incorporated into the black liquid from boiling over.

My mother, who saw my father's extravagant use of heaping spoonfuls of coffee as an affront to the taste buds as well as to the family's pockets, would lie in wait for him to step out of the kitchen for just a second, when she would skip over to the *finjan* to rescue a few spoonfuls of coffee, which she returned to the brown paper bag, before they had time to melt into the boiling water. She didn't always succeed, however, because as soon as Dad's eagle eye caught sight of the reduced coffee level in the *finjan*, he would replace the spoonfuls she had returned to the paper bag, plus an extra heaping teaspoon, to get his own back at Mom.

Mom was forever yelling that his extravagance was gnawing away at his daughters' dowries, but we always knew that, because of our father, neither of us would ever have a dowry, so what were we missing anyway—and apart from that, he had a knack of getting us on his side in all his quarrels with Mom. What did he want, after all? All he wanted was to enjoy life here and now; unlike Mom, who was forever thinking of her daughters' futures.

On Saturday nights we went to the movies. Every Saturday the whole family went to see a movie. It was the only thing my parents had in common—their great love for cinema. And they always took us along with them so that we too could soak up this culture.

When the movie *The Ten Commandments* arrived in Israel, Mom was sure she could make a small fortune. She went out a week before the first showing and bought up twenty cinema tickets; on the day, when a long queue had formed at the box office and most people had no chance of obtaining a ticket, Mom sold hers at an exorbitant price. In short, here in Israel and with no command of the language, my mother, who had once been a movie house owner, turned into a ticket scalper. How proud we were of her; even Dad was proud of her. Of course we were sorry we hadn't bought up fifty tickets; the demand was huge, and hundreds of people queued up in front of the movie house without a hope of getting in.

We saw the movie *Oklahoma!* three times. But the first time we saw it, we didn't enjoy ourselves at all. The movie was being shown at the Tamar in the Upper Hadar neighborhood, close to the Carmel and very far from Stanton, which was located on the slopes of Haifa's downtown region. By the time Dad, Fila, and I had climbed up hundreds of stairs and arrived, breathless and pale, at the entrance to the Tamar cinema, it became apparent that Dad had only enough money for two tickets and no more; it was a three-hour movie, and consequently the price of a ticket had been doubled. All of Dad's pleas and explanations—that we had come a very long way to be there, that he had no more money on him, and how could they allow two little girls to go into the movie house alone?—were of no avail. The stone-hearted usher would not relent; my sister and I went in on our own, leaving our father outside to wait for us. In the intermission we rushed outside to him, and with tears and pleas we tried to persuade the usher to at least let our father in to see the second half of the movie—surely he'd been punished enough, forced to sit outside for an hour and a half. The usher refused to relent, while we, our hearts breaking at the thought of Dad having to spend a further hour and a half outside, just didn't enjoy the movie. When it was over and we were making our way out, we cursed the usher with a visit to the grave of the black-hearted Hitler. At the tops of our voices, we said it, so he'd hear!

On Thursday our mother left us in the bath for a full two

hours—as if the longer you soak yourself in the water, the more likely you are to be thoroughly rid of all the dirt.

"We're expecting an important visitor tomorrow," Mom explained to us as we were falling asleep in the water, as usual. "The famous playwright, Eugène Ionesco, is coming to visit us."

"What's a famous playwright?" I asked my mom. And even Yosefa, who was wiser than anyone, didn't have an answer to my question.

"It's someone who writes plays," Mom explained. And I didn't understand how you could write plays. You watch plays, like you see movies, don't you? It's not a book that you can read.

"Why is Ionesco coming to visit us?" my sister asked my mom. She'd always been practical, my sister.

"Because he's a friend of Tante Marie's, and he's coming to visit her."

"And will he live here with her?" My sister went on being practical and suspicious, knowing that it was crowded enough already in Lutzi's house.

"No. He's a tourist. He's not immigrating to Israel. He's only coming for a visit," Mom replied, and left us too long in the bath.

The important guest arrived the following day. So important was he that even Tante Lutzi opened wide her red room, with all its chairs; she ran out the red carpet, as they say.

Tante Marie was my father's aunt, as well as Lutzi's and Vida's. When she immigrated to Israel to live out the rest of her life near her nieces and nephew, she was housed in the kitchenette, and when Dori, Lutzi's younger son, was recruited into the Israeli navy, she moved into the elegant room that faced the balcony; because she was elderly and because she was well educated, she deserved to have a room of her own.

Before World War II, Tante Marie had been a teacher of French in Paris, and it was there that she met her Christian husband, who was later appointed French consul in Tunisia. They had a daughter, Odetta, and Tante Marie continued to teach French to the children of the French colony in Tunisia. In time, she fell deeply in love with a Tunisian army officer and spent more time alone with him than was respectable for the wife of a consul. When her husband discovered her betrayal, he sent her packing and returned with their young daughter, Odetta, to Paris. A sad Tante Marie went back to Romania without her daughter, who had been torn from her suddenly; she obtained a decent position in Bucharest as headmistress of the French school for daughters of the Romanian aristocracy. She reverted to her maiden name— Franco—and when war broke out, she was known by that name. Franco, which had a non-Jewish ring to it, enabled her to continue in her post in the school for Christian girls, despite the war. She met Eugène Ionesco at the school in which she taught; he taught literature in the same school.

Now that she was retired, she had come to live in Israel to be near the only family she had left, her nephew Moscu and nieces Lutzi and Vida. Convinced that French was the international language that all educated people should be able to speak if they are to get along in the big world, she undertook the task of teaching French to the princesses of the house of Franco: Yosefa and me. She decided to instill in us—the last known members of the Franco dynasty—her accumulated knowledge and wisdom. Tante Marie told us that in Spanish the name *Franco* means freedom and generosity. She also told us that our family had been among the most established in Spain, and when the Spanish Inquisition began, the family had moved to Turkey and from there, one part of the family settled in Bulgaria and another part went to live in Romania.

Once we understood that Dad was the last in line of the Franco dynasty—since our mother didn't know how to make sons—my sister and I were riddled with guilt for cutting short this aristocratic line; so I agreed to learn French. Yosefa agreed because she wanted to learn everything.

Because we were having private French lessons, Mom forbade us to go around looking like urchins and insisted that we had to be suitably dressed.

So we got ourselves spruced up in the clothes we owned, washed our faces, and crossed the landing from our room to Tante Marie's.

Over ten lessons we learned to how to say "Bonjour," "Comment ça va?" and "Frère Jacques," until I rebelled and refused to continue with the lessons. Having to give up a whole hour of playtime out of only three at my disposal every afternoon between four and seven o'clock, coupled with the pungent smell of age that emanated from Tante Marie, just to learn a subject that was not included in the official school curriculum was just too much for me. Also, I had told my sister that in all the movies we went to see, they always speak English and not French, a sure sign that French was not so important a language as Tante Marie made it out to be. The lessons were discontinued. I don't know why Tante Marie didn't continue teaching my sister, who wanted to learn everything. She probably felt that teaching only Yosefa was too much like a private lesson, whereas having me there gave her more of a feeling of being in a classroom, which she must have missed.

My sister never forgave me; because of me she never learned French, because of our poverty she never learned to play piano, and because of the steep streets of Haifa she didn't know how to ride a bicycle.

And then Ionesco arrived in Israel in search of the stimulation he hoped to find in our tiny little country. As a famous playwright, he was sure that the post-Holocaust Jewish state would provide the perfect inspiration for a new play, and the new landscapes would expose him to materials he could never have found in Europe.

For five full days, my father took Ionesco all around Haifa step by step and on foot. Ionesco was shown the vista from the top of Mount Carmel, spreading down toward the sea. He saw the golden dome of the Baha'i temple, a source of pride to the city, and went down the myriad stairs and slopes that led from the Carmel to Haifa's downtown region, while the scent of coffee (from my father, no doubt) filled the air. Together they wandered among the laborers of downtown Haifa, a complex blend of colors, languages, and people; Arabic, Romanian, Yiddish, Polish, and Turkish ruled the street. And Moroccan—a lot of Moroccan.

And everyone was friends with everyone else, everyone went to the same place, even though they had not come from the same place, and most important of all, they were all Jews— well, apart from the Arabs, who in our eyes were also Jews.

Ionesco was very keen to know how a nation that had lost six million of its sons had succeeded in building such a state, albeit surrounded by enemies, but a homeland nonetheless. And Dad told him that he didn't for a minute regret having left the fleshpots of Romania, the movie house that the Communists had confiscated from him, so that his daughters could grow up as proud Jews in Israel; and it made no difference that, just for the time being, he was making his living selling cups of coffee.

After five days, Ionesco informed Dad that all the material he had accumulated would enable him to write ten plays about Israel.

In the end, after everything that he saw and absorbed and smelled and was impressed by in Israel, Ionesco wrote the play *The Chairs*, about my aunt Lutzi and uncle Lazer's front room. The room was described in great detail: the double bed at its end, the long table—about ten feet of heavy mahogany—with many, many chairs all around, as many chairs as such a long table can accommodate. And along the room's western wall, as if these chairs were not sufficient, there stood a further row of chairs belonging to the same dining room suite. The chairs were heavy, their edges decorated with a carved circular pattern, hand carved, of course. And most important, their red velvet upholstery had the soft, embracing feel of a loving chair. Like soldiers, Tante Lutzi and her husband Lazer's chairs stood regally along the wall, and this is what Eugène Ionesco wrote his play about. The play tells the story of an elderly couple setting up chairs, arranging and rearranging them like soldiers, in anticipation of the arrival of invisible guests.

The Chairs is 40 Stanton Street; at least that's the story that was repeated proudly in our home.

And my father, who spent five whole days taking Eugène Ionesco all over Haifa to provide him with inspiration, waited a long time for the play to be released, only to discover that he didn't get so much as a credit in the list of acknowledgments.

Mercedes was smiling broadly as she opened the door for them. "Hola," Mercedes said, and kissed her on the right cheek, then the left, then the right again. She recoiled, jumped back, not understanding exactly—since when was she supposed to be kissing strangers?—and the man told her that in Spain people say hello and give each other three kisses. To her, it appeared very odd, and he went on to explain that in France the habit is to give two kisses, one on each cheek. In Spain it was three.

At night, when she was introduced to Jorge, who also kissed her three times, she asked the man if she was supposed to kiss all the men in Barcelona, and he said that such was the custom, and it seemed a much nicer one to him than the limp handshake meted out by Israelis, as if they were doing you a favor. She agreed, recalling his firm handshake when they were first introduced and how impressed she had been by it.

"So why didn't you kiss me three times when we were first introduced?" She laughed.

"Believe me, I wanted to."

"Well, why didn't you, then?" she insisted, laughing.

"Because you would certainly have slapped my face."

Beyond the mandatory kisses, the two women were unable to exchange a single word. Like many Spaniards, Mercedes spoke no other language than Spanish and Catalonian. Mercedes was gorgeous and kindly and dressed in well-cut jeans, a button-up shirt, and killer heels, her taste exactly.

The man took her suitcase into the very small bedroom she would be using. Mercedes's room was much more spacious, and the living room was very pleasant. The apartment was extremely clean, and it was only after she'd learned to say a few consecutive sentences in Spanish and stayed for lunch with them a few times that she witnessed how the efficient Mercedes came home from work at lunchtime carrying shopping, stuck a chicken in the oven, washed down the floor, and served her boyfriend, Jorge, a glass of whiskey, straight to the armchair in which he was sitting watching sports on TV. When the meal was over, Mercedes would quickly wash the dishes and tidy up the kitchen; if Jorge was feeling horny in the afternoon, she would follow him into her bedroom and emit a few moans and groans before rushing off back to work, to unlock the office from four thirty until eight thirty in the evening. She could never understand where this pleasant

woman got all the energy to do so much work singlehanded-
ly, while her boyfriend just sat there watching TV, and even
to smile at him. Sometimes he'd get through half a bottle of
whiskey during a single afternoon break. On such occasions,
when he pushed Mercedes into their room, she would hear
her moaning—but not with pleasure.

She wanted to unpack her suitcase and hang up the
clothes she had brought for the next three months, but the
man said that his parents were longing to meet her and had
been waiting from the moment of her landing in Barcelona.
She felt guilty for the time she had wasted buying glasses.

She was hungry, a hunger accumulated over three months
of going without food in order to save enough money to fly
to the country of her bridegroom-to-be.

The arrived at a swish apartment block, and he pulled into
an underground parking garage, where he parked next to a
brand-new BMW. "This is my parking space," he explained,
"and that's my father's car," and when they stepped out of the
car and into an elevator, she felt she as if she were in a movie.

On the tenth floor, the man opened the door, calling out
"Mummy" and announcing in French that they had arrived.
She was sorry now that she had stopped her French lessons
at Tante Marie's, but she understood a little, because it
wasn't unlike Romanian. They entered a square hall, with
one wall covered in mirrors and green marble pedestals; the
other side had two shiny wood doors with painted flowers.
Next to the entrance stood a red-velvet-upholstered chair,

on which the man placed his briefcase. The hall was the size of her parents' living room.

A plump woman with ingenuous blue eyes walked toward them, smiling, and he went up to her to give her three kisses. Next, a distinguished-looking man with piercing blue eyes and a Kirk Douglas dimple in his chin came up to shake her hand. He introduced his parents, Luna and Alberto, and they remained standing, a little embarrassed, in the elegant hall. His father spoke fluent Hebrew and explained that he had learned the language when he belonged to the Hashomer Hatza'ir youth movement in Bulgaria. She spoke a stilted English with the mother, but the father and the man broke out in simultaneous translation as soon as she opened her mouth.

They entered the salon, and she caught her breath. It was very large, with two separate reception areas, one with a television, where they sat most of the time, and another, for guests, with wall-to-wall red velvet furniture. Leading off the salon was a dining area, containing a long table with enough room to seat sixteen. So there would be enough room for anyone wanting to eat.

She remembered that when they'd had all the uncles and aunts over for the seder, they'd had to spill over into the neighbors' apartment to accommodate all sixteen diners. The table was laid for a festive meal—a white tablecloth embroidered with delicate pale blue flowers and matching napkins, on which the cutlery had been laid. Each place setting consisted of a large plate under a smaller one and two kinds of drinking glasses, one for wine and one for water. A stainless steel bowl lined with a white napkin contained small slices of baguette; several other small bowls contained diced red pepper, tomatoes, cucumbers, and onion; and there was another bowl filled with croutons.

She looked up at the crystal chandelier hanging from the dining room ceiling, at the beautiful pictures hanging in the salon, at the large ceramic figure on the parquet floor in the corner of the room, and at the elegant dishes on the dresser and wondered if her gift would appear pathetic among all this splendor. Still, she put her hand into the bag she had carried close to her heart throughout the flight and pulled out a small blue porcelain figurine, which she had bought with her sister on Tel Aviv's Dizengoff Street. They had picked out the unique little piece simultaneously as soon as they laid eyes on it. The figurine was of a woman in profile, her head dropped sideways, a hand raised in doubt or pleading. Her body was soft, and her entire pose said, "Here I am, whether you want me or not." A gentle woman, powerful, her clay eyes filled with compassion.

The figurine pleased his parents, and his mother gave it a place of honor on the dresser in the dining area. She felt wanted, and they sat down to eat their lunch. His mother sat at the head of the table, her usual place, and his father to her left, her son to her right, and she next to him.

Laura, the housemaid, brought in a large stainless steel

soup tureen and laid it beside Luna at the head of the table. Luna served them all soup, first their guest, then herself, then her son and husband.

She was surprised to be served first; at home she had become accustomed to the men being served first, and only after them did the women get their food. Maybe it's because I'm their guest, she thought, but in the evening, when the extended family arrived for dinner, she discovered that his mother made a habit of serving the women first and the men later, which she thought was an excellent arrangement.

The first course was gazpacho, and it was accompanied by a detailed explanation from Luna that this was a Spanish dish, a cold soup made from all the vegetables on the table, finely blended, with added water, vinegar, and ice cubes. The red soup looked especially refreshing to her and was eaten together with the diced vegetables on the table and the fried croutons. She watched the man to see what he was doing and did as he did, exactly as her sister, who had accompanied her to the airport, had instructed her. So as not to make a fool of herself, she was to watch everything the others did and do the same; place her napkin on her lap, take up a small amount on her spoon—not so little as to appear insulting or so much as to appear a glutton—take note of the cutlery they were using for each course, and of course, not confuse the water glasses with the wineglasses.

The soup was delicious, but when his mother asked if she wanted a second helping, she was too shy to accept. She was glad in retrospect that she hadn't had another helping, because she was already full up after the second course, a Russian salad consisting of cooked vegetables in mayonnaise and coarsely cut pickled cucumber. Laura came around and collected the soup plates before handing the woman of the house the bowl of Russian salad, which she proceeded to serve first to her, then to herself, and finally to her son and husband.

The salad was tastier than the dish her mother made at home from cooked vegetables left over from the chicken soup. Here, obviously, the vegetables had been cooked especially for the salad.

"Is this a Spanish salad?" she wondered, and Luna explained that she cooked an eclectic variety of dishes from recipes she had picked up over the years. "The salad is a recipe I got from Ruth, my friend," she said, "and I always make my own mayonnaise." She didn't understand how you could make your own mayonnaise, rather than buy it in the grocer's shop.

The mayonnaise salad she ate with the small slices of baguette was so delicious that she was no longer annoyed at not being allowed to live with the man in a separate apartment.

Without asking, his father poured her a glass of wine, and they all said, "L'chaim." The man asked her if she liked the wine, and she said, "Very much," although she had no idea how to tell if a wine was good or not.

And again, Laura came in to collect the salad-soiled plates, and she didn't know if she should get up to help; as the man didn't stand up, she didn't either. She thought later that she should have helped, and at dinner she did stand up to clear the table in spite of the housemaid, which in retrospect salvaged her reputation in his parents' eyes.

Luna saved a portion of everything she had served for Laura, who ate her meal in the kitchen.

And again, Laura came in with a long stainless steel carving dish containing tender veal, which his father carved and his mother served out. Two small bowls, one with peas and the other with potatoes and onions, arrived alongside. The man piled her plate with generous portions of everything, as if suspecting that she was too shy to help herself; the veal was the most delicious meat she had ever eaten in her life.

She made a point of chewing everything carefully, as per her sister's instructions, and most important—but really most important—not to forget to eat with her mouth closed. With every bite, she repeated over and over not to forget to keep her mouth closed. It's very difficult to chew with your mouth closed. She didn't say a word, worried that if she opened her mouth, she would forget to close it again when she was chewing. In any case, she was quite shy about saying anything, so she sat there, meekly listening to those who were wiser than she. This too was in accordance with her older sister's orders to avoid making embarrassing gaffes in the home of a bourgeois family abroad, one of the pillars of the Barcelona Jewish community.

"Would you like to have some more garlic?" His mother interrupted her closed-mouth drill.

"No, why?" she said uneasily.

"Because I don't cook with garlic. Alberto doesn't like it, but I know that Romanians eat a lot of garlic."

"Bulgarians, too," added his father. "It's just that I hate garlic."

"Does your mother cook with garlic?" Luna asked.

"Yes, a lot of garlic," she said. "My mother starts her morning with three cloves of garlic. For her blood pressure."

"It's healthy, garlic," said Luna, "and really good against high blood pressure. I, personally, like garlic." Later, with time, she taught Luna how to introduce garlic surreptitiously into her cooking without her husband noticing it; after all, good meat really does need to be cooked with some added garlic.

"Alberto has diabetes, so nothing we eat contains sugar. . . ." His mother continued to share the family secrets with her.

As they finished eating the main course, they discussed the falling prices of gold ingots and agreed the time was not right for selling off those they had; she listened in silence, concentrating on the French and on his father's Hebrew translation and her man's translation into English; each sentence, as it was uttered, was translated simultaneously especially for her. After Laura had cleared away the dishes, and she had almost messed up by rising from the table—they had been seated for forty minutes and eaten three courses—Laura returned with a bowl of lettuce salad and fresh plates for everyone. She thought that Laura might have forgotten to serve the lettuce with the meat and now brought it to table, having just remembered. But it seemed that an experienced housemaid like Laura would never forget to serve something on time. Luna, who noticed her confusion, explained that in Paris they eat the lettuce salad after the main course, to ensure proper digestion. She took a little lettuce, which, of course was very tasty, but she was too shy to ask Luna about the dressing, which so enhanced the lettuce; and when the salad bowl had been removed and she was sure that this time they really had finished their meal, Laura returned with a wooden board on which pieces of every kind of cheese known to man were arranged. Various kinds of hard cheeses, Camembert, Brie, goat cheeses, every type of cheese except the regular yellow cheese she was used to at home. By this time she really had had enough and didn't even try any of the cheeses; she had had enough to eat to last her for the next two years. And this was before she even knew that there was still a dessert course to follow and that coffee and cake were yet to be served, and before she know that the entire process would be repeated in the evening—a meal that would last for over an hour, or if they were entertaining guests, two hours—with first courses, second courses, main courses, lettuce salad, cheeses, fruit, followed by coffee and cake. She had never in her entire life eaten so much in a single meal, with every course being a delicacy. And twice a day, even.

No wonder his mother was somewhat plump.

Another twenty minutes passed before a signal was given and the man stood up from the table, saying, "Thank you very much" in French, and she hurried to follow him in case someone brought in another final course that was good for the digestion, saying, "Muchas gracias." She thanked her hosts, not because that was what the man had done, but because it was what her parents had brought her up to do: each time you get up from the table, say, "Thank you very much," for the food that was prepared for you.

He took her on a tour of the house and showed her the large rooms; even Laura's room, which was attached to the kitchen, was a lot bigger than any of the rooms she had seen until then.

"Don't you have a balcony in your house?" she asked him.

"Of course we do," he was quick to reply, and led her to a fifty-foot-long balcony stretching from the dining area to the red velvet reception room.

The whole length of the balcony was filled with tubs of multicolored geraniums.

The balcony overlooked a smart office block without balconies. When she looked down from the tenth story, she saw cafés and bars packed to overflowing, with people milling around on the sidewalks waiting to get in.

"Don't you ever sit out on the balcony?" she wondered, renowned aficionada of balconies that she was.

"Not really," he replied.

"Pity," she said, "you're missing a connection with the outside."

He pulled her from the balcony to show her his own spacious bedroom, and when she saw that he had a suite all to himself, a lavatory for his own use, and a bath and shower that he alone used each morning, she remembered the once-a-week bath she used to share with her sister.

Dirty Thursday

Mom stood on the balcony, calling us loudly in Romanian to come up to eat. We always had to be called up to eat; it made no difference if we were busy and in the middle of an important game, or in the middle of playing hide-and-seek and not yet ready to reveal where we were. It didn't matter if the gasoline truck had just arrived and the intoxicating smell was driving us half out of our minds. It didn't matter if the driver of the ice van had just split a block of ice in half or in quarters and was selling the pieces to everyone who wanted to buy; nor did it matter that we had caught a ride with the horse-cart driver, sitting up behind him before being discovered and getting a lash of his whip.

Mom was calling us, and—if only to stop her shouting in Romanian—we hurried up the stairs to our apartment, although we knew that it was Thursday.

We were ashamed to speak Romanian, we were ashamed

of people knowing that we knew Romanian, and more than anything, we were ashamed of being Romanian. We always insisted to whoever wanted to know that we had a Sephardi father, and when people wanted to know what country he came from, we always answered quickly, He's from Romania, but he's a Sephardi Romanian. At home he speaks Ladino.

And we omitted the disgraceful fact that Mom was an Ashkenazi Romanian.

"Ooof, how I hate Thursdays," I said to my sister as we climbed up the stairs.

"Why, don't you like being clean?" she asked.

"No," I replied immediately. "I'll only get dirty again anyway, so what's the point?"

"Actually, I'd like to be clean all the time," my sister said to me. "I'd have a bath every day, if I could."

"Are you crazy?" I said, horrified. "No one washes every day. Not even rich people."

"I bet they take showers every day in America," she said confidently, "and they change their knickers every day."

"I don't believe that," I told my sister, who always knew everything and believed that there were people in the world who had a daily shower and even used it as an excuse to change their underwear.

We burst into the apartment through the kitchen. Mom was busy preparing *mamaliga* and told us crossly to go to the table. We entered the room and saw Dad peeping in from the other door, which led to Tante Lutzi's rooms. He held his finger to his lips, signaling to us to keep quiet, and tiptoed into the room and closed the door after himself, so Mom shouldn't hear. His hair was wet, and a large towel was draped over his shoulders.

I went to him and started sniffing, the way a dog sniffs at his master when he's just come home.

"You've been to the Turkish baths," Yosefa whispered to him, and I sniffed my father and told him that he smelled of roses.

He asked us not to tell our mother, and hid his towel behind the pile of bedding on the sewing machine. "You know how she doesn't like me spending money." We nodded our heads conspiratorially, prepared to defend him with our lives.

Dad asked us to lay the table and shouted to Mom, so she should hear, asking what she wanted him to do.

"I want you to stop wasting the girls' dowry," Mom shouted back without even putting her head out of the kitchen. "I can smell the roses on you from here. Have you forgotten that people who are hard of hearing have a heightened sense of smell?"

I took out four plates and laid them on the table, and my sister removed them and went to the cupboard to take out an orange tablecloth with a pale print. She spread the cloth over the table, and Dad asked her what the occasion was. My sister smiled at him and said that the cloth would protect the family photographs beneath the glass tabletop. I didn't understand how a cloth could protect photographs. Doesn't the glass protect them? But I said nothing. Dad smiled and patted Yosefa's head fondly, and I was jealous at the way my big sister always managed to please our father, whereas I only caused trouble.

My sister arranged the plates, brought over the jar of anemones we had picked the previous Saturday, and placed it on the table.

Mom emerged from the kitchen carrying a pot of *mamaliga* and asked my sister, "What are the flowers in honor of?" As if she already knew that there was no way I would ever place a jar of anemones on the table. My sister explained that she had seen it in last Saturday's movie. And Dad patted my sister's head again, glad that he had a daughter who shared his American dream.

"Keep your mouth closed when you're eating, and don't make any noise when you chew. It's not polite," my sister said to me when all the attention was on her.

"I'm not chewing the *mamaliga*. I'm just swallowing it. But it's terribly hot." I sulked.

She was always educating me. Stand up straight. Pull your neck up from your shoulders. Don't use bad language, and don't spit. Don't be rude, and don't look adults straight in the eye. They don't like it. Nod your head in submission as if you agree with them—and then you can do whatever you like.

"What else do you like in movies?" Mom asked my sister as she served out generous helpings of the yellow *mamaliga* bubbling in the pot. One tablespoon and then another until the plate was filled to the rim; then she added a dollop of sour cream to the torrid yellow mass, melting, blending, and folding it into the mountain of *mamaliga* until it got swallowed up, without a trace. She served Yosefa first, and then I received an equally generous helping.

"And his lordship?" Mom asked Dad. "What can I offer him? Margarine or yellow cheese?"

"Is there no cream left?" Dad asked, tempting fate.

"Whatever's left is for the girls for tomorrow. If you hadn't gone and wasted that money on your Turkish bath—as if we don't have a shower right here at home—maybe we'd be able to buy a jar of cream every day."

"You can shower in cold water," Dad said to her. "I like my water to be hot."

"We all know what you like," she retorted. "If you had a regular job, we'd be able to afford a boiler."

"As if you'd let me waste money on heating up water if we did have a boiler. You don't even let us waste water," Dad whined, looking at us girls to approve of his extravagances in the Turkish baths.

I looked at the half-full jar of sour cream and thought to myself, When I'm grown up, I'll buy up all the jars of sour cream in the world, just for him.

The pretty glass jar that held the cream was shaped like

a naked lady, like the oil refineries that could be seen in the distance from our balcony. The Haifa yogurt jars, we called them, and we wondered why they were yogurt jars and not sour cream jars. The heavy glass milk bottles were shaped like a slim woman and sealed with a chunky circle of silver foil, which Mom used to peel off very carefully so as not to waste a single drop of the *kaimak* that accumulated at the top of the bottle in a thick, dense layer that tasted of heaven. At first my sister and I used to quarrel over whose turn it was to get the *kaimak*. In the end we agreed on the sensible arrangement she proposed: me on even days, she on odd days. It was so logical as to prevent any confusion. Except that I didn't notice that the even days always added up to three, and the odd days to four.

"I look at everything in the movies. Their clothes, their makeup, the cars they drive, and especially the fancy houses they live in," my sister answered my mother.

I whispered to her that she was hurting our parents' feelings because we didn't have the money to own a grand house, and anyway, such houses exist only in America.

My sister tried to make up to our parents for the insult by telling them that her teacher, Hanna, had written in her notebook that she was a very diligent, responsible, and well-organized girl, and asked her to read her composition aloud to the rest of the class.

"What did you write about?" Dad asked, and my sister replied, "About what I want to be when I grow up."

Dad asked her if she still wanted to be a writer, and she said she did, "a rich and famous writer." Dad told her that people who dream usually get to fulfill their dreams, especially since my sister didn't lack imagination.

"A very diligent girl. Beautifully behaved and a real example to her peers," Dad read out of the notebook, once again stroking Yosefa's hair.

Fifth time in half an hour—I counted in my heart the number of times my diligent sister had had her head stroked by my dad.

"Your teacher didn't write that you were responsible and well organized," I said to my sister. "You were just showing off."

"No, I wasn't," she replied. "She said it to me herself."

Mom, who was pleased by the teacher's comment in the notebook, told my sister she didn't have to finish off her *mamaliga*. I took advantage of the moment and said, "So I don't need to either."

"We didn't get potato cakes for lunch today, and it's not fair." I tried to think of something more interesting than the teacher's praise for my sister.

"Why?" my dad obliged me. "Wasn't Dina there today to cook for you?"

"No. They told us that her mother had died. When are you going to die?" I asked, and Dad said that it would happen when they were very, very old, and we too would be old by then, but still not as old as them.

Mom tells us to get into the bath, and we get undressed. Two girls with their hair cut short and bangs; one's hair is black, the other's light brown; sad brown eyes and laughing green eyes. I throw my clothes on the floor, and Yosefa folds hers neatly and lays them on the wooden chair at the end of the bath, even though they are dirty. Probably to show me how responsible and well organized she is, and not just to show off.

I loathed Thursdays—cleaning day—because I knew that dirt wasn't going anywhere, as Mom was always saying to our Syrian upstairs neighbor, Bracha. Every day Bracha, mother of Sima, Rocha, and Yaffa, swabbed the floors of her apartment; after pouring out several bucketfuls of water, she would go over the floor with a stick and a cloth, poking into every dusty corner. Then she would squeeze the cloth and wring from it every drop of air and water, before going down on all fours and wiping the floor dry. On Fridays Bracha washed her floors twice, once in the morning and again in the afternoon, as a deposit for tomorrow's day of rest.

Mom often told Bracha off for keeping her floors so clean—and why for God's sake did she have to go down on all fours to wipe them dry?

"Anyone would think you were eating off the floor," Mom said to Bracha.

And Bracha told her that this was how she had done it in Syria. My mother never understood the logic, or more accurately, the lack of logic, behind daily housecleaning.

Bracha argued back that Mom also cleaned houses on a daily basis, and Mom answered that with her it was "to make a living, not as a hobby," like it was with Bracha.

We are naked, waiting for Mom to come in with the basin of boiling water she has heated on the Primus stove. She pours the hot water into the bath and adds some cold water. My sister measures the heat of the water with her little finger, and Mom puts in her hand and turns off the cold-water tap. We get into the bath and dive under the water and make sounds like ships and Dad puts in the paper boats he makes for us and goes out to lift up the entire house onto the beds.

The chairs, he places upside down up on the table, and he puts everything that can move about freely on the beds, together with the shoes and the vases. The carpet he had beaten that morning, he folds up and takes out to the balcony to hang over the banister. Thursday is the big washday for us, for our mother, for the weekly laundry, and for swabbing down the floors.

My sister reminds me that we have to soap ourselves thoroughly behind our ears, because tomorrow Fima will be examining us; I even scrub out the dirt under my fingernails.

As she raises her head from the water, I ask her anxiously if Mom and Dad are not already very old. Fila explain that

Grandmother Vavika was seventy, which was terribly old, but Mom and Dad are only forty-five.

"So how many years do they have left to live?" I ask and my sister asks me what's seventy minus forty.

"I don't know, I'm only in first grade," I say, annoyed with her for not understanding that in first grade they don't teach you how to subtract forty from seventy.

"Anyway, I've told you that Mom and Dad are not our real parents," says my sister, who has seen God and certainly knows how to do arithmetic.

"So who are our parents?"

My sister repeats for the hundredth time that Bianca couldn't get pregnant; it's a fact that she gave birth to us at a relatively late age, and I ask, "What's relatively?" and Fila, who is called Fila because I was unable to say a word as long as Yosefa, says that it's a man called Einstein, and I can't understand what that has to do with the fact that Bianca couldn't get pregnant, but I don't ask her anything else so as not to appear stupid.

Fila says that probably because Bianca couldn't get pregnant, Moscu, who wanted to make Mom happy and give her kids, kidnapped us from our real parents.

"So who are our real parents?" I ask my sister again, and she says that our father is a sea captain, and he's looking for us all over the world.

"And what about our mother?" I ask.

"Our real mother," replies my sister, "is sitting by the

window in the dark castle we own somewhere in England, surrounded by lawns, and weeping for her beloved daughters who've been kidnapped, as she waits for her husband the sea captain to bring them back to her."

I say that it seems stupid for our real mother to spend her time just sitting beside the window weeping and not doing anything about searching for us. The fact is that in the movie *The Man Who Knew Too Much*, Doris Day and her husband searched for their kidnapped son until they found him.

We hum the song "Que Será, Será" from that movie and sing the words *Whatever will be, will be, the future's not ours to see, que será, será,* and gradually fall asleep in the bathwater.

Later Mom enters the bathroom, pulls our heads out of the water, and we emerge soft, fluid, and wrinkled. She dries us, gives us clean underpants for the whole week, dresses us with a lot of love, and sends us off to sleep in our double bed.

"So how much is it?" I wake my sister to ask.

"How much is what?" she asks in reply, half asleep.

"Seventy minus forty-five," I tell her.

"I think it's thirty-five," says my sister, who is already in second grade.

Our mother strips off and gets into the bath after us. Into our water, of course.

When Mom has finished her mud bath, she puts the weekly wash in the tub and gives it a thorough soak. In the same water, of course. By the time all our dirty laundry has been washed in the grimy water and my mother has wrung it out thoroughly with her powerful hands, the water level in the bathtub remains the same as when we first entered it two hours before. Mom gives Dad the wrung-out laundry for hanging on the grand balcony that overlooks the port, fills buckets with the water from our joint ablutions, mine, my sister's, my mother's, and the laundry, and swabs down the floor of our room. Dad hangs the laundry outside, and my sister and I sleep.

When Dad is done hanging the laundry, Mom goes out to the balcony.

On the balcony she washes only our side. She doesn't touch the side belonging to Lutzi or her son, Dori.

After a tour of the house, they all sat in the living room to watch the TV news in Spanish, and Laura the housemaid served them coffee with cake that his mother had baked. His father nodded off in front of the TV, and his mother sipped her coffee, each time dipping a sugar cube in the hot liquid. Noticing her watching, Luna said that it was a Polish habit she'd had since childhood, to dip a cube of sugar in the bitter coffee.

The man informed her that they owned a chain of laundries and dry-cleaning establishments throughout Barcelona, which they managed together with his mother's twin sister and her French husband, Jean, and that his mother and her sister worked afternoons in the various shops.

Luna, who wanted her to feel a part of the family, told her that they had started the laundries and dry-cleaning establishments thirty years before, straight after World

War II, and in the days when no household owned a washing machine, their business boomed.

"It's harder nowadays." She sighed gently. "Everyone does their laundry at home, but they still hand in their clothes for dry cleaning."

"Where did you meet your husband?" She asked one of the questions that are of interest to all women.

Luna immediately obliged. "At the university in Paris. He had come from Bulgaria to study; we met and fell in love and were married within a year," she said, giving her a seal of approval to marry her son in less than a year. "And then war broke out, and we escaped here from Paris.

"It was love at first sight," Luna added, and looked adoringly at her husband, who was dozing in front of the television.

"It's understandable," she said to her, "he's very good looking."

"Isn't he?" His mother's blue eyes beamed at her sincerity.

"So you are Polish, not French?" she asked his mother.

"I was born in Poland. But when I was a year old, my parents took all their four children and moved to Berlin, and ten years later, we moved to Paris, and my children were born in Spain. We're a typical family of wandering Jews. My husband's father and grandfather also arrived in Bulgaria from Italy. It's down to them that we all have Italian passports. But we also have a real Italian in the family—

my sister-in-law, Paula, who's married to Alberto's brother. She's from Milan."

She thought it would take her a year to come to terms with all the foreign names in this extended family.

In the meantime his father awoke, smiled at her, and asked her, How's life in Barcelona? She smiled back at him bashfully.

Then his parents got up to go back to their work, informing her that the whole family would be there in the evening to meet her, and the man took her to Plaça de Catalunya. She fed pigeons in the palm of her hands and felt she was in heaven. Afterward they went to El Corte Inglés, Spain's largest department store chain, where she tried on three summer shirts and two pairs of cropped trousers at end-of-season prices.

"For this price, I'd only be able to buy one shirt in Israel," she said to the man, overjoyed. "How come the stores offer end-of-season prices at the height of the season?" she wondered, and he smiled at her, glad that she was happy. He went to the checkout desk to pay for the things she had tried on.

They walked through the Passeig de Gràcia, and he told her about Gaudí and his architecture. They sat in a café and ate tapas and she told him that her sister, who was studying architecture, would love to see Gaudí's buildings.

"Don't worry, she'll still be able to see them," he said, and she smiled at him happily.

"How could your sister have left such a beautiful city for Jerusalem?" she wanted to know.

"My sister is the clever one in the family," he said, and she thought to herself, Welcome to the club. "She always got top grades in everything. Every year she was awarded a 'Student of Excellence' certificate and all possible grants." He was obviously proud of her. "She graduated high school with the highest grades across the board. That's why no one cared when I got eighty percent, even though I'm the firstborn. She decided to study at the Hebrew University when she registered and was awarded all the grants. Apart from that, I've already told you that we are a very Zionist family, and it's always been clear that one day we'll go to Israel. My parents are happy that she has a boyfriend in Israel. Here the chances of her finding a Jewish husband weren't so good."

"Will she be coming here?" she asked him, a little apprehensive about this brilliant sister, whom she didn't know and had only heard over the phone, shouting at him in French on the eve of Passover.

"She'll be in Barcelona in a month's time with her boyfriend, and together we'll go on a tour of southern Spain." He was arranging her life for the next couple of months.

"Your sister will probably get on very well with my sister," she said, and he said he was sure she would with her, too. "Everyone loves her," he added.

That evening his mother's twin sister came to meet her, together with all the rest of the uncles, aunts, female cousins, and cousin Roberto. It was a close and warmhearted extended family, in which every possible language was spoken, from Spanish, French, and Italian to Bulgarian, Polish, and German. They all kissed her three times on the cheeks, and she, in spite of the kisses, which she found hard to accept, fell in love with them at first sight. She'd never been the yielding type. Even as a child, when her parents told her to kiss a relative of theirs, she refused. Her sister used to try to persuade her that it's not polite to refuse to kiss relatives, and she used to say that she didn't care, and she hated the feel of those wet lips on her face.

"And anyway, I don't like their smell," she would say.

"What smell?" her sister asked.

"Of old people," she replied.

They made love that evening when he returned her to the apartment she shared with Mercedes, and she asked him if he would be spending the night. But he said that didn't want to upset his parents, and he had to go home.

"I'll come by tomorrow morning to take you touring," he said. "I've taken a week off work to spend time with you."

She slept happily through the night. She had this feeling that something wonderful was happening to her, the same feeling that she had had when she was eight and her parents bought her a pair of new shoes for Passover, the first pair that were bought just for her, with no partners to share with. She fell asleep with joy in her heart, tempered by fear that it would turn out to have been only a dream. But when she awoke and saw the shining new shoes under her bed, she picked them up and placed them next to her pillow; she wanted to feel and smell their newness close to her head. Nothing equals the smell of something new.

She awoke at seven thirty to the sound of Spanish music on the radio and remembered that she was living a dream, and thought how happy her parents and sister would be for her.

Mercedes served her a cup of coffee and a fresh croissant, which she understood, from her sign language, had been bought earlier that morning. Mercedes tidied up the mess left by her boyfriend in the living room—whiskey glasses and a large empty bottle alongside saucers of nibbles—and left for work at eight o'clock.

She didn't know the man's home phone number, and waited until eleven, when he rang her to apologize and explain that he had overslept. In the car he told her that he had a problem waking up in the morning. Alarm clocks and telephone alerts were of no use; to awaken, he needed someone to give him a thorough shaking.

"Are you any good at shaking people awake?" he asked her.

"I'm not sure," she replied, wondering why anyone would need to be shaken awake. Indeed, what could be nicer than waking up to a new morning?

She remembered how, after years of shifting from one job to another, her father was hired to guard the gate at Autocars, the first and last car manufacturing plant in Israel. He was so pleased at having at long last achieved tenure that he woke up the cockerels at half past four every morning, and an hour later was already at his post, defending the factory against any possible intruder. From her bed on the balcony she could hear him getting dressed in the piercing, bone-chilling cold of a winter morning. Outside, the rain was coming down in torrents, and when he came to see that she was completely covered, although she was already sixteen years old, she pretended to be asleep, to avoid being saddened by her father having to go out in the cold. It was the same when she was riding in a bus and her eyes filled with tears at the sight of youngsters disrespecting an old person by not standing up; the tears rolled down her cheeks at the thought of her mother, laden with shopping bags from the market, having to stand in a bus, and no one getting up to offer her a seat.

The man took her to Park Goel and Sagrada Familia, and they hurried back to his place in time for the sacred two-thirty lunch. Laura opened the door for them, and his mother served them each a glass of freshly squeezed orange juice. This time too the meal was absolutely delicious and included a first and second course, a main course, a lettuce salad, cheeses, and a dessert; again, she was first to be served, like an honored guest. She looked at the statuette of the blue lady that had found its way to their dresser and felt herself wanted. His parents wanted to know if she was comfortable in the apartment he had found for her, and she assured them that she was. And again, they had their coffee in the corner of the living room opposite the TV and watched the news, which she didn't understand; his father dozed on the sofa, and his mother got ready for her afternoon work.

Afterward they went to Tibidabo, where she ate sugar-sprinkled churros, and at nine o'clock in the evening they went back to his home for dinner. She liked the fact that it was still daylight at that time of night, and that dinner was eaten then, or even at nine thirty, and it only started getting dark at ten. She pointed out that it was fun to be able to enjoy daylight until so late in the evening; in Israel it was already dark at seven, and because of the ultra-Orthodox, the government refused to advance clocks for daylight saving time.

That evening they were joined at dinner by Ruth and Nahum Lilienblum, who were described to her on the way to the meal as his parents' best friends and owners of Banca Catalana, the largest bank in Barcelona. Ruth was a very beautiful silver-haired woman, whose trim figure gave her a particularly young appearance. Nahum looked old for his age, slightly stooped, with wise eyes. He looked at his wife in adoration, and although they were sitting in company, it seemed that he spoke only to her and not to the others.

Nahum told her that she was a pretty woman, and she thanked him for the compliment. He asked her if she spoke Yiddish, and appeared disappointed when she said she did not.

"How can that be?" he wondered. "Your parents are Ashkenazis, aren't they?"

"Yes, but I'm a mixed Romanian," she told Nahum. "My father is of Turkish extraction, and although he was born in Romania, his family continued to speak Ladino, not Yiddish, like my mother's family."

"There's no such thing as a Jew who doesn't speak Yiddish," Nahum insisted.

"I'm Israeli," she told him proudly. When they were sitting in the living room, drinking coffee, Nahum told her that as a young man in a concentration camp he survived because of his ability to calculate accurately the number of items in the different piles of property belonging to victims of the gas chambers—a pile of wedding rings, a pile of chains, gold teeth, glasses.

He told her this offhandedly, as if to say, I'm here now in spite of them, and not merely here, but as the owner of the biggest bank in Barcelona.

"God created us perfect," said Nahum, who believed in God despite the Holocaust, looking at his wife and stroking her hand, and she watched him, fascinated. "Look at the female form—how perfect you are, except for one detail." He turned to her.

"What detail?" she asked, not understanding.

"What we are missing is an eye in the tip of our finger, so that we can push a finger under the bed when something falls under it, and we can find it easily." He demonstrated how an eye located in a person's fingertip could find any loss, both above and below.

She started giggling, and Nahum watched her with his wise eyes and said, "You're misleading, aren't you?"

"I'm misleading, why?"

"Because you're a woman-child."

She fell silent, embarrassed.

When Nahum and Ruth stood up to leave, they told her that they would surely see her in Haifa, which they visited at least three times a year because all their children had left Barcelona and settled there. They didn't give her the customary three kisses; they already had learned from their children that Israelis didn't like kissing every new acquaintance.

All that week the man toured Barcelona with her, showing her all the city's beauty spots, and she had to admit that Barcelona was much prettier than her hometown, Haifa. In the afternoon they made sure to turn up, in accordance with family tradition, for lunch at two thirty, with freshly squeezed orange juice, and to dinner at nine. Twice after dinner, they went back to her home early and stayed up chatting with Mercedes and Jorge, but he didn't stay the night.

She found it quite difficult to get used to the fact that she was required to show up twice every day at his parents' home for meals, but the food was always so tasty that she decided she shouldn't complain. She told him she wanted to learn Spanish, and he enrolled her at the university for a one-month intensive course for foreigners.

A month later she was already able to chatter whole sentences in Spanish; Mercedes was terribly proud of her and said that she had never encountered anyone who had learned to speak Spanish so quickly.

She reckoned that she had found Spanish so easy to learn because she knew Romanian from her parents, and the two languages are very similar. More than anything, she loved to talk with Paula, his Italian aunt, who also felt herself a foreigner, having lived in Barcelona for only ten years, and could sympathize with her occasional homesickness. She especially missed her sister.

His sister arrived with the French boyfriend she had met at the Hebrew University, and together they took their father's car and set out for a two-week tour, which covered the length and breadth of southern Spain. She was happy to be able to speak Hebrew all day long. His sister was very pleasant and modest, not at all the person she had heard screaming at him in French on the phone. They loved touring with her and watching her excitement at every new town and township they visited; it was, after all, the first time for her in the big wide world, whereas the man, his sister, and her boyfriend had been born there. She was like a small child discovering a wonderful world for the first time, and she infected them all with her enthusiasm.

The first time she walked into a church, her breath caught. They took photographs beside each and every town square, and she posed alongside every statue they saw of the Virgin

Mary or any of the many other Spanish saints; she pulled all kinds of funny faces to amuse her parents when she got home and showed them the pictures, so they could experience with her the wonderful time she had in Spain. In Toledo she was moved to tears at the sight of the old Jewish synagogue, which has remained in all its former glory; she was overcome with emotion and started crying, as if it were a place she had already been to in the past.

After a fairy-tale two-week trip, they returned to Barcelona, right in time for the Jewish New Year. She and his sister helped Luna a little in the kitchen, and more in laying the table. They were given precise instructions as to how to place the napkins and the best silver cutlery and, of course, the Rosenthal dinner service from the dresser, which was removed from the dresser for traditional holy days.

It was the most impressive meal she had ever participated in, and the food, naturally, was traditionally Jewish. The chicken soup was served with thin noodles or soup almonds that his mother always bought in Israel, since soup almonds are a purely Israeli invention. The second course was an excellent dish of gefilte fish, prepared by Luna with sharp horseradish that she bought in Perpignan. They used to go to Perpignan every four months to fill up their refrigerator with various French foods, such as fine salamis, mustards, cheeses, and of course, butter. His parents still missed French food, even though they had been living in Barcelona for nigh on thirty years. Thus, three times a year they traveled to Perpignan on the French border, and from there they often skipped over to Andora to pick up some duty-free electrical goods, and sometimes went on to Paris to visit Luna's brother and his delightful wife.

On Yom Kippur, they went to synagogue. Because the man fasted, she did too, to keep him company; in the Diaspora it would not have been possible to feel the day of atonement without fasting, since on that day life goes as on any other day of the year, as if we don't need to atone for our transgressions, and she loved him for it.

In the synagogue she was introduced to the entire distinguished congregation, and they all took an interest in the new Israeli visitor. Suddenly she noticed a glamorous woman showing more interest in her than were the others. Paula whispered to her that she was the man's former fiancée. She wanted to approach her and apologize for stealing his heart, but the woman turned her back as soon as she noticed her making a move toward her. And she thought to herself that in any case she would never have known to express her feelings in the sparse Spanish she had at her command. Moreover, she didn't really regret having stolen his heart. She was overjoyed.

But when the holy season was over and his sister returned to Israel and she didn't hear him mentioning anything about sharing his future with her, and she had done her part by learning Spanish and was even able to understand some of the news on TV and at conversation at the family dinner table, she told him that she was returning to Israel to start a new job, since she had run out of money after a stay that had lasted three weeks. He told her that he would be in touch, as if to say, Give me a little more time before I propose marriage to you, if at all.

She went back to Israel feeling a tad frustrated, and when her parents asked her, "Nu?" she showed them the pictures of her smiling all over Spain. They smiled and asked again, "Nu . . . ," and she showed them the new glasses he had bought her with the black frames and diamonds at the sides and all the European clothes that suited her so well. Her mother told her she had expected to see a diamond on her finger; she didn't respond, but found a job right away with a well-known Haifa architect.

Recycled Clothes

On Friday afternoon we get dressed in our best and climb all the stairs and slopes from our home up to the Upper Hadar neighborhood. My sister and I skip and jump in anticipation, with joy in our hearts and some anxiety—what clothes are we getting this time? Mom and Dad walk behind us with a heaviness typical of people who are no longer expecting anything.

Mom had cousins, Sammy and Fima, who had two daughters. They were considered middle class and lived in the Hadar HaCarmel neighborhood. Not only were Sammy and Fima in permanent employment, Fima as a school nurse and Sammy as a senior supervisor with the Port Authority, they also had relatives in far-off America; and it's a well-known fact that anyone who has relatives in America is one lucky person.

Nothing was superior to that secret address in America

from which you receive parcels of clothes and tins of preserves so the children in Israel will have something to eat in times of austerity. After removing the choice articles for themselves, they allowed us to choose what we wanted. Apart from the food, which they kept for themselves, naturally.

Fima checks Sefi's and my ears, nails, and of course, hair in a scrupulous search for lice; not for nothing is she a school nurse. And after we are found to be squeaky clean by her standards, Fima brings out the latest shipment, newly arrived from America. We fall on the pile, and I quickly pull out a brown blouse that looks good quality and tell my sister that I touched it first. My sister retorts that she doesn't want this particular blouse and pulls out the most beautiful blouse I have ever seen in my life. The blouse, which is made of a shiny deep blue fabric, is a wraparound style that ties at the back and has a stylized loop in a shade of red. And I can't understand how my sister's eagle eye always manages to spot the prettiest and fanciest item in the entire pile of used clothes. My sister, who sees that I envy her her blue blouse, pulls out a red vest from the pile that is getting steadily smaller and tells me that if I wear it under the brown blouse that I picked out, with the dark skirt, it'll look funny. I ask her why I should dress funny, and she tells me that if you wear funny clothes, people think you planned it in order to be funny, and that it's better to look planned than poor.

We look at Mom, who is standing in the middle of the room in an ugly beige suit, which hangs on her body and is several sizes too large for her. Fima says that it looks very nice, fits her perfectly. Mom says she'll take in the suit at the sides, and it'll be all right, trying to persuade herself and Dad that the suit looks pretty on her. Dad wrinkles his face and says nothing, and Fima says again, "It's a new shipment from America, arrived just this week." In all truth, she says, she had wanted the suit for herself, but it's absolutely huge on her, because Fima is petite and quite slim, even more so than Mom. And I think that in America there is plenty of tasty food to eat and everyone there is well built, and that is why clothes from America don't fit people in Israel.

Dad tries on a fairly hideous sweater, and Sammy signals with his hand that it looks "so-so," and I don't know why men are always more honest than women and have the courage to say, or signal, the truth when their wife isn't looking, and Dad takes off the sweater and returns it to the pile.

Fima tells Dad to take the sweater, at least for work, and Dad says that he doesn't go to work in a sweater like that, and in his line of business a man has to be dressed respectably.

Mom says to Dad that to hand out coffee off three-tiered coned trays in downtown Haifa a man doesn't need to be well dressed, and Dad tells her angrily that no one is going to see him in a thirdhand sweater.

Sammy asks Dad why he isn't talking to Niku, his brother-in-law from Hedera, who holds a very senior position in the local labor federation, and Dad doesn't understand how Niku in Hedera can arrange a job for him in Haifa. Sammy explains that the labor federation has connections all over the country. Mom asks Sammy if he can't arrange a job for Dad in the port, a job with tenure like she's always dreamed of, and Sammy says that he can arrange it easily, but only as a dockworker.

Fima asks Mom if she's done what they talked about last time on the matter of lice, and Mom says that she did exactly as she was told. Fact, she didn't find any nits, did she?

Fima tests Mom's memory with regard to destroying the lice while they are still in nit stage, and Mom replies expertly, one and a half cups of paraffin, half a cup of vinegar, a little salt and pepper, smeared on the head with a brush, combed into the hair in order to spread the mixture, wrap the head with a towel and wait for two hours. Fima tells Mom that she can laugh as much as she likes. There's no other way to kill them when they're small.

Mom asks Fima if she doesn't think that the paraffin and vinegar can seep into the brain and cause irreparable brain damage. After all, they are all pinning their hopes on Yosefa growing up to be a lawyer or a doctor. Fima the nurse dismisses Mom's question with a wave of her hand. We go into the girls' room to play with their dolls. Not only do they have a room to themselves, but they also have dolls.

I ask them when their mother is going to call us to supper.

I'm starving. Also, she makes the best omelets in the world. My sister says that anything except the *mamaliga* that we are fed every evening would taste good to us.

At long last, Fima calls us to come eat, and I pounce first but don't see any omelet on the plate. I look at Fima as she emerges from the kitchen, carrying a steaming saucepan; maybe now the wonderful omelets will arrive. But Fima says that she always makes us omelets, so this time she's decided to do something different and surprise us with some hot *mamaliga*.

She asks us if we like *mamaliga*. I don't reply, looking at my sister, waiting for her to tell Fima that we eat *mamaliga* every day. I know that Mom and Dad would never in their lives say something like that, but there are things that only children are allowed to say, because it's not polite to show dissatisfaction when you are getting free food, but Yosefa says only that of course we love *mamaliga*, except that today we're not all that hungry.

At night we leave Sammy and Fima's home and start the steep climb down Haifa's streets all the way to 40 Stanton. Mom, Yosefa, and I are carrying bags, and only Dad's hands are empty. In spite of everything, he never gave in and accepted the hideous sweater.

Dad grumbles to Mom about the dockworker's job he was offered by her cousin. Just like to see him working on the docks. And Mom replies that she didn't see anyone in Dad's family offering him anything better to work at.

"What's wrong, don't I go out cleaning houses?" she says, "Don't you think that that's the same as working on the docks? And who am I working for? So you can go out and buy yourself a new sweater to wear to your fancy business. A big genius who wastes his daughters' money, and let's just see how far it'll take them."

"Don't worry about them. They'll get on fine in life. I'm quite sure of that." Dad replies, picking us up in his arms, one girl to each arm, and galloping off down the town's slopes. Dad feels sorry for us because in the end we didn't get the omelet we had been looking forward to so much, and I am sulking at the fact that only because he had taught us not to hurt people, we didn't want to offend Fima by saying that we really didn't want to eat *mamaliga*.

That's it. The big shopping day was over. And with the joyous hearts that preceded such a day, we returned home happy with the thirdhand clothes we had received, and that were later rinsed out in Thursday's dirty bathwater. And all this was before we knew anything about the hole in the ozone and that everything had to be recycled. In fact, we, who recycled ourselves, our clothes, and even our water, could have become rich only from this.

She worked for the architect from eight in the morning until four in the afternoon, and at five o'clock she turned up at Duchovny's bakery to sell high-quality rye bread to anyone who wanted bread other than the government-subsidized uniform bread.

She worked for Duchovny not because she needed the extra income, which never did any harm, but because he had called and almost begged her to come back to work for him because he couldn't find any salesperson he could trust not to steal from his cash register.

Duchovny was a lonely, childless old man who owned and ran a flourishing bakery business from home and had no one to leave it to. She felt obligated to him because of all the money she had pilfered from his cash register; even though she knew that he knew that she had pilfered and was therefore not obligated to him, still she felt obligated.

And maybe she just liked him and wanted to help him out.

She had started working for Duchovny when she was seventeen, during her final year at high school. He had been part of her life during all the upheavals of her move to Jerusalem. He loved her so much that he concluded with her that whenever she wanted, whenever she had an hour to spare, she would come to sell bread, but never for less than two hours. When she turned up for work, he was able to go up to his apartment for a break from his work, which began every morning at four o'clock. He trusted no one except her, even though she had no doubt that he was fully aware of the fact that she was nicking ten liroth from the cash register whenever she felt like going to the movies. On two occasions he even asked her the following day if she'd enjoyed the movie. And sometimes she would even tell him herself, as if to inform him that the cash register lacked ten liroth. She always took ten—exactly ten—liroth to cover the cost of two movie tickets, never a single lira more, not even for popcorn. After all, she had been brought up by her parents to love the cinema, and she took the money only so that she and her poverty-stricken friend who went to Haifa's Reali High School could soak up some culture. But if she'd pinched some money for popcorn too, that would be proper theft.

Duchovny was happy to have her back, after she'd left him for Jerusalem after finishing her studies, and then for

Tel Aviv, and lately, for Barcelona, even if it was only for two hours a day, and he wasn't upset on her behalf that she hadn't received a proposal of marriage, which as far as he was concerned would have meant final desertion. To each his own.

When she went back to work for him after a two-year absence, he told her that he'd had an acquaintance who used to steal from the cash register between one and two hundred liroth a day, as if to say that her ten liroth were peanuts.

He said this and went up to take a rest, feeling that his bakery store was in good hands. And she, who now worked for her living as a draftswoman, was fully able to fund her own movie tickets and didn't nick another agora off him. Duchovny was so moved by the fact that his money remained intact that later, when she got married, he gave her a check for three thousand liroth, the same sum that would have accumulated to her credit if she'd helped herself to ten liroth every day, and even more. He always told her that he would have adopted her if, God forbid, she hadn't had parents of her own, and she always replied that she had the best parents in the world.

When she started working for Duchovny at the age of seventeen, her loser of a boyfriend Israel used to come sometimes to pick her up, and Duchovny would look at him in disapproval. She could see that he hated the youth, just as her parents and sister thought that nothing good would ever come of him. And even when she went back to him with her tail between her legs after Israel had deliberately got her pregnant so she wouldn't have to go into the army, Duchovny didn't say, I told you so, just as her parents and sister didn't say anything, only sighed in relief that the affair between her and Israel was well and truly over.

Whenever irritating customers complained about her hurrying them along to decide whether to buy rye bread or three onion rolls instead of wasting hours of her time and taking up valuable space in the small shop as if it was the most fateful decision of their lives, he would nod his head and explain to them that she's just a kid, and when they left, he would pat her head and say, "Don't pay any attention. They probably have hard lives, and the decision over which loaf of bread to buy is not an easy one for them." But one day a particularly grumpy women came in straight from the hairdressing salon—with an elaborate hairdo piled on her head like a tower, held together stiffly with tons of hair spray—and shouted at her in Yiddish that the bread she had given her was apparently not fresh. She explained to the woman that she didn't speak Yiddish, and the woman threw the loaf of bread down on the counter and asked, apparently, for it to be changed. She changed it and wrapped the bread in brown paper, and when the woman bent below the counter to place the loaf in her shopping bag, she gathered up all the bread crumbs on the counter and flung them at the grumpy woman's hair-sprayed tower hairdo. There's a limit, after all, to the amount of other people's hard lives she can put up with without answering back. Her life too was hard—what with her man in Barcelona and her selling bread in Haifa.

He used to call her at least twice a week and talk about his yearnings, and she said nothing, not understanding why, if he missed her so much, he only called her on the phone. She missed him terribly, even though she was having an affair—nothing stormy or wonderful, but enough to soften her longing—with her boss, the architect.

"I've got a boyfriend, and I love him," she told her boss when he started showing interest in her beyond the bounds of their working relationship.

"And where is he?" he asked.

"In Barcelona!" she replied.

"Barcelona is a long way off," he said, and she thought, Out of sight, out of mind, and it wasn't as if she had left Barcelona with any kind of commitment or even any talk in that direction, so she didn't feel that she was cheating on him, unlike her boss, who was cheating on his wife with her.

"How can you cheat on your wife like that?" she asked, with the naïveté of a twenty-three-year-old.

"When you are in my place, you'll be doing the same thing," he told her with the assurance of a forty-year-old.

"I would rather get a divorce than cheat on my husband," she said, and he explained that he got married at a very young age, and by the time he was twenty-five he already had three children, and that life erodes and routine gnaws away at everything good and we are only passing through this world, and blah, blah, blah.

She decided that she had to do what was good for her and she wasn't employed by her bosses to be the guardian of their morality, and anyway, if he wasn't having it off with her, he'd be cheating on his wife with some other woman. And at that point in time, the affair suited her. It was close by, it was available, it was noncommittal, and it was pleasant to while away the time. Although she had suitors who were her own age and unattached, she was genuinely in love with the man in Barcelona, and her heart was not free for courting. Her married boss wasn't really courting her, and he wanted only one thing, sex; and since he was extremely handsome, she was happy to go along with it. But when he told her about the Distinguished Service Medal he had been awarded in the Six-Day War and the way his best subordinate had been killed, he wept like a child and touched her heart that was full of yearnings for afar. She admitted to him that she was in the east while her heart was in the west, and it was pain that connected between them.

After a three-month separation, the man called and asked her to arrange their wedding for the following March. She asked if this was a proposal of marriage, and he said that it was. When she went, full of joy, to announce to her boss that she was getting married in March, she was certain that he would share her happiness, but he was obviously too depressed.

"You'll soon find someone else for a fling," she tried to console him, but he looked at her with even more pain and asked her, was that all he was to her, a fling?

"Yes," she replied. "Wasn't it?"

"Who knows where it could have led to?" he replied, and she looked at him in astonishment.

"Lead to what?" she asked. "I'm getting married in three months' time to the man of my dreams."

"I have feelings for you, don't you understand?" he said, and she didn't understand, and resigned from his office without understanding.

Old Duchovny took her on gladly for an eight-hour working day at the same salary she had received in the architect's office. She didn't want to work for longer than eight hours, so as to leave her time for her wedding arrangements.

Since her sister was living in Tel Aviv, she was helped by Johnny and Rosi's daughter, Batya, who had already been married for two years and most probably had plenty of experience in weddings and even had a little girl who went with her to all the function halls in Haifa until they chose one that she considered the most suitable.

When she told the man over the phone that she had found a lovely function hall, he immediately said that he and his parents would settle only for "Carmel Halls."

"It's expensive," she said.

"So what," he replied over the phone, "you only get married once in your life."

Over the phone, they decided that they would invite two hundred and fifty guests: one hundred from her side and a hundred and fifty from his, since he had a large family in Israel too, and it seemed quite logical to her, considering the fact that his parents would most probably pay for this wedding, in the fanciest hall in Haifa, just as, two years before, her brother-in-law's father had paid for the wedding of her sister and his son with a hundred guests at a prestigious restaurant in Tel Aviv. Her sister and brother-in-law had refused to get married in a hall and insisted that only close relatives should participate in the event.

When the groom's parents came to meet her parents a fortnight before the wedding, her father told them that he would pay for his own guests. He said this out of politeness, and also out of self-respect. Perhaps he hoped that they would dismiss the proposal out of hand, since it was not he who had suggested holding the wedding in the most expensive function hall in Haifa. But they didn't refuse, and her parents rushed off to take a second mortgage on their apartment in order to pay for the wedding of their younger daughter in a venue that was far beyond their means.

It was lucky for them that only a hundred guests had been invited from their side. They flatly refused to accept from her the small sum she had managed to save over the last six months; better it should stay in her bank account, for any eventuality.

Later, they all took the Carmelit to the Carmel Halls to choose the menu, and when his parents chose an open buffet, which made the wedding even more expensive, her parents looked at her in vague desperation, too embarrassed to say that they were unable to pay that kind of money. Happiness is an expensive business, she thought suddenly. Sadness is a much cheaper commodity; for this only homemade tears are needed.

The groom's family, including the groom, went to Jerusalem, and the future bride and her parents stayed in Haifa and gnawed their nails.

She canceled the dress she had wanted to buy because of the price, caught a lift from her father's work at Autocars in one of the vehicles that went to Tel Aviv, and landed at the home of her cousin Yael, whose wedding had taken place six months earlier. Two months before, Yael had kindly offered her the use of her wedding dress, but she thanked her and said that she wanted a dress of her own. All hers, not shared.

She took Yael's dress, which was two sizes too big for her, and returned to Haifa, straight to the dressmaker, to take in the dress.

When she came back from the dressmaker, Fima and Sammy were at her parents' to hear how the first meeting with the in-laws had gone and to relate excitedly that they had taken the train from Tel Aviv to Haifa, after their weekly visit to their granddaughter and daughter, and struck up a conversation in Yiddish with a very nice couple of tourists, and what a small world—it turned out that they were from Barcelona, and here a relative of theirs was also getting married to a young man from Barcelona. Maybe you know him? they asked Ruth and Nahum Lilienblum, who told them happily that not only did they know the groom, who is the son of their friends, but that they were visiting Israel this time especially for the wedding.

"She's a beautiful woman, the bride," said Nahum to Sammy, who explained that even as a child she had been beautiful, "but she's too willful," he added.

"What do you mean by willful?" asked Ruth. "I found her to be a very gentle girl."

"She's charming, and she has a good heart, but she's rebellious," Fima explained, "She does only what she wants to do."

"That's what is so nice about her," concluded Nahum, the Pole from Barcelona, who had been captivated by the future bride the first time he met her. "She seems a strong woman, and I am sure she'll make an excellent *balabusta* and housewife."

"He loves her, and that's all that matters," added Ruth.

Fima and Sammy told her all this in her her parents' home, adding that when they got off the train, excited by the chance meeting, they agreed between them that this was a Cinderella-style love story.

When the man called her in the evening from Jerusalem and asked if the dress she had bought was ready, she didn't tell him that in the end she'd be getting married in a second-hand dress, lent to her at the last moment by her cousin, and only said that the dress fit her figure perfectly.

She told her sister about the exorbitant price of the meal that her parents had committed themselves to, and said she felt like calling off this whole wedding, which had become unbearably expensive, and instead getting married as her sister had, by the rabbinate, with only close family present.

"Too late. Tell him the truth," suggested her sister, but she explained that if her sister had seen the way they live there, she would understand how impossible the truth would be to tell.

The designated day arrived, and he came to pick her up to go to their wedding in his sister's VW Beetle, dressed in a deep green velvet suit and a blue bow tie. He was the handsomest bridegroom she had ever seen, and she was so proud that he was her bridegroom.

They entered the hall where his parents awaited them, festive and elegant, and her small parents beside them, slightly lost in the fancy function hall.

His mother told her that her dress was very beautiful, and his father asked with anger in his eyes who had changed the catering they had chosen together from a free buffet to a sit-down dinner with waiter service. She wanted to tell them that they hadn't decided together, and that it had been more their decision, but she didn't know what they were talking about and looked straight at her mother.

Her mother told her that they had made the change because they felt that people were naturally bashful and would therefore refrain from going up to the free buffet to serve themselves.

"I'm sorry I took it upon myself to change the catering. But you aren't familiar with the mentality of people in Israel. They are used to being served at the table, not standing in line to get their food," she said, attempting to excuse the last-minute change she had decided on without involving any of the others.

"But how did you have the nerve to change things without even telling me?" she asked her mother quietly afterward in Romanian.

"I've cleaned a lot of houses to arrive at this moment, and no one is going to take it away from me. You know I'm right, and that it's much more respectable to be served at the table by a waiter."

His parents were furious at her mother, and his father didn't exchange a word with her throughout the wedding, except for a "Mazel tov" after the chuppah. His mother was more forgiving. And she herself, by the time everyone came up to her to kiss and congratulate her, had forgotten the unpleasant incident.

After the chuppah, she and her husband were lifted up in chairs, and they looked into each other's eyes from the heights of their wedding hall, and she thought in her heart, For better or for worse. The food seemed to have been good, even though very polite waiters served it straight to the tables, but they didn't taste any of it because they were too excited to eat. And when everyone had loosened up from the wine that flowed like water, his father handed out cigars to the men. It was a complete surprise, and all her friends went around with cigars in their mouths, feeling like men of the world. She looked at her parents, who had given birth to her at the age of forty in order to arrive at this moment when they could boast about their daughter and her impressive bridegroom, and especially because they had not been able to boast about their older daughter's wedding, which was only a meal in a restaurant without a chuppah and a wedding service and all their card-playing friends. And when had they ever been to a wedding where they handed out cigars?

When the rabbi came up to her, because he could see that the groom didn't speak Hebrew, and asked who was paying, the father of the groom or the father of the bride, she said, "Whoever has it," and pointed to the father of her new husband from Barcelona.

The last of the guests left at one in the morning, and they drove to the nearby Dan Hotel, where he lifted her up according to tradition, and when they crossed the threshold they spread the checks they had been given all over the bed and the floor. They lit a cigarette and enjoyed calling each other "my husband" and "my wife," and she wanted him to stay in his green velvet suit because he looked so handsome in it.

But when he wanted to have sex with her, she said she wasn't able to.

"Why, are you menstruating?" he asked, disappointed.

"No. It's just that I can't have sex in a regular way, going to bed before going to sleep. I hope our sex will be a surprise, and not in the evening, at the end of the day, before falling asleep."

She had surprised him suddenly with this response. Maybe if he'd known that this is how she felt, he wouldn't have married her.

"For example, if I'm frying schnitzels and you come up to me and hold me and pull my panties off me and then, you know, surprise me. In the middle of my frying schnitzels."

"In our home, Laura fries the schnitzels. Would you like me to surprise her?"

She burst out laughing, grabbed his hand, and rolled him over the floor over the pile of checks, all the while pulling off his green velvet suit and he removing her cousin's wedding dress.

The following day they went to say good-bye to old Duchovny. On the way she met Batya and her little daughter, who promised her that they would come to visit them in Barcelona, since her husband was a seaman, and they could join him on one of his voyages.

"Is she a friend of yours?" her husband asked her, and she told him that she had no idea what their family connection was, but that Batya had been a part of the landscape of her childhood.

Operation Sinai

At night, my sister and I dreamed the same dream. Exactly the same dream.

In our dream we found a coin on the sidewalk. We bent down happily to pick up the coin and found beneath it another coin. We took that one too and, again, found another coin underneath it. That's what they mean when they say you've got a penny in your pocket. We stood up to leave and suddenly stopped, went back to the spot of the hidden treasure, and began digging. We dug further and found another coin, and then we found coins of greater denomination, a huge pile of coins. Like someone who wins the jackpot in a casino and jumps in the air with victorious cries of joy; that's how we felt in the dream, except that we had to dig in the ground to find our jackpot.

Two sisters with a single dream.

And so we wandered the length and breadth of Stanton,

playing, inventing stories, and jabbering our childhood gibber, conducting our lives along the line that separated imagination from reality and everything that came in between.

Fantasy plays an important role in poverty. It has the ability to slightly soften the deprivation, and I believe my parents were aware of this and never tried to bring us back to "reality." I think that when they called us, for example, back for supper and we didn't respond, Mom and Dad knew that we were in the midst of our fantasy time. Like today's children have their "story time."

I loved my father's story about the two fishermen standing on the edge of the pier, catching fish. One of them is exceptionally well dressed, the other very simply. The elegant fisherman asks his down-to-earth counterpart what he's doing. The man replies that he's doing what the other guy's doing, fishing for fish. Says the elegant fisherman: since you're here already, wasting your time with your fishing rod, waiting patiently for a fish to bite, why don't you do as I do and set up two fishing rods; that way you'll be able to catch twice as many fish.

The simply dressed fisherman replies: And what will I get out of it?

Says the elegant fisherman: You'll have more fish to sell, and you'll have more money to spend.

The simply dressed fisherman asks: And what will I get out of it?

The other fisherman replies: With the additional income, you'll be able to buy a good fishing net; you'll be able to spread out your net and catch a lot more fish.

The simply dressed fisherman asks: And what will I get out of it?

The elegant fisherman says: You'll have even more fish, and then you'll be able to buy yourself a big fishing boat, to employ thirty people to work for you, and you won't have to work anymore.

And what will I do all day? the simply dressed fisherman asks the elegantly dressed fisherman.

I know, says the gent; you'll be able to sit all day and fish to your heart's content.

The plain fisherman responds: And what am I doing now?

Dad used to tell us all the stories until Rosi came and replaced him. Rosi was an amazing storyteller. She remembered every detail of every story and never left out a single magic princess, locked by a wicked stepmother in a narrow, windowless turret, with a tiny slit in the wall that only an eagle's beak can get through.

The Rosenberg family consisted of Rosi, the mother; Johnny, the handsome father; and Batya, their skinny daughter. Either Rosi or Johnny was a distant relative of my dad's, and after they had scoured the country in search of work, Dad arranged a job for Johnny as a dockworker at the port and persuaded his sister, Lutzi, to rent the Rosenbergs

Tante Marie's kitchenette. It was out of respect for the elderly, Dad explained to his sister, and Tante Marie moved into the spacious room that faced the balcony, the room that had become vacant when Dorie went into the navy. Batya, Sefi, and I crowded ourselves into the Rosenbergs' narrow bed, because the windowless kitchenette had no room for two beds, and floated off on a broomstick fueled by Rosi's magic spells.

We rode away on Rosi's stories to cold and far-off lands, with kings and counts, princes and frogs, and knew that only love could save the world from evil.

Smiling from ear to ear, we all fell asleep in the narrow bed, happily dreaming our dreams, certain that tomorrow morning our lives would be much nicer.

In the morning we awoke to hear Rosi screaming and yelling. Johnny, her husband, had come home as drunk as a lord, exuding stinking alcoholic fumes, and full of inebriated cheer, he rounded off his evening by beating his wife to a pulp for daring to ask where he'd been all night.

Batya, who was thin to the extent of plainness, used her small fists to separate her mother, the storyteller, from her father's murderous fists. But Johnny shook her off as only general security agents know how to shake off people and started beating her to a pulp, too—taking it in turns, laying off one to lay into the other. We stood aside, watching, our bodies trembling with fear and, especially, insult. We felt insulted to the core; how could anyone be so cruel? We had gone to sleep with hope in our hearts and awakened to this horror.

Fila and I tried to push Rosi out of reach of Johnny's blows, but we didn't succeed even in tickling the ends of his fingers, and he pushed us off with the ease of a sumo wrestler flicking off a feather.

The noise and shouting drew our father, and he too caught a blow from the inebriated Johnny.

We had no telephone with which to call the police, and my sister and I ran to the balcony and started screaming at six in the morning, "Help! Help! They're murdering our dad."

It was a warm morning, and all the windows on Stanton Street were open; from each house, there suddenly appeared a large number of heads, eager to see the source of our cries that our father was being murdered.

The first to arrive on the scene was Nissim, our Syrian neighbor from the floor above, and since he was a big expert at domestic violence and not a day went past without him taking his belt to all five of his children, he managed easily to release our small and beloved father from the terrifying fists of Johnny.

Dad told Johnny to take his wife and daughter and bugger off out of his sight as far as possible.

Beaten half to death, Rosi got down on her knees and begged Dad to forgive Johnny, because he didn't really mean it. He had accidentally drunk a little too much and lost control of himself.

"It won't ever happen again, I promise you," Rosi swore to Dad.

Dad refused to listen and said that it was enough that people were beating each other in every other house on the street. In his own house, he wasn't going to put up with a man beating his wife and children.

Johnny lay on the small bed and wept like a child admonished. He said he was sorry and that he would never raise his hand again to anyone and that he had nowhere else to go.

"That's the reason you've been wandering all over the country. Everywhere you go you get thrown out after you've beaten the living daylights out of everyone there." Suddenly my father understood why Johnny and his family had never managed to settle down in any one place.

"I only beat my wife and daughter to let off steam," Johnny said in his own defense.

Bruised, tearful, and sad-eyed, Rosi looked at our dad the hero and whispered that if he threw us out of the house, Johnny would murder her and her skinny daughter.

Then Dad said to Johnny that they could stay, but the next time he beat Rosi and his skinny daughter Batya, he'd have him put straight in jail. "In jail you won't have anyone to beat. And you won't have anything to drink, either."

Then Dad took us, his beloved daughters, to our own room and hugged us close to himself, where we fell asleep in his arms, protected from all evil.

The following evening, Rosi came into our room with her

skinny daughter Batya, and as we lay in bed, she told us her wonderful fairy stories.

When we fell asleep, she took her daughter and went back to the windowless kitchenette.

That night we heard the rise and fall of an air-raid siren.

Fila cried that Johnny was killing Batya again, but Dad said this time it wasn't Johnny. It was a siren, and we were at war.

The war in the Sinai Peninsula had begun.

A police car drove through the street with a loudspeaker, calling on the inhabitants to go down to the shelters. Haifa, our city, was being bombed.

Within seconds, Johnny appeared in our room with his daughter in his arms, took my sister and me by the hand, and led us down to the shelter. Dad took Grandmother Vavika, who was still alive but died a year later, and our sensible mother grabbed some blankets.

In the shelter, I discovered that one of my slippers had slipped off my foot during the great escape down the stairs, and I broke into an anguished wail—"I want my slipper. I'm going back up to look for it"—and tore myself free of Johnny, who was still holding on to the little girls as if he could protect them against the bombs.

The adults' pleas that the Egyptians were bombing us and that I would have no use for slippers if I were killed on the stairs had no effect on me.

Johnny offered to go up and bring me the slipper, and Mum asked him, if he was going up anyway, to bring some

Turkish delight down from the closet, second shelf to the left, where it was hidden for exactly such occasions. So we can at least die with something sweet in our mouths, Mum said to Johnny, and he went back upstairs.

After what seemed like an eternity, Johnny returned with my slipper and the box of Turkish delight.

"What took you so long?" my mother complained.

"You hid the Turkish delight so well that you yourself don't remember where you left it," Johnny said. "I turned over the whole closet until I found the box on the bottom shelf on the right."

We gobbled up the Turkish delight, and I said I was thirsty.

Johnny went upstairs and returned with two bottles of seltzer.

After drinking, all the children started crying that they needed peepee.

Johnny went back up and returned with a potty, and we all lined up for a pee. When the children had finished, the adults took it in turns to use the potty.

When the sirens went off again the following night, Dad said we might as well stay in our nice warm beds rather than spend the night chasing after a potty. Luckily for us, the war ended a few days later, and we went back to hearing Rosi's fairy tales at bedtime, until Johnny had earned enough at the docks to move his wife and daughter to another apartment, where he could continue beating them without my dad's constant interference.

All she wanted during the honeymoon in Greece was to call her sister to tell her about the wonderful things that were happening to her.

"We were in a hotel on a cliff overlooking the sea, and all the signatures in the guest book were of famous movie stars. I saw Paul Newman's signature and Glenda Jackson's," she told her sister breathlessly over the phone. "Truth is, my heart aches at the thought that one night in the hotel costs the same as Dad's monthly salary."

"So why does your heart ache?" her sister asked.

"Because we spent six nights there, and I couldn't stop thinking what Dad and Mum could have done with the equivalent of six months' labor."

"You'll get used to it," her sister told her, as if she knew all about the lives of the wealthy.

"Do you know how much one picture of the newlyweds

on their honeymoon cost, taken by the hotel photographer?"

"How much?" asked her sister, the student whose life wasn't easy financially.

"The same as the bespoke dress you had sewn for your wedding."

"You don't say. I hope it was in color, at least?"

"Black and white. But big. We placed it in a silver-plated frame in the living room."

"And how much did the frame cost?" her sister asked.

"As much as your entire wedding," she replied.

"Nice," said her sister. "You'll get used to this, you'll see."

"Get used to what?" she asked her sister.

"To a better life," she replied. "The main thing, though, is that you behave nicely and don't make a fool of yourself."

After the honeymoon they landed in Barcelona, straight into a huge apartment with wall-to-wall parquet flooring. Above them on the fifth floor lived his uncle with his Italian wife and two children. The apartment was empty so that they could furnish it together, and he showed her proudly where he planned to place the living room, the dining room, the master bedroom and his study, and a further two rooms that he designated for guests from Israel and perhaps for their children, too.

When she saw what he intended to be their master bedroom, an enormous room that could be traversed on skates, she said that she felt the room to be too large and lacking in intimacy, whereas the room next door, which he had designated for his study, would make a perfect bedroom.

She didn't like his plans for the giant living room, which was divided into two unequal spaces, and thought that the smaller would be more suitable for sofas and a TV. The larger space, she thought, would best hold a dining table, around which they planned to entertain his family and friends.

He didn't agree with her, and in order to prove his point he took her up to the fifth floor, to show her that at his uncle's, too, the larger space served as the living room, and the large bedroom was used by his uncle, while the smaller bedroom belonged to their son, Roberto, and their daughter had the one that was smaller still.

"So what?" she said. "They have children."

Paula took her aside in the kitchen and tried to persuade her that his plan was compatible with interior design in Barcelona. But when she realized that she didn't agree, she summed up the matter in one sentence: "That's what it's like in a marriage."

"It doesn't have to be like that. I, too, have an opinion," she said adamantly.

"But it's his profession. He studied five years for this," the aunt insisted.

"So what? I'm a woman, and I know what I like and what I don't like," she replied, and thought to herself that even if

Paula thought she had some nerve, after being brought to such an elegant apartment, not accepting the majority decision over where her bedroom and the living room were to be located, she still couldn't bring herself to agree with them, in spite of her sister's request that she behave nicely.

They continued to argue for a week, until she told him that she felt a little lost in all these huge spaces, and she needed, at least in her own bedroom, to be able to get inside herself. I'm not used to a bedroom that measures more than three hundred square feet, she explained to him. At home my bedroom was the closed balcony, five by six feet, and she added that she was accustomed to the warmth that comes with overcrowding. He capitulated.

When she went down in the elevator and the uniformed doorman stood up and hurried to reach the door before her to open it for her, she felt terribly embarrassed and told him in Spanish that she was quite capable of opening the door for herself, but he just smiled at her politely and continued to hold the door open. When she entered the building carrying bags of shopping from Court Inglés, the doorman took the bags from her and made for the elevator quickly so that she wouldn't need, God forbid, to wait, and she wondered what her parents would have had to say at the sight of the courteous doorman treating their daughter like a princess.

But when she told his parents at a dinner at their home that she was embarrassed by the doorman opening the door for her as if he was her servant, his father admonished her slightly and said that this was his job, and she had to adapt herself to life in Barcelona and behave like a lady, and not embarrass the doorman by preventing him from doing his job.

But she screwed up yet again. When his mother lent her Laura for one day a week to clean her apartment and cook whatever was necessary, she refused to allow the maid to cook for her. It's enough that she was cleaning; she should sit down with them to a lunch that she herself had cooked. But she could feel that Laura was unable to swallow anything in their presence and that she was embarrassing her, too.

One evening his parents announced that they were planning to celebrate their wedding in a swish function hall in Barcelona with all their friends from the Jewish community. She asked if it wasn't odd to celebrate twice, and they explained that the entire community was expecting to join in their happiness and to bring them wedding presents.

True to form, they prepared a wedding list in Barcelona's most prestigious department store, one that included everything they needed for their new home, and the wedding guests were invited to choose the gift from the list that was most compatible with their means and their own taste. This very logical arrangement meant that everyone came away satisfied. Instead of giving a check for an amount that you can never be sure is enough, and which simply dissolves into the pile of checks that all the other guests have given, you are given the opportunity to bring a wedding gift that is to your taste and to the taste of the receivers, and the newlyweds receive a personal gift from each guest. Of the stylish list of gifts they picked out and with which they furnished their apartment, from the refrigerator to the sofas and down to the toaster, the only thing she chose in the fanciest store in Barcelona was a set of bathroom scales for weighing herself at home. When the man who had become her new husband said that it was a cheap gift, and who the hell would choose a set of scales, she laughed and said that it would be someone who wanted to bring some balance into her life.

"But really," she replied earnestly, "with my very own set of bathroom scales I shall feel that I'm a wealthy woman, the kind that weighs herself whenever she feels like it." Of all things in the prestigious Barcelona department store, it was the bathroom scale that symbolized her new economic status; a kind of luxury that you don't need, but want.

The scales remained almost alone in the store until two days before they were married for the second time in Barcelona, when Kushi arrived suddenly on his way to the United States to visit her. When she asked Kushi why he chose the scales for her, he replied, "My dear, for someone who grew up in Wadi Salib and marries a guy from Barcelona, a set of bathroom scales is the epitome of wealth. It's the epitome of showing off. I thought it was just like you to wake up in the morning and say to yourself: 'Hey, I've got my own personal bathroom scale. I no longer need anything from anyone.'"

"Where did you get that knack of always being able to

read me so accurately?" she said. "So you're not angry with me anymore?" She referred to having slept with his brother during the Yom Kippur War.

"I was never angry with you," he told her, knowing exactly what she meant. "I simply didn't understand why you did it, and I'll never be able to understand," he said and dropped the subject.

Her sister and brother-in-law also stopped off in Barcelona to see her before flying off to New York to continue their studies, and she admitted to her sister as they stood together in the kitchen of her expensive home that she was beginning to feel a little lost.

"You're just not used to being married," her sister explained, and deserted her with her new family in Barcelona.

They corresponded; her sister never forgot in any of her letters to teach her decorum and to remind her to eat with her mouth closed, to chew and not gulp food down, to hold her knife in her right hand and the fork in her left, and to distinguish between fish and meat knives.

"Do you think the roast chicken on my plate will be offended if I cut it with a fish knife?" she wrote to her sister.

"The roast chicken won't mind, but your mother- and father-in-law will," said my sister, who was smarter than anyone else.

And in another of her letters she wrote to her sister about an interview she had with the architect Koderk. He's the most highly thought of architect in Barcelona, she wrote. So his son explained to me that to be hired by him, you need to be clean and orderly. Do you see, he didn't ask me if I know how to draft, or how many years experience I have. He only wanted to know if my work is clean and orderly. What do they think I am, their cleaner or their draftsperson? He explained that at the end of the day, each draft has to undergo two kinds of erasures, and then to be thoroughly cleaned with a piece of cotton wool soaked in benzene before being rolled up, ready for laying out the following day on the drawing board.

She remembered Leon, the bleeding-heart liberal from Istanbul whose drafts were the best in the class. He had an inherent talent for the profession that she had had to learn in spite of herself. She had met Leon at engineering school when she was studying architecture, and he spoke little Hebrew. At that time she invited a few South American students to her home, where she read out the material in easy Hebrew, before the exams.

Leon shared a rented apartment with a woman from Colombia who had immigrated to Israel after her younger brother had been abducted by the Colombian authorities and his body had never been returned. She had enjoyed visiting Leon's rented apartment, which he had furnished with his good taste, and how, while he prepared tomato soup for her out of a packet, she taught him words in Hebrew.

Once a fortnight she would go with him to visit his mother and younger sister in Tel Aviv. She loved seeing the compassion in his eyes when he looked at his mother, whose husband had left her for his young secretary. He was full of anger for his father and had only sympathy and tenderness for his mother and lovely sister.

Later, having decided she wanted to study at the Hebrew University of Jerusalem, and not having been accepted, she felt an emotional need for a change of scenery, and Leon had helped her hunt for an apartment in Jerusalem. The prices were exorbitant. Eventually they found the apartment with the two women who were renting out the doorless lounge at an affordable price, and Leon bought a sheet of plywood and built a room divider with a door that opened and closed, so that what she actually got was the best room in the apartment at a reduced rent. When the other women saw her capacious private space, they insisted she should share it with them, but, waving her lease at them, she sent them to hell.

She and Leon agreed that if she decided to stay in Jerusalem, he would join her, and in the meantime she started working for Ackerstein and traveled to Haifa on the weekends to visit Leon and her parents. Then, when he wanted to join her in Jerusalem, she had betrayed his love with her relationship with the man from Barcelona, who trumpeted in her ear in English.

In her heart she thought that if Leon had known how to trumpet in English, she might never have left him, but she admitted to herself later that she had been bothered by the fact that Leon was thin and almost the same height as her, and when he held her in his arms she felt she was being embraced by a boy and not, as she wanted, by a man. Go tell a silly twenty-two-year-old girl that a tall, Spanish-speaking man is no more masculine than short, Turkish-speaking Leon.

"Did you get the job with Koderk?" her sister asked in a letter from New York to Barcelona.

"I did," she replied, "but not before asking him if I needed to come to work with a green surgeon's mask on my face. My Israeli chutzpah must have pleased him, because he started to laugh."

"So everything's all right," her sister wrote back. "What are you doing with the money?"

"Save it for hard times and send some home to Mom and Dad."

"Why bother?" her sister asked. "You know they'd never touch your money."

Their lives in Barcelona took on a regular routine. They worked in the mornings; at two o'clock in the afternoon he would come to pick her up for lunch at his parents', until she rebelled and they agreed to eat at home twice a week. In the afternoons he was busy with his Final Design Project, which took many months to complete, and she couldn't help comparing him with her sister, who had taken two months to complete her project for the Technion.

Any time she felt like doing something different with him in the afternoons, he would argue that he couldn't spare the time to leave his project, and he asked her to refrain from tempting him to do so. Sometimes she went out with Mercedes, her much-loved Spanish friend. Sometimes it was with a few of her workmates, and most of her time was spent with Paula and her children, or his parents, while he allowed himself a weekly outing with his friends.

His mother taught her how to cook dishes from her vast repertoire of recipes and shared many of her culinary secrets. In time, she learned to cook so well that she sometimes invited his parents and all his uncles and aunts to eat at their home, and her food was always warmly complimented. When Ruth and her husband came to dinner, they were served an eggplant salad with a lot of garlic, and rice-stuffed vine leaves with a yogurt sauce on the side, and Nahum said he'd always known she would turn into a good *balabusta*.

"How did you know that?" she asked, charmed.

"It's all in your eyes," he said, "especially since I have an eye in my own finger and I can wander about with it, in the tops as well as in the bottoms." He laughed, and she answered him by saying that there isn't a Romanian woman alive who doesn't know how to cook, it's inherent in their genes.

Rummy

Damn. Next Friday is rummy night at the Markovitzes' house.

I hate going to their place. They live so far away, and if Dad loses at cards he won't feel like carrying me home in his arms, and I am fed up. I am fed up having to schlep home with them at two in the morning because of their stupid card game.

Why can't we have rummy night at our place every Friday?

Why should I have to be dragged along with them, just because Fila is frightened of being left alone at home? I'm not afraid of burglars. What can they steal from us, anyway, except for our rummy tiles, which are shinier and more lovingly polished than all the tiles owned by any of the others?

I told my sister I wasn't going to the Markovitzes' next week. Not after what happened to us with their daughter,

Shila; I said that she should stay at home with me. My sister promised that it would be just one more time, and Dad promised that we'd be allowed to paint the rummy set on Saturday.

By the time she was twelve, Shila Markovitz was already five feet eight inches tall, a fact that gave her a huge inferiority complex, because of her height and because of her pimples. It was because of her pimples that Shila slapped on packs of makeup, in the staircase so her parents wouldn't see when we went out. And her height, together with her makeup, made her look sixteen.

Shila, who was an only daughter, went to great lengths to please the boys, because of her inferiority complex and because her parents didn't really love her.

The last time we went to their home, my sister told my dad that she wasn't going down with Shila to play hide-and-seek because in any case Shila didn't really play with us. Mom persuaded her to go down to the street anyway; otherwise the "little one" (in other words, myself) would go crazy with boredom and frustration watching them playing rummy. Shila soon joined the chorus pressuring my sister, because she knew that her parents wouldn't allow her to go down alone, and she was desperate to be considered cool. My sister agreed grudgingly, angry with me because it was my fault that we had to go.

"And it's only because of you that we are here at all," I answered her at once, which shut her up.

We walked out of their apartment, and the first thing Shila did was to sit herself down in the staircase for a whole hour to smear makeup all over her face to hide her pimples, and it was my job to turn on the light whenever it went out.

As soon as we stepped out on the street, we were surrounded—or to be more accurate, Shila was surrounded—by four large sixteen-year-old hoodlums.

I suggested playing tag and didn't understand why they were looking at me in disdain and saying that tag was a game for five-year-olds.

"I'm eight and a half, and I love playing tag," I protested, but they only wanted to play hide-and-seek, and Shila said they were right. Tag was a babies' game. I gave in and agreed, so long as I got to be the seeker. I stood next to the wall and counted, one, two, three, up to fifty. Anyone before and after me, to my sides and underneath me, is caught.

I opened my eyes and started looking for the others. I found my sister within a second because she was always afraid to wander too far away; she was also afraid of dark places.

We started looking for Shila and couldn't find her. As we approached the empty and deserted space that we didn't usually dare go anywhere near even in daylight, we heard whispering, and on the street corner we saw the four boys all over Shila, fumbling with her breasts.

We stood aside so as not to be seen. Now we were hiding from them. We thought at first that she was giggling along with them, and thought of going back without her.

As we were turning to leave, we heard her crying and telling them, "Leave me alone."

We watched as they dragged her toward a truck at the edge of the field, and one of them stayed nearby on the outside. Fila said we should hurry home and call Shila's parents, and I said that Shila's parents would probably beat her when they discovered her hanging out with those hoods.

"Let's go talk with them," I said to my big sister, and forced her to come with me.

We went up to the one who was waiting outside and were pleased to see that it was Ya'akov, who was a member of the Abbas family that lived on our street.

I told him to tell his friends to let Shila go immediately, and he asked, "Why?"

"Because if you don't, I'll tell your dad that you stole chewing gum from Avram's grocery store, and your dad will beat you to death with his belt. Even more than usual." Ya'akov was almost convinced, because everyone knew that his father had a whole lot of self-respect and didn't allow his kids to steal.

"Anyway, we're on our way to the police right now." My sister suddenly found her courage.

Ya'akov, who was a bit more afraid of his father's belt than of the threat of the police, climbed into the truck and brought out a crying Shila.

"Your mascara has smudged all over your face," I told her, to make her laugh, but she didn't stop crying.

She didn't have to ask us not to tell her parents. We took it for granted that we wouldn't snitch on her. My sister only told our dad, after making him swear not to tell Shila's parents. And he really didn't, because he knew that the poor girl would get another whipping, and my dad hated it when parents beat their children.

When Shila graduated from grade school, her parents sent her to work as an office clerk. My mother argued with Shila's mom that she should have let her daughter go on to high school, or at least do a secretarial course, but Shila's mom said that she had supported her daughter until she was fourteen, and that was enough. It was time for Shila to support herself, find a husband, and leave home. Apart from that, high school costs a fortune, she said—I mean, not only will there be no more money coming in, but we'll have to scrimp and save for another four years before our not-too-bright daughter finds herself a decently educated husband. And who's to say she'll find herself a better husband; what guarantees are there in life? "Look at yourself," said Shila's mother to my mother, "you're an accountant, and where did your education get you? Here in Israel you're cleaning houses to support your children; that's a life?"

Mom said she didn't care. She was definitely sending Yosefa to high school. As for me, she wasn't quite sure. "But between you and me," she whispered to Shila's mother, "she's so pretty, she'll know how to get on. But your Shila, you know . . ." And my mom fluttered her hand in a "so, so" gesture. "Shila should at least get herself some useful skill," my mom added.

Friday it's our turn to host the rummy game. I love it when it's our turn. The entire house is up on its hind legs, and with the eager anticipation of seriously heavy gamblers, we set up the three card tables for our distinguished guests. We spread out the green baize card cloths that Dad brought from Romania and collect the red-upholstered chairs from Tante Lutzi. We then help Mom with food; a variety of sandwiches with *kashkaval* cheese and black olives, Romanian red eggplant with a lot of garlic, *ikra* that Dad prepared himself with finely diced onion on the side, and slices of plain Shabbat challah. Salty Bulgarian cheese with sliced tomatoes on top, to soften the saltiness. Sometimes there are *burekas*, served with brown hard-boiled eggs, fruit and watermelon, and of course, my mom's fabulous *cozonac*.

On Thursday, when it's our turn for cards, I'm even willing to forgo playing downstairs, if it means I can help my mom with the *cozonac*.

Mom separates the egg yolks from the whites, careful not to break them; even a tiny speck of yellow in the whites could cause the foam, which is Dad's job to whisk, to break. With her fingertip she scrapes out the very last scrap of white from the half eggshell, leaving it shiny in its emptiness. Even when it's only an ordinary fried egg or omelet being cooked, a finger has to be placed inside the shell to draw out the white to the very limit of its ability.

The yeast dough is left to rise overnight, wrapped in two layers of toweling, like a child who can't go out with a wet head after being shampooed. The wrapped parcel is placed ceremoniously in the warmest spot in the house, next to the Primus stove. When the dough has risen to three times its original size, we roll it out together and add the delicious filling that Mom has prepared from cocoa, sugar, cinnamon, and ground nuts. We tried to get out of using raisins; never liked raisins.

When the dough is rolled and filled, we place it gently in the round baking pan with a hole in the middle and join the two ends. Mom covers the pan with its lid—as they say, every pot has a lid—and we wait a few more hours for the dough to rise once again. Only then does Mom place the pan on the flame, and we wander around it, checking every five minutes to see if the cake is rising as it should and sniffing the glorious smell of *cozonac*.

When the guests arrive, Mom shoves some *dulceata* into their hands (good job she doesn't push it into their mouths) to get their appetites moving. As if you know a lot of people whose appetites are static, apart from anorexics. *Dulceata*, accompanied by a glass of cold water. My mother places this very sweet delicacy, a jam she prepares herself some time earlier, in beautiful small crystal bowls that she brought from Romania, with a glass of cold water to wash out the intestines.

No self-respecting Romanian home would welcome you without an offer of *dulceata*, and I always said no. I refused to even taste it.

"Try it at least—otherwise, how can you tell you don't like it?" Dad tries to coax me.

"I know, because it's brown," I reply, and refuse to touch it.

Once the players are seated at their game, we take up positions to the side, carefully scrutinizing everyone's cards.

I enjoy sitting next to Dad and learning from him how to play. Dad likes to take chances, so there's always a lot of tension surrounding him. At the end of the evening, my parents count up their money. Between Mom's caution and Dad's risk-taking, they usually come out quits; indeed most of the time they win more than they lose, which makes my sister and me very happy.

The food is served at about ten o'clock in the evening. For this moment my sister and I have been waiting for six weeks, for our turn to come, when Dad and Mom get up from the card table to do the final preparations and we take their places in the game. We play instead of them with real money—not make-believe—and we get to keep whatever we win. Anything we lose is our parents'. Even in a game of cards, our mother and father trust us not to lose.

It takes about half an hour for the food to be served to the tables, and we take full advantage of this time. When we win, the guests complain that we use a code language to reveal to one another what cards each of us needs. It's a lie, but we are used to hearing adults lying to save face. That's why we don't care, as long as we win.

After the food and after clearing away the plates, we still have a few minutes left to play while Dad prepares the strong coffee, as only he knows how. Only when he takes his seat and the *finjan* is heating on the stove does Mom hurry over to rescue a couple of spoonfuls of the excess ground coffee that Dad put in and return it to the bag, before the coffee manages to boil over slowly and the liquid starts to froth.

After coffee, Dad goes back to the game, and I am happy that he is in a good mood. The following morning, my sister reminds my father that she's willing to stay behind with me at home next Friday, on condition that she gets to paint the red and yellow rummy pieces on her own.

"She can paint only the black, and you can do the green ones." My sister tries to squeeze as much as possible out of her negotiations with Dad.

"Why does she get to paint two colors, and I get only one?" I go straight in, complaining. "So let me at least paint in the higher numbers."

"It doesn't go by numbers, stupid. It's by colors," my sister butts in. "And it's only four colors."

Dad takes me aside and asks if I want to go with them to the Berkovitzes' the following Friday.

"You know I don't," I snap.

"So give in to your sister this time, and next time you'll

get to paint more pieces than she does," he coaxes me—which in the end turns out not to be the case. Next time, too, my sister paints two colors and I only one.

"So I'll paint the green and you the black," I bargain with Dad. I don't like black. And, besides, I don't want to paint the blacks, just because my sister says that this is what I have to paint. I have always been contrary toward my sister, so as to stop her showing off for being a year and eight months older than me.

"Why don't you like black?" Dad asks me.

"Because people who wear black are always sad"—I find an immediate excuse—"just as you were sad when Grandmother died."

So we shouldn't quarrel, Dad let us paint the rummy tiles every couple of months, even though they didn't need painting more than twice a year. Romanian tile rummy is not played with plain old cards, as it is by the Poles, but with tiles, and the color of the numbers engraved in them fades with time. We had two good sets of rummy tiles from Romania, and didn't use inferior, bought-in-Israel ones. Ours were heavier, made from much better quality stone.

Dad soaked the tiles overnight in soapy water. When we got up in the morning, the tiles were soft and faded, giving themselves up to the devoted care they were about to receive. We dried them off thoroughly, picked up a fine brush, and carefully opened the four jars of paint—red, green, yellow, and black. We dipped the brush in paint, just a little so it wouldn't smudge, and painted in the number on the tile, each with its own color, giving renewed color to its cheeks. When the paint had dried, we used a razor blade to scrape off the excess color from the edges and polished the tile with a little benzene, to bring back its natural shine.

Only because of us were the rummy tiles shining and new-looking; my sister and I were forever arguing over which of us would get to paint more numbers.

When her husband allowed himself to lay aside his project for a few hours to take her out for an airing, they went to visit friends of his who bored her—especially Jakob, a Jew who had inherited a fortune and made another from his extensive business ventures. He was always dressed in the height of fashion, without so much as a speck of dust on any part of the dark suits he favored, always with a matching tie. Even when they visited him at home, he was always dressed in a suit, and his wife, a Jackie Kennedy lookalike, matched her style to his as a good wife should. Their house was furnished entirely in white leather that you were afraid to sit on in case it got dirty, and their children were never allowed into the lounge, so as not to make a mess. They were allowed to play only in their own rooms, and then only between five and six, after which they were washed and fed in the kitchen by their nanny, because they were not

allowed into the dining room adjacent to the white lounge.
She thought to herself, How miserable those rich kids are,
growing up in a white house, where they are not allowed to
touch anything and where they lead lives as disciplined as in
a military academy.

After a year in Barcelona, the man informed her that they
would be flying to Israel at Passover for a visit.

She was happy, but made it clear to him that she intended
to have the seder with her parents.

"But we want to be with my sister," he said.

"And I want to be with my parents," she told him, "and
I have no problem with you being in Jerusalem while I'm in
Haifa."

He looked at her dumbfounded, incapable of understanding how she could propose such an arrangement for a family
seder.

"You are my wife, and I want you to be with me," he said.

"I was my parents' before I became your wife," she retorted childishly, but capitulated in the end and agreed to
be in Jerusalem for the seder, and go to her parents the next
day. Otherwise, she knew, her parents would be made anx-
ious by her wealthy husband and go out of their way to impress him.

The first thing she asked her parents was what was happening with Batya.

"What's supposed to be the matter with her?" her mother
replied cagily, not looking her in the eye.

"I've written her three letters already and she hasn't replied, and I couldn't phone her because I've lost her number." She went to the telephone and asked her father for Batya's number. Clearly embarrassed, he told her that Batya had died ten months before. "Shortly after your wedding, she was diagnosed with jaundice and passed away within a month."

"Why didn't you tell me?" she asked, and her parents told her they didn't wish to hurt her, knowing that she could just as well get bad news in Israel. It wasn't necessary to send such painful messages all the way to Barcelona.

"How can anyone die so quickly from jaundice?" she asked her father in anguish, and her husband held her hand firmly.

"No one knows. She just died very quickly," her father said.

"I bet it's because of those thrashings she got all her life from her father. And how did Johnny react to her death?" she asked.

Her father looked at her mother, who said that Johnny had shot himself on his daughter's grave. "He must have loved her after all," her father said.

"And Rosi?"

"She's still telling fairy tales to everyone who's willing to listen and to anyone who isn't. She's slightly out of her mind. We go to visit her every week and take her some food. She'd have died of hunger, otherwise."

Their meal was a sad affair; she said she needed some
air and left the house. Maybe if she went to the same place
where she had met Batya a year ago, the day after her wedding, she might still see her, she thought. Maybe she wasn't
dead at all. She didn't see Batya, but met a girl she had been
to architects' school with. The girl told her that Leon was
married and the father of twins, and he was now living in
London, where he was a very successful architect.

"You know, life goes on," the girl said smugly.

"So it does," she replied, happy that Leon seemed to be
doing a lot better with his life without her.

She hurried back to her parents' home, where her man
was waiting for her. He was worried about her, and she
asked him to trumpet for her in English. Two weeks later
she was happy to return to Barcelona.

That summer they went to the Costa Brava resort of
Lloret de Mar with Mercedes and Jorge, who were happy
to share their vacation in the house owned by his parents
and uncle. She ate paella, drank sangria, peeled shrimp, and
gobbled squid and various other kinds of seafood as if they
were sunflower seeds. He husband laid aside his Final Design Project and allowed himself to spend the entire vacation with her, and she remembered why she had fallen in
love with him. He brought her flowers in bed, just for the
sake of it, and carried her on his back like a sack of flour
up the steep stairs of the house, which was built on the side
of a hill. In the sea, he dove beneath her and raised her to

his shoulders before throwing her behind him back into the water. They frolicked and laughed like a couple of kids in love, and only when his parents came for weekends did he suddenly become serious and behave in a way that befits a European man of constraint.

On her twenty-fifth birthday, which fell on Rosh Hashanah, the first day of the Jewish New Year, her husband surprised her by taking her to the airport without telling her why. She thought they were flying to Rome or Paris, until she saw her little parents walking toward her with their suitcases.

Bianca immediately took over her Spanish kitchen and cooked them a few choice Romanian dishes, which his parents also enjoyed, once she had pointed out to her mother that she would have to reduce the amounts of garlic she used.

She enjoyed showing her parents the wonders of Barcelona; even more enjoyable was to see their enjoyment, even though her mother spat out the seafood, unable to understand how her daughter was able to eat that nonkosher, *treif* food. Her father loved everything he was given and chatted with their doorman in Ladino.

After a month in Barcelona, her parents flew to Paris, since not only had her husband wanted to surprise her on her birthday, he also wanted her parents to enjoy a taste of the big wide world, and for a whole week they were guests in the home of his uncle and aunt, who showed them all over the City of Lights. Her parents returned to Israel like two people awakening from a dream, and she loved her husband all the more.

When her friends Gingi, Amiram, and Moshe came to visit, her husband took them to see a bullfight, and she took them to an amusement park and the Las Ramblas boulevard.

But when winter came and everyone had gone home, her husband returned to his Final Design Project for the next six months, and once again she felt alone in a foreign land.

One evening they were invited to dinner at the home of Jakob and his wife. The meal wasn't particularly filling, but the plates it was served on were impressive. She was hoping that the dessert course would provide some compensation, until the maidservant arrived—in that home it was most definitely a maidservant—bearing four unpeeled oranges and placed one on each of their plates, as ceremoniously as if she was dishing up the finest Russian caviar. She looked down at her orange, then watched Jakob pick up a knife and fork and peel his with amazing dexterity, using a single set of cutlery. He didn't touch the fruit with his fingers, and when the orange was peeled, he cut each segment in half with his knife and used his fork to pop them into his mouth. Her husband did the same, and so did Jakob's wife.

"Don't you like oranges?" they asked her.

"Of course I do, I was brought up on oranges," she said, and picked hers up with her left hand, peeled it, and ate each segment separately with her hands, ignoring her knife and fork.

The three looked at her silently, and she said, "Where I come from we eat oranges with our hands. Like chicken, with our hands only.

"By the way, how are Marc and Gabi?" she asked suddenly, wondering why she hadn't had a glimpse of their children.

"Marc is in his room, grounded for two weeks," Jakob replied.

"Why, whatever has he done?" She always wanted to know everything.

"He went into our room and dismantled all the drawers in the closet," Jakob said, and she thought to herself that the kid must have gone crazy, justifiably; but she said nothing and made a silent oath that her own children would be brought up in Israel.

On their way home from the dinner party, she told her husband, "Look how unhappy their children are." He disagreed with her, saying that children need a framework in which to be brought up.

"Children need love," she protested.

He agreed that Jakob might be a little too strict in raising his children, but was sure he loved them. She wasn't so sure, and she wondered to herself if Jakob's children loved him, their own father. She was sorry she had never asked Batya if she loved her father in spite of all the beatings she suffered at his hands.

"I want to go back to Israel," she said.

"Aren't you happy here?" he wanted to know.

"That's not the point. I want to live a small apartment in Tel Aviv with four children who eat oranges with their hands," she said instead of replying to his question, and later over the phone, she told her sister that she was suffocating.

"What are you suffocating from?" her sister asked, realizing that she must be suffering if she was phoning her rather than sending a letter.

"From the rules. There are too many rules here. Too many politenesses. All day long I find myself having to work out what I can and what I can't do. What a lady is permitted to do and what she isn't. I am not allowed to laugh with the owners of the local grocery store, and certainly not with the doorman, because I am a grande dame and it is not done here for a grande dame to consort with the lower classes. All those knives and forks are driving me nuts, and I even have to use them for eating an orange. An orange, do you get it? An orange, that's all. And the kids here are miserable."

"Aren't you exaggerating just a bit?" her sister asked her.

"I am not exaggerating at all. I am getting so pissed off."

"Maybe you're just bored?" her sister suggested.

"Maybe," she replied.

"Get yourself a dog, like I did," her wise sister advised her, and she went out and bought herself a delightful cocker spaniel puppy and named her Medi, which is short for Meidale. Now she had a reason to wander the streets in the afternoon with her new puppy. Except that his parents had to know what she needed this extra burden for.

"I love dogs," she said, "and besides, I'm pregnant," she announced to everyone at lunch, after Laura had brought in the lettuce salad.

Her husband looked at her, as did her mother and father-in-law, and silence reigned.

"How nice," said her husband, and went up to her and hugged and kissed her.

"Isn't this rather too soon?" Luna asked, and his father said nothing.

"Soon for what?" she asked.

"You know," Luna stammered, "you're young and only just embarking on your careers, and," she went on, "you're not even established yet."

"We'll get established as we go along," she replied, and looked into her father-in-law's silent eyes.

"We're both working, making good money," she added quietly.

Her husband continued to hug her and said nothing. In the end his father said that they had been married only a year and a half, and that it was a good idea to give the matter some serious consideration. "Look here," he added, "you've got a dog." And it sounded like, "What do you need a baby for? You've got a dog to keep you amused."

"Children like dogs," she said, and added that she was tired and wanted to sleep.

She called her sister in the evening, and then her parents, who screamed with joy at the news. Paula the Italian aunt came down to their apartment and told her emotionally that Luna had already reported the pregnancy; *"Bracha tova,"* she said, "and I'm really happy for you. Children bring joy." She started telling her what she should do to handle her morning sickness.

Later Luna called to apologize for their chilly reaction that afternoon and that she thought that she had every right to decide whatever she decides.

She said that she had made up her mind, and that was that.

That night she told her husband that he had six months to complete his Final Design Project if he wanted to be with her, because she was going back to Israel; she was taking the pregnancy and Medi, and she hoped he would be with her as well. "I want to have my baby in Israel, with my parents and my sister by my side," she told her husband.

Our National Pride Day

I stood on the balcony watching Ya'akov being beaten by his father with a belt and feeling terribly sorry for him. Someone must have snitched to his father that he was stealing from the grocer's. My sister came out to the balcony with a glass of milk and told me that I ought to drink milk, too.

I told her I didn't want to, and she said I must, or I would never grow.

"So what," I said and continued to feel sorry for Ya'akov, whose father was beating the life out of him. My sister told me that if I didn't drink my milk, she'd pour hers all over my head.

"I dare you," I replied, and she poured a whole glassful of milk all over me.

That evening I ran a high temperature, and my mother told my sister that it was because she poured milk over me, but on the way to the doctor's the next morning Mom explained that it was probably because I had caught tonsillitis again, and she hadn't meant it when she told my sister that it was because of her, but she was cross with her for wasting a glass of milk.

There was a long queue in the doctor's office, and we got number eighteen even though we'd arrived there first thing in the morning. Mom tried to fib by saying that she was number nine in line, but someone else was number nine and people started shouting at Mom that she was a liar. I was terribly ashamed.

When we left, we saw a policeman, and he asked me why I was crying. I told him I was sick, and that I was afraid I wouldn't get well before Independence Day.

He said of course I'd get well, because there's a whole week to go until Independence Day.

Because I was sick, Dad bought me a blackboard and colored chalks and my sister immediately called Sima, Rocha, and Yaffa down from the floor above us and said that she was the teacher and she was going to teach us how to write our names in English.

English is an easy language to write. All you do is scribble up and down; here and there you draw in a circle, and you have to take special care to join the letters together and leave a reasonable space between them so the words are separated and there you have it, English. Easy peasy. Not like Hebrew, which is a hard language to handle.

My sister wrote down her name and said that from now

on she would be known as Josephine, because she had decided that her name should be the same as that of the heroine in *Little Women*. After all, she explained to us, the name Josephine is the equivalent of Yosefa, which she shortened to Sefi, except that people who call their daughters Josephine are not Jews, and we are. She even started showing off how she could enunciate the *J* in Josephine the way they do in American movies, and forced us to do the same.

Dad explained to my sister that you can't just go around changing your name, and that she had been named for her grandfather, Yosef, and it's not their fault that she was born a girl and not a boy, and that a person's grandfather's memory has to be honored. And anyway, he said, names have to come from the Bible; you can't just invent all kinds of other names. My sister complained that all she'd ever wanted to be was special and different from everyone else and it's not fair that they had to give her a boy's name and that it's she and not they who'll have to bear that name for the rest of her life.

Sima wanted to be teacher too, but my sister wouldn't let her because the blackboard belonged to me.

"Then I want to be teacher," I piped up immediately, but my sister said that I've got tonsillitis and am therefore not allowed to talk.

In the evening, after they had forced me to eat some chicken soup, Mom leaned over me and recited the witches' prayer in Yiddish, spat three times, *tfu, tfu, tfu,* and forced me to say the words after her, words in Yiddish that I couldn't understand, and in the end, Dad and Sefi as well had to say Amen and Amen to the entire House of Israel. Four days later my temperature dropped and I was able to join in the Independence Day celebrations, the best holiday of our year.

On the evening before Independence Day we went up to Herzl Street in the Hadar neighborhood to watch all the youth movement kids dancing the hora, our hearts full of pride for having achieved a sovereign state of our own, despite all the tyrants and in spite of all the enemies that surround us on all sides.

We went to bed early so there would be no problem getting up at five o'clock the following morning.

The annual Israel Defense Forces parade, pride of the Jewish nation, was being held this year in Haifa. One year it's in Tel Aviv, the next in Jerusalem, and once every three years it takes place in Haifa.

We all woke up in time. Mom and Dad had already prepared the sandwiches, and we hurried off to grab a good spot in the middle of Ha'azma'ut Street, where the parade passes at ten o'clock; we had to be in the front row so no one could block our view of our national pride. We clapped our hands when the tanks rolled by, and we shouted for joy when we saw our soldiers, so proud and so handsome, and just see where we are now, despite Hitler, may his name be cursed for all of eternity, *tfu, tfu, tfu*—spit three times and

grasp a bunch of your hair, waiting for the first bird to arrive to save us from the curse so it shouldn't come back on
us, heaven forbid.

After all, every toddler knows that when you place a curse
on someone, you have to spit three times, grab a clump of
your hair, and wait for the first bird that comes your way.

My ever-practical sister explained that I should try not to
do any cursing unless I was sure that there were birds flying
in the sky; otherwise I might find myself holding on to my
hair the whole day long, and when there is no bird, you get
stuck with the curse. It's the same when you see a black cat.

There was a sudden downpour, and although Dad wanted
to stay to see the end of our national pride parade, Mom
wouldn't let us, because of my tonsillitis and the fact that
my temperature had gone down only a few days before.

Her water broke at eight o'clock on Friday evening at their home in Rishon le Zion. The man was so excited as he tried to pack her a bag for a three-day stay in hospital that things kept falling out of his hands. "But you're only thirty-seven weeks gone," he said, trying to cover his fears.

She asked him to make her a cup of coffee and calmly packed all the things she'd need for a three-day hospital stay: slippers, underpants, nursing bra, a dressing gown, and pajamas, since she hated those green polka-dot hospital-issue pajamas. She wouldn't have minded wearing the blue pajamas that male patients received but couldn't really imagine the hospital maternity ward providing her with men's pajamas. She was happy as she packed her bag. Happy that she was going to give birth to her baby, and even happier for being spared an additional three and a half weeks of a heavy and cumbersome pregnancy.

She placed all her makeup in the bag, but not before quickly smudging on some black eyeliner to emphasize her green eyes, and coloring her lips in a shade her husband favored. It took him all of ten minutes to make her a cup of muddy black coffee, not the real Turkish coffee her father would have prepared for her, and when he brought it to her in a mug—who for hell's sake drinks Turkish coffee out of a mug?—his hands were shaking. She felt her first contraction at that very moment. It wasn't quite as weak she had been led to expect by those experienced in this kind of thing. On the contrary, the contraction was aggressive enough to send her hurling from her seat on the bed next to the packed bag. The coffee spilled, turning her white duvet into a muddy brown sludge. She stood beside the bed, grasping its sides, and the man took the soiled duvet and removed its white cover. A dark stain remained on the white duvet.

This is not a good omen, she thought to herself, and she was scared. It would have been a luckier sign if the cup had at least been broken. But it's in the nature of a mug not to break easily, and only the muddy coffee spilled out and stained the white duvet her mother had bought her as part of her marriage dowry.

She wailed and laughed at the same time, thinking of the dowry the man had brought to their marriage: the apartment, the car, the furniture, a TV, a washing machine and dryer, dishwasher, kitchen utensils, an assortment of mixers and blenders, and a machine for making coffee; whereas the dowry her mother had given her consisted of the white duvet that she had paid for with the sweat of her brow, cleaning the homes of strangers on Mount Carmel.

They reached the hospital that evening at nine o'clock. In spite of the increasing contractions, she was happy to be giving birth on a Friday, like the Sabbath bride, divinely inspired by God. She was told to walk up and down, up and down, in order to intensify the contractions, but she had no cervical opening. With a two-finger opening you get sent back home.

Over and over she marched the length of the long corridor while her long-legged husband struggled to keep up with her. She was determined to give birth to her baby as dawn broke, and the swift walk was no more strenuous now than her daily routine with her cocker spaniel, Medi.

"Where's Medi?" she asked the man; she remembered that she hadn't said a proper good-bye to her beloved dog, in the heat of the spilled coffee and the premature contractions.

"At home," the man replied.

"What do you mean, at home? I could be held here for twenty-four hours." It didn't occur to her that her labor could take even longer.

"So I'll nip back home to take her down," the man tried to reassure her.

"And leave me here alone?" She was alarmed. "Where's my sister when I need her?" she murmured to herself.

"In New York. Would you like me to call your mother?" he asked her, hoping she'd refuse.

"No," she replied at once. "I don't need her here to spur me on in Romanian."

"Voy a dar a la luz"—she said the sentence in Spanish that she had liked when she discovered she was pregnant. *To give to the light.* What a nice way to describe the act of giving birth. "You only need to add the letter *y*, and you'll be giving your baby light as well as air." She huffed and puffed and took longer steps, her energy at boiling point.

"Where are you running off to?" He chased after her on his long legs. In her design for their wedding invitation, her sister had drawn a pair of long legs and the train of a wedding gown. "Come on, sit down for a moment. You've been marching for three hours already. Drink your coffee," he said, holding out a cup of coffee he'd taken from the vending machine.

"What's the time?" she asked.

"Five past midnight," he replied. "Shabbat."

She gave in and sat down to drink their machine-made Shabbat coffee. She loved that cappuccino they sold in hospital vending machines. It's the only thing you can put in your mouth in a hospital; everything else is utterly inedible.

"Do you know the Hebrew word for a machine that's become obsolete?" her man asked her, trying to distract her from another contraction that was so powerful as to almost draw the very life out of her body.

"Contraction after contraction and no opening," she said, disappointed. "The whore, she swallows," she added quickly.

"Who swallows?" He was focusing on the contraction.

"The machine. You asked for a word to describe a machine that's become obsolete. I hope I won't become obsolete after giving birth to this baby." She was suddenly gripped by an obscure fear, remembering the mug of black coffee spilling all over the white duvet her mother had given her as a marriage dowry.

A religious couple came and sat next to them, and the religious woman told them that this was her fourth baby but the first time she was giving birth on a Shabbat; she was happy as she said this.

At two in the morning they took her into the delivery room. The religious woman had been taken in half an hour before. She would no doubt give birth first, as she had plenty of experience and knew how to do it.

In the delivery room they could see the religious woman's husband in the cubicle next to theirs. She could hear the woman screaming at him, "What have you done to me, you bastard?" and was surprised to hear such language from an observant Jew. Where the hell did she learn to use such words? Her husband was embarrassed for her and told the man who was about to become a first-time father that he was used to his wife pouring out her anger on him with every contraction. She uses such profanities only when she's giving birth to a baby, he said, defending his wife.

In sorrow you shall bring forth children; and yet your fury shall be on your husband, she thought to herself as she competed with the other woman over which of them could shout the louder.

"I should be pregnant all my life, if that's the only chance I get to curse the whole world and its wife," she said to the two men standing nearby. "But on second thought, with pains such these I don't wish myself more than one more birth. It's far too painful," she said, trying to amuse herself and her baby's father.

He held her hand, blew on her tormented face, wiped the sweat from her brow, and caressed her.

"Would you like me to massage your feet?" he asked, and she said no, her feet didn't hurt.

A good man, she thought to herself. I'd marry him, if we weren't already married.

Noa was born at five in the morning. Five minutes later, the religious woman also gave birth to a baby girl. It was as if the two women were in competition, and her Noa had beaten the religious woman's baby, to be born on the holy Sabbath.

"It's a girl," her man said to her, and there were tears in his eyes.

"Why are you crying?" she asked him. "Are you disappointed?"

"If you'd seen the scissors that doctor used to cut you up like a chicken, you'd be crying, too," he replied.

"Ay, ay, what does the pain matter now? The baby's out, isn't she?" She looked at the man suspiciously; maybe she wasn't out?

"It's the placenta. Push down hard," the doctor ordered, his face in front of her wide-open legs.

She pushed hard and screamed like a banshee.

"The placenta's out. I'm cutting. Don't move," said the doctor. "I'm starting to sew you up."

"Will it hurt?" she asked, exhausted.

"Even if it does, you won't feel a thing," the doctor said as he was stitching her up.

"My mother would never do any sewing on the Sabbath," she whispered to her man, who was holding her hand, burrowing into her, at one with her agony.

"He's stitching you up exactly as you do with your rice-stuffed chicken dish," he said.

"With pine nuts and raisins," she added.

"Best in the world, the way you do your stuffed chicken." He had learned her idiosyncratic, ungrammatical way of speaking, and sometimes spoke Hebrew the way she did.

"You like my stuffed chicken," she stated.

"It's you I love," he said and gave her a long kiss on her lips.

When he let go of her lips she told him that stuffed chicken would be the first thing she would teach Noa to cook when she took her first steps in life. "I have a Romanian recipe that is passed down from one generation to another," she explained, and he placed his long fingers on her mouth. "Don't talk now; just rest," he said to the woman who had just given birth to his baby daughter.

"Is he still sewing me up?" she asked, feeling nothing except his fingers on her lips.

"I'm almost done," said the doctor, "you can close your eyes and fall asleep."

"How does she look, my baby girl?" she remembered to ask her husband, with her eyes closed.

"Perfect. Beautiful, just like you," he replied.

She drifted into blissful sleep.

New Shoes

I awoke in the middle of the night happy with the knowledge that something good had happened. I tried to think what it could have been, and then remembered; I peeped under my bed and saw my new shoes, sparkling away even in the dark of night. I stroked my shoes and smelled their new smell and then laid them down carefully on the floor so they wouldn't get dirty. I fell asleep again, happy.

Yesterday the whole family had gone down to the wadi, near the movie house, to buy me and my sister shoes for the first time in our lives.

I wanted black patent leather shoes like the ones my sister's friend Chaya had, because they had a permanent shine; and my sister wanted red shoes.

Mom tried to persuade her to go for black or white shoes, because they go with everything, but my sister was adamant that red goes with everything too.

The shopkeeper measured my foot on a metal shoe gauge with numbers running up its middle and told my mother that I was a size 28.

"So what size shall I bring?" he asked. Dad said to bring a size 29, but Mom wanted 31, so they'd last for the next three years, as my feet grew.

They compromised in the end on a size 30. The shopkeeper brought out a pair of black patent leather shoes, pushed a lot of cotton wool into the shoes so they wouldn't fall off, and let me try them on. He brought a pair of red shoes for my sister, not patent leather.

"I don't have red patent leather," he apologized.

"So what?" My sister snatched a shoe from him and sat straight down to try it on. "I don't like shiny shoes," she said, and looked at me in disdain.

I stroked my black patent leather shoes, and my sister stroked her red shoes, so that Mom and Dad would see that we loved our new shoes and wouldn't suddenly change their minds and decide not to buy them for us.

Dad told the shopkeeper that he would pay for the shoes in nine installments, and that he needn't worry.

"I'll have the money to pay for the shoes," he said; "don't forget there's a general election in November." And the man nodded his head in understanding and straight away wrapped up our shoes with no misgivings whatsoever.

It was the first Passover in our lives that my sister and I had new shoes that had been bought especially for us.

In subsequent years, they bought new shoes for my sister, whereas I got to wear her castoffs.

It was also the first Passover that my sister and I were each given a new white pleated skirt. Instead of being paid in money for shortening dozens of such skirts, Mom had received two new white pleated skirts that just needed taking up, for her two daughters.

Mom packed our new skirts and new shoes in a suitcase, and we took the train to our uncles and aunts in Hedera for the seder.

She was pleased that her daughters were dressed in new clothes for this seder and proud that she was able, at long last, to show them off to Niku, her brother, and Eva, his wife.

We arrived at the railway station and joined a very long queue at the ticket counter. The train carriages were also already packed with people traveling to Tel Aviv.

Dad squeezed me, my sister, and the suitcase in through the open window and we saved seats until he and Mom could buy tickets.

When the train set out at last from the station, I stuck my head out of the window, and Dad shouted at me that I would get my head chopped off by a telephone pole. But I didn't care. I loved the feel of the wind on my face, and to watch all the houses seeming to fly past as we gathered momentum; sometimes I'd see people waving to the train from inside their homes, and I would wave back enthusiastically.

A bus waited for us at the station when we alighted in Hedera, and I didn't understand why an entire bus would be waiting for only four people, or even a few others, getting off the train, or how the bus driver knew the time of our arrival with such accuracy, so that we didn't have to wait for it four hours as we sometimes had to wait for a bus in Haifa.

My sister explained to me that the bus knew in advance when the train was due to arrive, just as in Haifa we knew when the train was setting off in the direction of Hedera, but I didn't really understand what she was saying.

Niku and his wife, Eva, had immigrated to Israel in the 1930s. Before obtaining a senior position with the Histadrut, the General Labor Federation, Niku had been a *ghaffir* with the Jewish Settlement Police. After doing their bit drying the swamps, Niku and Eva settled in Hedera, where they built their own little corner of heaven and raised their three children. Niku and Eva believed that if they couldn't succeed in turning Mom and Dad into instant Israelis, then at least we, the girls, would rid ourselves of all our Romanian mannerisms and become prickly little sabras with all the necessary Zionist idiosyncrasies built in. They were annoyed with Mom for not taking the trouble to learn Hebrew, when she should be speaking only Hebrew with us. Mom argued with Niku that he should have taught his children another language; if not Romanian, then at least Yiddish, since it's always important to know another language, apart from Hebrew.

But Niku was adamant—only Hebrew! So my mother, who never once went to an *ulpan* for learning Hebrew, and in any case was hard of hearing, spoke to Niku's children in a mixture of a little Hebrew, a little Yiddish, and a little sign language. And they all understood her.

Of course, Rivkale, Itzik, and Yossi had been nurtured from birth on a love of Zion and were perfect Israelis. We townies from Haifa, from Wadi Salib, no less, envied them. We envied them first of all because they lived in a lovely house, with a garden and flowers and trees and a lawn; and most important, they had fruit trees—orange, lemon, plum, and loquat. They even had an orange press in the shed in the garden, which they used to squeeze fresh orange juice for us and supply us with vitamins. Altogether, the ability to pick as much as we wanted, to eat as much as we could until one night we twisted and turned with agonizing stomachache from stuffing ourselves on plums, made us feel we were in the Garden of Eden. And second, we envied them because in their home they spoke only Hebrew.

At night we slept in Yossi's room. His parents opened out his steel bed, raised the bed beneath it, and joined the two. Sefi was first to grab the better side—the one next to the wall. Yossi slept on the other side—the one taken by people who get up early in the morning; at five thirty that hyperactive kid was already awake. I was stuck with the crack along the center of the bed, which was actually a gap measuring several centimeters across between the two beds, because of the significant difference in height. I didn't sleep a wink all night because I was terribly embarrassed about sleeping with a boy, even though he was my cousin, and anyway, I was frightened of farting in the middle of the night and not being able to keep it quiet. All night I lay there like a statue, not breathing or turning over. Rather like porcupines making love—very, very carefully.

When we went to Rahamim's grocery store in the morning to pick up a few things the grown-ups had forgotten to buy for the seder, I saw Yossi push a packet of candy and a bar of chocolate into his pocket. Rahamim asked Yossi what to jot down on his mom's account, and Yossi told him just the things we'd been sent out to buy. "Are you sure that's all?" Rahamim asked Yossi, and the little thief said that he was one hundred percent certain.

I snitched to Dad that I'd seen Yossi stealing stuff from Rahamim's grocery store, and Dad said that he wasn't a thief.

"Yes, he is," I told my dad, "he stole candy and chocolate."

Dad told me that even if Yossi thinks he's stealing, Eva pays for everything later, because Rahamim also writes down everything he's seen Yossi putting in his pocket, so as not to shame him.

That evening we wore our new white pleated skirts and I wore my new black patent leather shoes and my sister wore her red matte leather shoes. My sister wore the close-fitting blue top with the red buckle, which of course went beautifully with her shoes. I wore a brown top, and it didn't match, even though I had black patent leather shoes that were supposed to go with everything.

We sat down ceremoniously at the perfectly laid table, as befits a traditional kosher family seder. Although Niku and Eva were secular and did not even fast on Yom Kippur, as my parents did, they never skipped so much as a single letter of the Passover Haggadah; we waited patiently for God to bring forth the Children of Israel out of Egypt with clenched fist and an outstretched arm.

I was waiting only for the *afikoman* and watched Niku's every move to see where he was hiding it. I noticed nothing suspicious about him, and when the time came to look for the *afikoman*, we all spread out across the length and breadth of the room. My sister searched the sofa, Itzik moved all the cushions aside, Yossi searched in all possible cracks, and I made straight for the pile of records in the dresser. I flicked through all the Russian records that were there and that Eva loved to listen to because she had come from Russia. When I discovered a record in Hebrew, by Yaffa Yarkoni, I pulled it out of the pile and felt the lumpiness of the *afikoman*. Yes!!! I'd found the *afikoman*. Now I could ask for anything I could think of.

I wanted to ask for a bicycle. But I was embarrassed to, because I knew that it cost a lot of money, and anyway, with all those hills in Haifa, no one could ride a bicycle.

I wanted to ask for a football, but was embarrassed because I was a girl.

Most of all I wanted to ask for a blue top with a red buckle, but I knew that such tops exist only in America.

"What shall I ask for?" I whispered to my sister.

"Ask for a book," my sister advised me quickly; "it makes the best impression."

So, to defy my sister, who wanted a book for herself, I asked for a coloring book. "One for me and another for my sister," I added.

My mother glowed with pride at this demonstration of sisterly love, never suspecting that I was only being contrary not asking for a reading book because this was what my sister wanted.

She awoke to see the religious woman nursing her baby. The girl had been named Rivka.

"Here's Rivka for you to feed," said the ward sister to the religious woman and attached a black-haired baby to her breast; which is how she knew that the religious woman's baby was called Rivka.

Two days later, when she walked into the room they shared with two other women, she heard the religious woman refer to her behind her back as "that poor thing. She delivered a sick baby. Praise be to God that my own baby was born healthy." She was nursing her Rivka and talking to two ultra-Orthodox women who were sitting on her bed. The three women fell silent as soon as they noticed her climbing onto her bed and turning her back on them.

She didn't understand at first why she was being ignored,

not having Noa brought to her to feed. When she saw the religious woman nursing Rivka for a third time, while she herself was still without a baby in her arms, she asked the sister about her Noa.

"Why aren't you bringing Noa to me so I can feed her?" she asked; could it be construed as an eccentric request, to be allowed to feed the baby she had given birth to more than twenty-four hours earlier and whose perfect face she had never even seen?

"I don't know," the sister replied. "Ask the doctor," she added, and walked out.

"Where's my husband?" she shouted at the sister.

The sister poked her head in and pointed out that some new mothers were asleep, and would she please keep her voice down. "Your husband is waiting outside until Rivka has finished nursing."

She fumbled for her slippers and went out in her pajamas to the hospital corridor. She hadn't been able to find her robe and couldn't remember where her husband had told her he'd placed it. It was freezing cold in the corridor, and she was shivering all over, although it could also have been out of fear.

He was waiting outside, unaware of the storm raging in her soul.

"Have you seen her?" she asked him immediately.

"I haven't had a chance yet. They told me they'd talk to us soon."

"What do they have to talk to us about?" she attacked him.

"I haven't a clue. Isn't it accepted procedure?"

"No. It isn't accepted procedure," she replied, as if, after giving birth for the first time in her life, she cared what was accepted procedure and what wasn't. Besides, even in school she had never liked those people who were "accepted." In fact, she quite loathed them, and everything that was "accepted" tended to raise her anxiety level.

"Let's go and see her." She dragged him, tottering in her slippers at a speed that would have graced a participant in the Tel Aviv marathon. They reached the nursery and asked a nurse where their daughter was.

After checking the baby's name and that of her parents, the nurse went from bassinet to bassinet, only to return with the information that their baby was not there.

"Where is she, then?" she asked, her stomach doing an about-turn, feeling as if any second she would collapse right there.

"When did you give birth?" asked the pleasant nurse.

"Yesterday," she replied.

"And they haven't brought her to you to nurse?"

"Yes, they brought her and I lost her," she screeched in response. "Where on earth is my baby?"

The man supported her and asked if there was someone there qualified to tell them where their baby had disappeared.

"Maybe she's in the Premature Babies Unit?" replied the nurse, who may have been raised at home on 1950s tales of kidnapped Yemenite babies and realized that something was not quite in order here. "Maybe she was born prematurely? Did you give birth early?"

"Is a birth weight of five and three-quarters pounds considered premature?" her husband asked.

"No," said the nurse, "a little small, but certainly not a preemie."

"Premature, preemie, where the hell is the Premature Babies Unit?" she asked.

"At the end of the corridor," the nurse offered.

This time he was dragging her along quickly, her slippers slip-sliding relentlessly off her feet. They reached the end of the corridor and pulled up in front of a reinforced door with round windows, like a ship's. The door was locked. They knocked on the door, and the ward sister, who was dressed in operating theater greens and had a surgical mask on her face, came out to them with a warm smile on her face. They introduced themselves, and the nurse immediately said she would call the department head. Dr. Mogilner, according to the identity badge on his white coat, a silver-haired doctor with a heavy South American accent, informed them that their baby was suffering from respiratory difficulties.

"What do you mean, respiratory difficulties?" They both caught their breath at the same time.

"The baby turns blue, and we are unable to find the reason for it," the doctor said and led them gently into his office. He asked her about the pregnancy and if it had been normal.

"She was absolutely fine," her husband said at once, as if

to make it clear that she had made no problems and that he had been with her all the way.

She looked at him and said she wasn't quite certain that the pregnancy was completely normal.

"What do you mean?" he asked.

"I mean I was under terrible stress because I had dragged you to Israel and I was afraid you wouldn't be able to make it here and you'd have to give up a lot of the things you were used to, and maybe you wouldn't find a job and then your back ached and I had to do a lot of the house moving myself, even though I was pregnant, and then your aunt died . . ." She spoke in a stream of words, as if spewing up the last few months clean out of her guts.

"But everything is all right now," he said, as if telling her not to worry. "I am glad we made aliyah and that our daughter was born a sabra."

"Can emotional stress affect the health of an unborn baby?" she asked Dr. Mogilner, who replied, "Absolutely."

"And what about the delivery, was it normal?" the department head asked gently.

"I gave birth here, in this hospital. Don't your records tell you anything about my delivery?" she asked. Maybe something had happened in the course of the delivery that she had been unaware of.

The doctor scrutinized the report in front of him and told them that the delivery had passed without any particular hitch.

"Would you like to see her?" he asked, and they both jumped out of their seats and followed him. They wanted to go in with him but were told that they would first have to wash their hands, put on a green gown that had to be tied at the back, cover their shoes with green covers that also had to be tied carefully, and of course tie a mask carefully over their faces, so as not to introduce a single germ into the preemie unit. When they first tried, they got confused with the back and front laces, but in time, over the three long months that their baby was hospitalized, they became very practiced and were always ready to enter the sterile room within seconds.

They looked down at her in wonder. Their baby was lying there like the most perfect angel they had ever seen in their lives. Every organ and every limb was in place; nothing was missing. She was naked.

"Isn't she cold?" she asked the blue-eyed nurse, to whom she had immediately taken a liking, because she had gone straight to the incubator and turned Noa, so they could to see her in all her glory.

"No. She's not cold." Zohara smiled at her. She had noticed the nurse's name tag on her green uniform. "The incubator is the warmest place in the hospital," she reassured the concerned parents.

She remembered the weekly visit in eighth grade to the Kfar Galim agricultural school, for a whole day working in the fields. That year winter had been particularly cold and wet, and when the town kids were given the choice of jobs—they had, after all, volunteered; or more accurately, their services had been offered to the agricultural school—every one of them had chosen to work in the fruit harvest. As Haifa townies, they wanted to eat as much as they could off the trees. She asked their instructor if there were any other options.

He suggested work in the kitchen or harvesting potatoes, but she shook her head.

"Don't you want to be with all your classmates in the fruit harvest?" The instructor appeared to despair of her.

"I see enough of them all week," she said.

"I have an incubator full of chicks," he told her.

"What would I have to do there?" She was instantly interested. On a cold wet winter's day an incubator sounded good.

"Nothing much," he said. "Just keep an eye on the chicks, make sure they don't get cold."

He took her into a kind of dwarfs' hut, where she had to bend her head in order to get in and then could only either sit or lie on the straw that had been spread over the hard dry earth. It was nice in there. Not for nothing was the place called a hothouse for chicks, which scurried around tickling her feet, since she had immediately taken off her shoes. The place made her feel like Gulliver in the land of the little people, and she loved the sensation of all those chicks climbing over her body as if she was a sack of straw. She watched them for hours; at first they all appeared a uniform yellow, but she gradually learned to distinguish between them.

She identified the cock of the coop, the arrogant one, the

pampered one, and the lazy one. When she noticed the runt, the one who didn't know how to push his way to the food, she adopted him for herself and gave him a special portion of food, just for himself, so he'd grow big and strong. The next week she brought a book with her and read it out loud to her chicks, as if telling them a story. She took special care of the little runt she had adopted and made a point of feeding him before various other pushers-in could get to the food. According to the laws of nature, the weak survives only if it has someone to look out for it. Over six weeks, her chick grew to be like all his peers, and in the meantime the skies had cleared, and it had become too hot for her inside the hothouse. She told the instructor that she wanted to work in the groves, and she was able to bring home lots of freshly picked apples. Everyone was happy. Watching her beautiful baby lying naked in her incubator, she remembered that time at agricultural school and thought suddenly that the instructor must have devised this job especially for her so that she would learn how to take care of that weak little chick.

Noa opened her eyes wide.

"They are blue. Like your mother's and your aunt Anna's," she said to her husband.

"The color can change," another nurse said as she walked by them—as if what mattered to them was whether the baby's eyes were going to change from blue to brown or to green or amber, and not the respiratory problems she suffered from, for which the doctors had no explanation.

August Disasters

A month later two very sad things happened to my sister, and she spent all her time crying. Dad was unable to console her, not even when he explained that disasters always happen in August, because that was the month in which the destruction of the Temple took place. Our dad wouldn't even let us go to the beach on Tisha b'Av, because it's a day on which a lot of people drown, even though there were plenty of lifeguards around, because they weren't on strike at that time.

My sister's best friend Chaya, the most popular girl in the class, left Israel for America after her uncles who lived there had managed to persuade her parents that the future was much greener for the Jews in New York, and besides, it's cheaper to give a doll as a gift without having to mail it to Israel and pay postage; and Hanna, my sister's beloved homeroom teacher, was killed in a road accident.

The sudden and simultaneous loss of the two women she admired most was an unbearably heavy blow to my sister. Moreover, Chaya took with her all her dolls and the piano that my sister loved to run her fingers across the keys of. And for Hanna, who nurtured the neighborhood's children even though she herself was from the Carmel, to suddenly disappear from her life was a terrible loss. Young people in those days got killed only in wars, not in anything as banal as road accidents.

In order to console her, Dad took us for a ride on the newly opened Carmelit light railway through all the stations from downtown Haifa and right up to the top of Mount Carmel.

Only after all four of us (yes, Dad agreed to take Mom, too) had watched to see that nothing bad happened to any of the other people did we muster the courage to step onto the escalator. It was then that my new shoe—one of the pair my parents had bought me for Passover—got caught in the escalator, and I watched it as it bounced over the stairs and was squashed on the other side. Brokenhearted, I cried for those stairs to stop moving so that I could go and rescue my shoe, but it was no good. The stairs continued to move, mangling to death one shoe of the first pair of new shoes I had ever owned.

I was still wailing when my sister burst out laughing, and Mom and Dad joined her; pleased to see her forget for a moment her tragic losses, they were keen to encourage her to laugh more.

We walked around the Carmel neighborhood for a while and then went down, on foot of course, with me hobbling along on one shoe, holding the other, ragged and ruined by the escalator in the new Carmelit light railway. My lovely new shoe had lost all its patent leather shine.

The next day we wore our new white pleated skirts from Passover even though it was a regular weekday, and Mom took us to the head office of the Carmelit light railway, with me grasping my disgraced shoe in my hand.

The manager looked at my sad eyes and explained to Mom that he couldn't reimburse me for one new shoe. If I had been injured, or squashed to death, for that they have insurance. But not for a single shoe that got mangled because I didn't know when to step on that modern escalator that moves of its own accord and doesn't have to be operated.

"Still," he said, in reparation, "the girl will get ten free rides on the Carmelit."

Mom immediately told him to make it ten free rides for the whole family, and when, to her surprise, the manager agreed, she was quick to add, "Round trip. So we won't have to walk down from the Carmel to Wadi Salib." The manager agreed to this too, and we went away satisfied, determined to celebrate our victory.

On the street corner an Arab kid was selling prickly pears. We went over and joined the queue to buy some. In front of us stood a fat man who ate one and then another pear and yet another and another and another. And every time we thought he had finished eating, the glutton's sharp eye picked out our prickly pear, pointed to it, and the Arab kid picked it up in his scratched hands and sliced it, peeled off the prickly skin, and handed it to the fat pig who stood in front of us in the queue. By the time my mother shouted at him to give pears to the girls as well, the fat slob had put back at least forty already. The boy peeled two nice juicy prickly pears and handed them to us. But no sooner had Mom pointed out other pears for him to peel than the boy noticed an approaching policeman, and since he had no license to sell prickly pears at the entrance to the Carmelit, he quickly gathered all his goods together and disappeared to the right, down the alleyways of the Turkish market. We were devastated because the fat man had eaten all our prickly pears, and hadn't even paid for them; Mom reckoned that it was certainly he who had called the policeman, but not before he'd finished gobbling down all the prickly pears.

The policeman walked up and asked us if we'd seen the direction the Arab kid had run off in. The prickly pear thief pointed in the direction of the boy's escape. Mom told the policeman that the man was lying and that she'd seen with her own eyes how that that man had stolen all the prickly pears off that poor kid who was only trying to make a living, and anyway, the boy had run off in the opposite direction. The policeman, who had no illusions about the ability of adults to lie, turned to my sister and asked her if she'd seen where the prickly pear seller had disappeared to. He must have decided that a nine-and-a-half-year-old girl in a white pleated skirt wouldn't lie.

My sister pointed in the same direction my mother had.

The policeman hesitated for a moment, and I waved my mangled shoe and asked him why should he believe that liar who ate all our prickly pears and was also very fat.

The policeman set out in the direction Mom had sent him, and we made slowly to the right, where we found the Arab boy with the prickly pears and bought another one each, paid him, and went on our way.

We were very proud of our mother for misleading the policeman and defending the Arab boy. Not only did that fat bastard eat up his entire livelihood, but that he should do time in jail for it as well?

But Dad decided that a round-trip ticket on the Carmelit was not enough to make up to a girl for the loss of two important women in her life and a few days later he came home carrying a large cardboard box. We all gathered around it, trying to guess what was inside.

My sister was first to guess and said: "It's a radio!"

Mom hoped it might be a small manual washing machine, one with a handle that has to be turned and then the laundry comes out clean and would relieve her of the revolting Thursday-night laundry burden. I thought it was a large doll that Dad had decided to buy for us to share, now that he had some money, because soon, in November, there'd be a general election, and Chaya had taken all her dolls with her to America, but it was indeed a radio. It was a brown radio with a plain wood case and rounded corners and a green dial that lit up when the radio was switched on and words that come out of it with music. Most of the time the radio was switched off, because electricity costs money, and once a day Mom and Dad listened to the news in Romanian.

And there was another surprise from Dad at the end of the month, when he took us to be filmed for an American movie. It was a real movie; and he even made some money out of it. For this he had needed nepotism, *protekzia*, and the party arranged for Dad and his family to be extras on the movie because this time, just before the elections, they were buttering him up more than usual after learning that our house had been the only one to avoid being sprayed with stones during the riots in Wadi Salib, unlike all the other Ashkenazi houses.

It was a movie about a thirtysomething American woman who realizes that her childhood sweetheart has survived the Holocaust and is living in Israel, and she has arrived on a ship from America to meet the love of her life, whom she hasn't seen for about fifteen years. Of course she had refused to marry in America, because in her heart of hearts she had always believed that her beloved had survived the horrors of the Holocaust. And he hadn't married in Israel, but had listened ardently to the daily radio program *Seeking Relatives*, until he'd managed to locate her. They meet on the wharf as she disembarks from the ship, dressed in a pale pink suit and pink hat and holding a white bag. Her beloved is waiting for her at the bottom of the gangway, holding a bouquet of fresh flowers. We were extras, waiting for our relatives who had just arrived in Israel on the same ship. The actress held on to the railing, trying not to pass out in anticipation of meeting up again with the man of her dreams. According to the stage instructions meted out by the director, we were required to applaud each time any of the travelers walked down the gangway. Over the course of several hours we watched as the actress went up and came down the ship's gangway to the applause of the extras, until she was finally reunited in a passionate kiss with her beloved who was waiting below. They kissed time and time again, and each time the actor was provided with a fresh bouquet of flowers. Sefi and I soaked up every word that was said in English, relished every moment in the presence of genuine American actors, and prayed that it would never, ever end. Our happiness knew no bounds. Besides, we knew that Dad was making money just from our standing there. But the fact is that we would have stood there for days on end for nothing, the director need only have asked. In the end we even took all the bouquets back home with us.

For a long time they stood gazing down at their perfect little baby; then Noa began suddenly to turn blue and her tiny fists beat at the air as if asking, Whence would my salvation come? Her mouth was pursed tightly, and her entire body appeared to be struggling against something they couldn't see. In the incubator, all the instruments started beeping. The nurse tried to lead her out, but she refused to budge. The nurse pushed her lightly and inserted more oxygen into the incubator, but Noa turned bluer; she was twenty-six hours old.

The baby opened her mouth wide as if trying to shout, changed her mind, and started crying, a long silent wail. It wasn't the demanding cry of a hungry newborn baby, but the silent cry of a newborn wanting to live; a sad cry. The instruments stopped beeping. Her breathing gradually returned; her tiny, perfect mouth was slightly open. She looked at them, and she felt that her baby was reassured and knew she was safe with her parents nearby, although this had been their first meeting. She inserted her sterilized hand through the round opening and stroked the baby's soft head. She loved her so.

Zohara said that it was about time she tried feeding her baby.

"Hasn't she eaten anything until now?" she asked, slightly vexed that they had been starving her so-tiny baby.

"She's been given fluids intravenously." Only then did she notice the tube that was connected to the baby's minute foot. "We still don't know what is causing her respiratory problem, and we've run all kinds of tests on her, but we still don't have any explanations. Let's make a first attempt at feeding her."

"With a bottle?" asked the new father.

"Through a tube," replied Zohara, and tried inserting one into the baby's right nostril. After several attempts, Zohara, with her magical smile, called Dr. Mogilner and told him that she was unable to insert the tube through the baby's nostril. Dr. Mogilner stood next to the angel in white, watching her trying to insert a new tube, this time through the left nostril; again, she failed.

They were terrified, since it was at this very moment that they were beginning to realize that for some unknown reason their baby was unable to breathe, and it was also impossible to feed her. The man held her hand with all his strength, as if trying to draw courage from it. But Dr. Mogilner seemed very troubled. He asked Zohara to take two new tubes and try once again to insert them into the baby's nostrils. Zohara tried again, but failed.

"The nostrils are blocked." She looked at the doctor in desperation.

"Excellent." For the first time Dr. Mogilner seemed to shine. "That's the reason for this baby's respiratory problems."

He turned to them, pleased. "The baby's nostrils are completely blocked, and that is what is causing the blueness. This is the first such case I have encountered personally in the twenty years I have been a specialist in premature babies."

"Is that good or bad?" she asked at once.

"It's solvable," he said, and appeared extremely excited. "Now we can start treating the problem."

Dr. Mogilner asked Zohara to bring an airway device, and with utmost gentleness, inserted into the baby a kind of small hollow tube whose sides were fixed to her mouth. "Now your baby will be able to breathe," he said to the worried parents and watched her until her breathing was regular and relaxed. The device held the baby's mouth open and enabled her to breathe through it.

They looked in wonder at the child's regular breathing and her extraordinarily beautiful face.

"This is the most beautiful baby we've ever had in this preemie unit," said Nurse Zohara, and Dr. Mogilner immediately agreed with her.

"She's the most beautiful baby we've ever had," said the man, his eyes shining.

"You are looking at a miracle," said Dr. Mogilner.

"A miracle that you discovered the problem?" she asked.

"No. A medical miracle that the baby has managed to remained alive for twenty-six hours without being able to breathe." As they watched her wordlessly, the doctor explained that newborn babies don't have the instinct to open their mouths in order to breathe. "Only at one month old, sometimes only two months, do they develop the instinct to breathe through their mouth. I have no explanation for the miracle that your baby, with her nose completely blocked, has managed to survive all those hours without air."

Hand of God, she thought to herself, and realized that she had given birth to a little angel with enormous blue eyes and God by her side.

According to standard procedure, she was released from hospital three days later; Noa remained in the Premature Baby Unit for an indefinite period.

"You have a very sick baby," the doctor said, trying to explain the gravity of the situation. "Fortunately we have successfully solved the issue of the blueness, but the blockage of her nose is only a symptom of another fundamental problem that we haven't yet managed to locate. Her blood tests lead us to suspect a problem in her autoimmune system, but we still have to check other things, and she has to be under observation twenty-four hours a day."

"Can I come back every two or three hours to nurse her?" she asked.

"Right now you have to rest at home," Dr. Mogilner told her in his heavy South American accent, with the gentleness that is apparently typical of heads of Premature Babies Units.

"Why?" She was offended. "Isn't my milk good enough?"

"She's breathing through her mouth," her husband pointed out at once.

"She won't be able to breathe if she's at the breast," the doctor explained, when she still didn't understand that Noa's mouth mustn't be closed over a breast or the teat of a feeding bottle.

"The only way she can be fed is through intubation," said the doctor. "We'll supply you with a breast pump so you can express your milk, which we'll then feed to your baby through the tube. There is no substitute for mother's milk if the baby is to get all its immunities." And he added, "All the mothers in the preemie unit express milk so that we can feed their babies."

"And when will Noa be released?" She insisted on knowing his prognosis.

"I haven't a clue," the doctor told her candidly. "Certainly not in the near future."

She went back home with the things she had packed for the birth, and on the way to their car, they saw the religious couple about to drive off, their fourth baby in its mother's arms. They looked on enviously.

Leaving their hearts in the Premature Babies Unit, they returned to an empty house. A large coffee stain graced the mattress of their bed. He put fresh sheets on the bed and inserted the white duvet into a blue cover, so she wouldn't see it in its shame. He knew how fond she was of blue. He filled the bath with hot water and mineral bath salts and wanted to help her undress, but she preferred to be alone with herself when she washed the hospital off her body, a term that turned over the years into a catchphrase they both used when they returned from hospital after a long day of treatments—to take a shower in order to wash away the hospital and to vigorously scrub off the germs they had brought with them. Completely immersed in the warm water, she lay quietly, motionlessly, checking how long she could lie underwater without air. She was a heavy smoker, so her possibilities for airtime without air were rather limited. It's no wonder that since the telephone companies took control of airtime, they've been charging so much money for it. It's an expensive commodity, air. She surfaced from the water all at once with a cry of agony. At that very moment, the man came into the bathroom with a pair of clean underpants and pajamas and laid them on the side of the sink. He knew her aversion to mixing up clean and dirty clothes in the bathroom—it reminded her of poverty—but he didn't want her to step naked out of the warm bathroom; February is the coldest month of the year in Israel, and in the empty house, without their baby girl, the cold penetrated her soul. In spite of the hot bath, she shivered all over as she climbed in under the blue duvet, unable to control herself. She consoled herself with the knowledge that the preemie unit was centrally heated, and in the incubator, her Noa wasn't suffering from the cold.

"How is she going to breathe, our baby?" she asked the man from out of the furnace of her body.

"Like deep-sea divers," he replied. "She'll get used to it, she's a strong baby."

"I wasn't able to just now, in the bath," she said.

"You had a choice," he told her.

"Have you tried it too?" she asked him.

"Three days already I've been holding my nose closed with my fingers to see what it's like."

She fell asleep and awoke in the middle of the night, her entire body shivering and her teeth chattering uncontrollably. She was burning up with fever. The man brought her a thermometer; her temperature had shot up to 104 degrees Fahrenheit.

"I think you might have pneumonia," he said.

"What's it like?" she asked.

"Pneumonia?" he asked.

"Stopping up your nose and not breathing?" she asked back.

"A nightmare," he replied.

For nine days she lay in bed with a severe case of pneumonia, a raging fever, and a terrible sense of guilt for being unable to stand beside her daughter's incubator. Her husband visited the preemie unit every day and didn't bring back any encouraging news. Anything Noa was fed through the tube, she vomited back up again; she continued to lose weight, and still there was no clear picture of what she was suffering from, except for a mother deficiency. Because of the pneumonia and the antibiotics she had been obliged to take, she was unable to express her milk, and her breasts shrank as her milk dried up. She felt like an empty vessel, utterly useless.

Her mother came from Haifa for a few days to care for her, leaving her sick husband in the care of a good neighbor, even though she herself suffered from extremely high blood pressure.

Bianca recited her silent prayer, words in an unknown language, spit three times at her burning head and Amen, three times. But her temperature didn't drop.

Bianca was extremely depressed, what with her husband sick in Haifa, her daughter consumed by fever and a severe case of pneumonia, her newborn baby granddaughter hospitalized in a serious condition, and her witch's prayer not proving itself.

Between one hallucination and the next, she tried to make her mother laugh with stories about her father, when his senility had already passed the brink of tears and there was nothing to do but laugh at his antics. She had visited them unexpectedly in their home in Haifa when she was in the eighth month of her pregnancy, and her mother ran off to the market to buy food so that the fetus inside her would become familiar with Romanian cuisine. Her father, who seemed uncharacteristically angry, complained to her that Bianca had thrown away his black shoes that he had only just finished polishing. During the last year of his life, he had loved polishing shoes. He would sit for hours, completely focused on his shoes, brushing them forward and back, back and forth, with the polish and the cloth from side to side, then with the brush, polishing them to a high shine, as if the shine he gave to his old shoes reminded him of the shining highlights of his life.

"She's probably trying to get back at me for throwing away all her *shmattes*," her dad explained to her with the healthy logic of an absolutely demented mind, the result of the multiple strokes he had suffered over the last year.

"Mom can't have thrown away anything of yours," she tried to explain to him, with a logic that really was healthy. "Did she throw away the toilet paper from the attic?" she asked her father.

"Not that," he replied, "but those black shoes that I just finished polishing, she did throw away," he insisted.

"So, quick, before she gets back from the market, let's throw out all the toilet paper." She wanted to take the edge off her father's anger, by disposing of those rolls of toilet paper that her mother had pilfered from the customs when she cleaned there fifteen years before and saved in the attic for a rainy day.

This time too Bianca had arrived from Haifa bringing with her about five toilet rolls, so as not to waste hers. Her sister used to get angry at their mother and tell her that she had enough money to buy toilet paper for her too, but Bianca would say, "Pardon me, but my bum doesn't need that soft pink papers of yours. It falls apart in my hands. My bum"—when she said "my bum," she always qualified it with "pardon me," because she thought it sounded like a rude word—"is used to the coarse paper I got from the customs." She realized that it was not going to be possible to change the habits of a lifetime and bowed to her mother by placing the toilet rolls in the bathroom, for Bianca's own private use. But as soon as her mother left the house, she was quick to get rid of the ancient toilet paper she had left in the bathroom.

"Are you crazy?" said her dad fearfully. "She'll kill me if I throw away her toilet paper." In his befuddled mind, he understood that it wouldn't do to annoy Bianca now, since she was the only one left to take care of him.

She and her father began searching for the perfectly polished black shoes. They looked under the bed, under the blankets, on her mother's sewing machine, on top of the closet, among all the albums, and there really was no sign of the shoes. She showed him his newly polished brown shoes. He fumed and said that he was referring to the black shoes that he had only just finished polishing. He remembered very well that these were the black shoes, and as proof, he produced the black polish and cloth, which quite clearly had just been put to use shining up a pair of shoes. She moved all the exhaustingly crowded furniture in her parents' apartment and found nothing. She even checked the garbage can outside, not the one inside the apartment; maybe her father had been right for a change, and her mother had indeed thrown away the shoes. In the garbage can she was surprised to find a lot of carelessly discarded food, not even wrapped in plastic bags. There was an almost full container of cottage cheese, a wedge of the unsalted Canaan sheep cheese that her mother ate a lot of because of her hypertension, and even cucumber peelings that her mother saved in a bag in the fridge and used to place on her feverish brow. It seemed odd, but all the tenants in the house used the garbage can, and maybe one of them had cleaned out his fridge. She went back to her parent's place and opened the fridge. It was completely empty. There wasn't a thing in it. She opened the freezer door, and there, standing on the shelf, were the black newly polished shoes in all their glory.

"Why did you throw out all the food?" she asked her father, who of course didn't remember a thing.

"So there'd be room for the shoes," he replied.

"But why in the freezer?" She wanted to understand his thought processes.

"It keeps longer in the freezer, like meat," her father explained.

Difficult Language, Hebrew

Quick as the wind, I slid down the banister on the way out of school and felt my flesh being slashed by the tiny pieces of glass stuck to it. I reached the end of the banister dripping blood. My bum was full of glass fragments, and I couldn't remove them because they were stuck in my behind.

Knowing that there was another hour before my sister finished school, I made for the office where my father worked. At that time he was a realtor, but at this too he made no money. Dad took me to the clinic, where they quickly put stitches in my bum. This time I didn't need a tetanus shot, because I'd already had one only three months before when I had jumped over a railing and landed on a metal pole.

The nurse recognized me and chastised my dad for not taking care of his little savage, and Dad said that a scar on the bum of an eight-and-a-half-year-old is quite sexy.

We went home, and my sister flew at Dad, asking what Mom was doing at the school today.

"She's taking over from another cleaner who's off sick," Dad explained to my furious sister.

"And why does it have to be in my school?" she asked.

"Because maybe there she'll finally get permanency," Dad said, and my sister shut up.

Accountant looking for a housemaid's job, or any other exhausting physical labor, where knowledge of the Hebrew language is not required. Fluent in Romanian and Yiddish, some French, hard of hearing. This, no doubt, was the notice that Mom would have composed, had she chosen to seek employment in the classified ads in the daily papers. To her, the most important thing was permanency. She was permanently seeking a job that would give her permanency, and permanency was something you could get only if you worked for the authorities.

She dreamed of permanency so she could at long last be able to take a day off work without having it docked from her wages. But to her the most important aspect of permanency was that it gave a person pension rights. A woman with a pension was a woman with status. A pension meant having security for thirty years ahead. It meant that she could easily save for her daughters' dowries, because now that she's got the matter of her old age sorted, she'll get her pension, and she'll never be a yoke around the neck of her two daughters.

After school the following day, my sister and her friends Malka and Tova waited for me at the school gate so we could go home together. Dad had made her swear that she would always come home with me so I wouldn't slide down again and open the stitches in my bum.

Tova asked my sister if our mother was cleaning the classrooms now.

My sister was ashamed to say yes, so I said to Tova that yes, she was, "and they've even promised her permanency if she does it well."

When I saw Mom arriving at the school with the last bell, I went into the first classroom she had to clean and helped her place the chairs on top of the desks so she could swab the floor.

Those kids, no matter how many times they are asked to show some consideration for the cleaners by placing their chairs on top of their desks at the end of the day, just hear the bell and make a mad dash outside before the teacher can even think of giving them any more homework to do.

My sister pretended not to see our mother cleaning in our school and quickly made her way out with her friends. I, who had never cared what anyone thought, stayed behind to help my mom. According to my sister, it was because I was pretty that I could allow myself not to bother with what other people thought.

The next day too I stayed behind after school with Mom and lifted all the chairs while she washed down the floors with a lot of water, because it wasn't costing us anything. Those were the days when we didn't spend all day worrying about the level of water in the Sea of Galilee.

My sister left with her friends as usual, and after saying good-bye to them at the end of our street, she returned to the school, entered the classroom quietly, and helped me pick up chairs and place them on the desks.

On the fourth day of our mother's cleaning job in our school, both of us stayed behind after the final bell, lifted up the chairs, and swept out the classrooms.

Floor washing was something that Mom didn't allow us to do until we were seventeen, so as not to ruin our hands— not at home, and certainly not where she worked. Your hands are your dowries, she always said. And I had thought that towels and cooking pots made up a dowry. For the same reason, she wouldn't let us wash the dishes at home. Anyway, dishwashing was Dad's job.

Mom resigned from her cleaning job at our school at the end of the week, even though they had promised her permanency. She didn't want her young daughters cleaning classrooms after school hours. Or at all.

Mom was given a job at the customs service and was happy. At the customs, not only could she say at least one day a month that she was sick, but she was also able to take things away to her heart's content.

Every place where Mom worked, she used to steal something. She didn't when she cleaned private houses, because people always suspect the cleaning woman, and besides, people were always very generous toward her and gave her all kinds of things for her cute little girls. A government place, on the other hand, is something else altogether. The Establishment has money, and it's no problem stealing from them. So Mom pilfered a few pencils, some pens, papers, several teacups, a little sugar, some saccharin, coffee; all for our own personal domestic use, of course.

From the customs, Mom made a regular habit of taking away toilet rolls. Every day she'd come home with two rolls of toilet paper in her bag. After two years of work for the customs, there wasn't a corner in the apartment that wasn't packed with toilet rolls. The attic was already stuffed with enough toilet rolls to save us from a third world war.

Mom worked at the customs from six in the morning until midday, and when she came home she sat down to take up white pleated skirts.

This was her second job, shortening hems on pleated skirts. These skirts required special dressmaking skills, and Mom was not really a dressmaker. It was necessary to unpick the belt with the lining at the top of the skirt, not the bottom, where the skirt was pleated. She then had to cut off the required length before arranging all the pleats into the belt with the lining, and then sewing together all the pleats on her sewing machine.

At five every evening, Mom hurried off to her third job in a café on the corner of Hanevi'im and Herzl, where she worked in the kitchen, making sandwiches, washing dishes, and picking off the heads of the rolls so as to allow the insertion of frankfurters into the decapitated rolls. At eleven o'clock, when the café closed for business, she lifted the chairs onto the tables and washed the floors so the place would be clean for the following morning.

At midnight Mom came home on all fours with a large plastic bag full of heads. The heads of the rolls that had been decapitated in order to insert wieners into them were the treat my sister and I waited for all day. We gobbled down so many heads that we went to sleep with a terrible stomachache. Sometimes, in order to shake things up, Mom would fry the pieces of bread and sprinkle sugar over them. American toast heads, Mom used to call it, and we often called Sima, Rocha, and Yaffa from upstairs to share and enjoy our fried heads.

At school, after the government had stopped providing us with a free ten o'clock meal, my sister and I took out our heads and were the envy of all the others.

But Mom had a knack for making us embarrassed. When she brought my raincoat into the classroom because I had forgotten it at home—or more accurately, I had refused to take it because it was monumentally hideous—Mom knocked on the door and apologized in a heavy Romanian accent, "It's for Ifale, so she won't be wet in water."

Needless to say, I wanted the earth to swallow me for the rest of my life, and never to be exposed to the ridicule of my classmates, for not only was I Romanian, but at home they call me Ifale!

We were ashamed when Mom pulled out the sandwiches in the middle of a movie, handing them out to us, rustling the wrapping paper and the plastic bag with the rubber band, to keep it all fresh so it shouldn't get dry; with her cries of encouragement in Romanian, everyone in the audience knew not only that we were Romanian but exactly what we had in our sandwiches.

And of course we were mortified on the bus when she took off the best years of our lives to get the driver to let us travel for free. And if the driver insisted, Mom would ask us to do our eye trick. Practiced and genuinely ashamed, we looked at the driver with piercing pain-filled eyes; his sympathetic Jewish head wouldn't allow him to put us off the bus, and he made do with the children's ticket that Mom handed out to him. We really did have sad eyes, if only from the thought of having to climb up all those hills in Haifa on foot, instead of the luxury of traveling by bus. When she didn't get away with it, we hissed quietly, "Nazi," to make him know exactly what we thought of him; but he was upset at us for calling him a Nazi, and we hadn't really meant to hurt him.

When we arrived at our stop after having traveled for free on the bus and Mom saw a street beggar, she used to give him all the fare she had saved from the journey and tell us happily, "You see, we made that beggar's day; now do you understand why it's so important to steal your way onto the bus?"

When we were finally accepted into the summer school run by the nepotistic Israeli Labor Party, Mapai, it was only after Dad had carried out so many missions for them, "lending" them the apartment for their party gatherings and lectures and filling it with all the neighborhood's Moroccan and Kurdish inhabitants and everybody else from Wadi Salib who could fit into our single room (Dad told them simply that there'd be good food to eat, so it was worth coming, and they could take home whatever was left at the end). Election time was a time when Dad flourished, and during the two months preceding the elections he'd earn enough money for the whole year. But Dad got most of the money out of the party during the very last week running up to the elections. And that is how we got the fancy residential summer camp, with board and food and activities and macramé and ceramics—in short, Club Med gratis for Franco's daughters.

Mom accompanied us to the pickup point for the summer camp, where she shoved everyone aside, lied that she'd been there before but left for a moment, and pushed us onto the bus first. She thought that if you're first on the bus, you get the best beds, and certainly the best food. Mom didn't forget to tell the counselor in perfect Yiddish to make sure that we ate everything we were given, because she was paying a fortune for the summer camp.

We were ashamed of Mom in the long queues for the doctor when she regularly forged her number in line, or when she said in a voice full of confidence, after making sure of the number that was in with the doctor, that hers was two numbers hence. She took the risk of someone else saying that he had that number, when she would say, "Oh, so sorry, my mistake!" And so, when we were number ninety-eight in the queue, we'd go in instead of number forty-three, when it was exactly his turn to go in.

We were embarrassed when Mom didn't hear what was being said to her because she was hard of hearing, when she didn't understand what was being said to her because she didn't know Hebrew, or when she pretended not to hear or understand when it suited her not to hear or understand.

When Mom shook her head vigorously, we knew that she didn't understand a word of what was being explained to her, and we were obliged, in a loud voice and, of course, in Romanian, with all the world's eyes on us, to explain to her what every baby understands in Hebrew.

Most of all we were ashamed of our mother for not knowing Hebrew. Because the fact that she didn't know Hebrew meant that my sister and I were forced to speak Romanian.

Since in our house there were many more Sephardi friends than Ashkenazi, they learned in time to speak with Mom in Romanian, especially about food, of course. In our home no one quoted Bialik or Alterman; people weren't familiar with the works of Shalom Aleichem, and apart from the occasional reference to Ben-Gurion, they all spoke about food.

When Mom called us from the balcony, "Fila, Renutza, vinu smanchetz," the whole of Stanton would mimic her. To this day it's possible to wander through Stanton, which is now occupied only by Arabs, and hear my mother's voice calling us in to eat in Romanian. We were so ashamed, and Mom couldn't care less.

Whenever Yael, our cousin on Dad's side, came to our place for lunch, she was always served the smallest drumstick, and we were ashamed of Mom and of Yael's small drumstick. It made no difference even when we used camouflage tricks to swap our plates because Mom, as if suspecting something, would sit down next to us until we'd finished eating everything on our plate, and we'd swallow and suffer and choke and swear that one day we'd compensate Yael for all the pieces of chicken that our mother had denied her.

On the other hand, when Yossi, our cousin on our mother's side, came to visit us from Hedera, he was always given a piece of meat equal in size to ours; sometimes his portion was even larger than ours, and we were so pleased. Not only was Yossi from our mother's side, he was also her oldest brother Niku's youngest son, the child of his old age. Still, my impression was that Mom was doing her usual cold calculations, and taking into account the frequent vacations we spent in Hedera, she wanted to avoid a situation whereby in Hedera, we would be allocated the smallest drumstick.

After she'd been nine days at home with pneumonia, and twelve days following Noa's birth, the man returned, grim-faced, from the hospital. Noa had contracted an infection in her blood. They had changed her blood but were unable to overcome the infection. Her condition was serious.

That evening her sister, who had just flown in from New York, came to visit and was horrified by the way she looked.

"What's happened?" she asked, suspecting that her sister had been to the hospital and was shocked by Noa's critical condition.

"You look like a shadow," her sister said, and apologized for not having been able to change the time of her flight home to be with her through these difficult times.

"It's all right, Mom took care of me," she told her sister.

She climbed on the scales in the bathroom and discovered she had lost twenty pounds in nine days. More than two pounds a day; as if in solidarity with Noa, who wasn't gaining any weight at all.

The following morning they made their way to the hospital with the terrible feeling that there might no longer be anyone for them to caress through the windows of the incubator. For twenty-five tense minutes they didn't exchange a word, all the way to Kaplan Hospital in Rehovot. It was if any unnecessary chatter would put their baby's life in even greater danger. Out of breath, they arrived at the Children's Department, and the man helped her tie on the green gown and fixed a surgical mask over her mouth, all the time propping her up to prevent her from collapsing; she had still not recovered from her pneumonia.

Dr. Alkalai informed them that Noa's condition was terminal. The airway that had been inserted in her mouth to allow air to flow in had become infected and caused gangrene in her face and oral cavity. The liver was distended, and the kidneys were not functioning. The baby was bloated from an excess of fluids, and if she did not pass water within the next twenty-four hours, she would not survive. Lack of oxygen was causing her to convulse, and it was hard to tell if there was any brain damage. He explained that she was receiving three types of antibiotics intravenously as well as plasma. "We are doing all we can; your baby is now in the hands of God," the doctor added.

They stood by the incubator for a long time, knowing that Noa was not aware of their presence. "Your baby is in good hands. There's nothing more for you to do here today," Dr. Alkalai said to them with unexpected gentleness for such a large man. "Her chances for survival are very slim, maybe only one percent. Only a miracle can save her. I hope you believe in miracles."

"What is the miracle supposed to look like?" she asked.

"If she passes water during the next few hours, we'll consider that a miracle," Dr. Alkalai said again.

The man wanted her to go back to her warm bed, but after some brief hesitation, they decided together to stay with their baby in the hospital. They went to the canteen for some tasteless, lukewarm coffee.

When she called her sister to come to be with them, her brother-in-law informed her that her sister had gone to Haifa because her father's condition had deteriorated and he had been taken to the hospital. With infinite selfishness, she thought only of herself; now she wouldn't even be able to ask her mother to come to be with her.

"Maybe it's just as well we don't have a telephone," she said to her husband.

"Why?" he asked.

"Because that way you don't get bad news," she said. "We didn't have a telephone in my parents' home because we couldn't afford one," she told her husband as she sipped at the vile coffee, "and the only time someone called the neighbors and asked for me, it was to tell me that Varda's sister had managed, finally, to commit suicide."

"Who's Varda?" he asked, as if this was the most important question.

"Do you remember the mother of a friend of mine that you donated blood for when they couldn't find a vein in my arm in Hadassah Hospital in Jerusalem?"

"So that's Varda."

"No. That was her mother, who became very sick after her daughter, my friend Varda's sister, had succeeded in killing herself. For a whole year she had been trying. Twice she walked into the sea and tried to drown herself; once she jumped from the third floor and only sustained some injuries; once she stood on the railway lines but lost her nerve at the last minute. The final time, she took an overdose of sleeping pills she'd been collecting for a year without her parents' knowledge."

"But why?" he wondered.

"She wanted to die," she replied. "I was the only one that Varda told about her sister's suicide attempts over the year. In the end she succeeded, and Varda called my neighbor to tell me that her sister had managed to do the deed. Those are the words she used to tell me."

"Did you get to go to the funeral?" he asked.

"No," she replied. "We had a SAT test the next day, and I hadn't even started reviewing. So straight after that call, I sat down to study and didn't stop until the exam. We had a break during the exam, and all the smokers dashed into the toilets to light up. Suddenly the principal walked into the girls' lavatory, and we were all in there with cigarettes, and he asked us to step outside. As we started to walk out, ter-rified that he was planning to cancel our exam because he'd caught us smoking, he told me to stay behind, and after everyone else had left, he asked me how Varda was doing, knowing that I was her best friend.

"I told him she was all right, and I was thinking only about how I could hide the waves of smoke that were rising from the cigarette I was hiding behind my back. I was hoping he might not notice all the smoke emanating from me.

"'Are you sure?' he asked me.

"'Maybe things will be easier for them now,' I said with the stupidity of an eighteen-year-old.

"'Do you think I could go to the shivah?' the principal, who imposed his authority on the entire school, asked me.

"'Under different circumstances I would have said they'd be glad,' I replied.

"'Thank you,' he said, 'you can go on smoking.' And he walked out of the girls' toilets. The school principal that a whole school was terrified of had revealed himself to be a sensitive and considerate person when asking me about Varda. It turned out that he genuinely cared for her and her family; and do you know what's even sadder about this whole story? That school principal, who was quite old, had only one son, and that son died of cancer when he was only eighteen. An only child," she said quietly.

"Let's talk about happier things," he said to her.

"What, for example?" she asked.

"For example, that my parents are arriving next week to be with us," he said.

"Lovely," she said, and in her heart she hoped she could cheer up for them.

They were spending the night on a bench in the waiting room next to the Premature Babies Unit, locked in each other's pain, when Dr. Mogilner shook them gently awake at four in the morning to tell them that a miracle had happened and Noa had passed water.

"And what now?" the man asked the doctor.

"Carry on praying," he replied. "That germ has caused havoc, and we're now going to have to repair all the damage. We seem to have overcome the infection in the blood, but the germ has settled in the face, because of the plaster that was holding the airway in place, and caused gangrene in the baby's cheeks and oral cavity, which created a cleft in the palate and a severe ear infection."

Over the next three weeks, she turned up every morning at seven in the morning at the preemie unit, with the man joining her later after he'd finished his work; depressed, they returned home together to an empty house. He would fill a bath for her and massage her back, but he no longer trumpeted in her ear. Most of the time they were alone with the paralyzing fear and pain of the long wait. Her sister came for brief breaks from her father's bedside—he had suffered a major stroke—to be with them; sometimes his sister stood next to her by the incubator but was no less helpless. His parents arrived for a ten-day stay, looked at Noa in the preemie unit, shook their heads, and said nothing. It was as if they feared that anything they said would only worsen the situation.

All day and every day she sang to her daughter the song, "The prettiest girl in school has the prettiest eyes in school and the prettiest braids in school," and it made no difference that Noa had no hair, and her braids hadn't grown yet. Noa was the prettiest girl in the preemie unit, in spite of the bandages on her face, and she never stopped singing her that wonderful song. She wasn't particularly familiar with the words of other songs, never having been a great fan of all those sing-alongs, and on school trips when everyone sang their beautiful-Israel folk songs, she would quietly hum Beatles tunes or Cliff Richard songs. Then Yudit Ravitz appeared on the scene and restored her self-respect with "The Prettiest Girl in School" and provided her with proof that she too was prepared to sing songs whose words touched her soul.

The doctors and nurses treated Noa with a devotion that was nothing short of heartwarming. Five times a day they performed suction on her, draining the pus from her vocal cavity and ears, but sometimes they had to prick her three or four times a day before they found a vein for an intravenous dose of plasma or antibiotics, or just for a daily blood test. It is inhuman for a young mother to have to watch her minuscule baby, less than seven pounds in weight, being subjected to needle pricks in her head several times a day. It is inhuman even for an experienced mother. In time, she learned from the intensity of Noa's crying which of her caregivers had a magic touch that caused her less pain, and firmly refused to allow any inexperienced intern to stick needles into her baby.

Every such prick and every cry cut straight to her soul. She thought to herself that if it were possible to examine someone's soul under a microscope, they'd find in hers a myriad of cuts and scratches, equal in number to the times that Noa had been pricked.

One day when Noa opened her mouth wide as if trying to shout to everybody to stop hurting her, she noticed suddenly that her daughter had no uvula.

"She has no uvula," she pointed out to Zohara, the head nurse.

"No uvula?" asked the nurse.

"That little grape in the very back of the mouth," she said, reminding the nurse what a uvula was.

"Ah, yes. That's right, we'd noticed. But don't worry, there's no medical significance to a uvula."

Still, she asked Dr. Alkalai about the uvula's role in the human body, but he too insisted that, as far as they knew, the uvula had no medical significance.

On Friday morning, three weeks later, she entered the ward and stopped still as a block of salt. The space in which Noa's incubator had stood was empty, and she already knew from all those weeks in the hospital that an empty space meant that the baby hadn't survived the night. She remained standing in the empty space. Frozen. Until Zohara, the charming nurse she had taken a shine to from the very beginning, noticed her. Zohara was feeding a baby girl or boy in an incubator near the widow. Noticing her puzzled expression, Zohara smiled and called her over to join her by the window.

"We've moved Noa to be near the window so she can soak up some sun. Come, you can finish feeding her through the feeding tube." She walked to the window hesitantly, trying to bring herself back to life, and saw the sun's rays painting Noa's naked body with a pinkish tinge, as if only half an hour in the sun had already given her a slight tan. Even her bandaged face had taken on a pinkish hue.

"She feels a lot better today, so we decided to move her to the light," Zohara explained, and passed her baby to her.

"Thank you," she said to Zohara, but she was talking to God.

She glanced at the lawns outside the window and prayed for the day when she would be able to dance out there with her Noa, who would no longer be connected to pipes and tubes and blood transfusions.

That evening was Purim, and they went to her sister's for a holiday meal. Her sister had brought their mother over from Haifa, to give her some respite from sitting vigil at their father's hospital bedside. Bianca told them she had spent the morning at the cave of the Prophet Elijah, where she prayed for the safety and full recovery of her sick husband and baby granddaughter.

When they arrived back home, she told her husband that she wished to donate the thousand-dollar gift they had received from his aunt and uncle in Paris for Noa's birth to the Premature Babies Unit at the hospital. He didn't object, even though she knew he had wanted to use the money to buy a video camera.

The next morning, a Saturday, five-week-old Noa smiled at them for the first time. It was only on them, her parents, that Noa bestowed her grateful smile. Whenever anyone else approached her, a doctor or a nurse in a green surgical gown, Noa would start crying, as if knowing that she was about to be pricked again.

"Well, they all look like something from outer space," her man said to amuse her. "I too would be crying all day if I had all those green people wandering around under my feet."

She picked her daughter up in her arms and glanced toward the round window of the preemie unit, where she saw a clown waving at her. She looked at him and thought she must be hallucinating; how did a clown land in the hospital straight out of the blue? The clown waved his arms at her and pulled some funny faces. He signaled to her to come up close, and when she stepped out toward him, he handed her a very shiny blue balloon. She saw that the letters on the balloon read, "I love you, Mommy."

"This is for you," said the clown. She stared at him in disbelief and saw three more clowns wandering around the wards, handing out balloons and candy to the children. And then she remembered that today was Purim. She returned to the preemie unit and tied the balloon to Noa's blood transfusion stand.

Noa smiled at them again and at the bright blue shining balloon.

At midnight their neighbor knocked on the door and said that there was an urgent phone call for them, and when, with trembling hands, she picked up the receiver, her sister told her that their father had died. She started to cry, and when her husband grasped her shoulders, afraid she would collapse, she said that it was a relief—a relief that it wasn't Noa, and a relief that her father's share of suffering was over.

Circus Madrano

At long last, the Circus Madrano arrived in town. Every year it went first to Tel Aviv, then to Jerusalem, and finally, to Haifa, even though Haifa is the most beautiful city in Israel.

It was the same as the military parade on Independence Day; first it went to Jerusalem, our capital city, then to Tel Aviv, before ending up in Haifa.

My sister and I wanted to wear the clothes we'd received from Fima and Sami's last shipment from America to the circus. But Dad said he was very sorry, because the butcher who had promised him two tickets to the circus in return for the lovely sign he had painted over the door of his store hadn't been able in the end to obtain the tickets that he was supposed to have received from his brother-in-law who worked for the municipality.

My sister was crestfallen, and I straightaway lied to my dad and said that I couldn't care less about that stupid circus, so he shouldn't get heartsick for not having the money to take his darling daughters to the circus. I looked him straight in the eyes, to stop him from feeling that I was really disappointed to death.

The next afternoon, as we were outside playing our usual game of hide-and-seek, Fila told me that we were going to the circus on our own.

"But we're not dressed nicely," I said.

"We can't get in anyway. We'll just walk around, maybe get a glimpse of the elephants," my sister told me.

Back and forth we circled, until suddenly we saw a tiny hole in the fence.

A hole in the wall is an open invitation to a thief—that's exactly what that hole looked like.

We couldn't make up our minds what to do. Should we continue circling, or should we steal our way into the circus? Suddenly my sister grabbed my hand hard and dragged me after her through the hole in the fence.

I was horrified. Of the two of us, Fila was the coward. Where did she get the nerve to steal into the circus, when it's obvious to everyone that the place is crawling with police all waiting just to nab kids who have stolen in illegally and take them back to their parents and make them ashamed of themselves? My sister ordered me to keep my back straight, the way she forced me to practice at home, walking with books on my head so I wouldn't develop a hunchback like Avram from the grocery store. We walked through the circus like a couple of robots, taking tiny steps like Japanese ladies and pretending not to be looking from side to side in fear. When we reached a water faucet, we rinsed our faces and passed damp hands through our hair and clothing so as to smooth over the poverty, and continued walking straight-backed and trembling with fear, mingling with the happy crowds.

There was an intermission, so everyone was wandering around with cotton candy, balloons, nibbles, and red toffee apples, and all to the magical sound of the music that they always play in circuses.

Suddenly we saw Auntie Lika and Uncle Max looming up in front of us. Auntie Lika was Mom's oldest sister, and they lived in a house in Givat Olga with a garden full of fruit trees. My sister made me swear not to reveal the fact that we had stolen in, so they wouldn't tell on us, and when they asked us if we were enjoying ourselves so far, my sister exhibited amazing acumen and I nodded my head briskly, not uttering a word.

Then my wise sister told them she'd run out of patience and couldn't wait to see the second half of the show, which was absolutely true.

Max took some money out of his pocket and gave it to us to buy ourselves some cotton candy or a lollipop.

I was over the moon with joy; not only were we getting to see the circus without its costing our dad any money, but we were also going to have some cotton candy. It was the absolute fulfillment of all our dreams.

We said good-bye to Auntie Lika and Uncle Max, and I

made straight for the cotton candy stand. But Fila pulled me back hard—she was, after all, a year and eight months older and therefore stronger than me—and explained that we still weren't out of danger, and anyway we looked suspicious in our faded clothes that came from the parcel Sami and Fima had received from their relatives in America, and any minute a policeman could turn up and catch us out as soon as he asked to see the tickets we didn't have.

"So what are we going to do?" I asked my older sister who had stolen us into the circus, and she explained that with the money we had received from Uncle Max, we had to buy a shiny silver balloon, the kind of balloon that is very expensive and prestigious and only rich people can afford, and with a balloon like that in our possession, she believed, no one would ever suspect that we were underprivileged and had stolen into the circus.

Sadly I said good-bye to the cotton candy stand, and we went to buy a fancy silver balloon that would remove all suspicion from girls who steal into the circus. My sister immediately picked out a red balloon, and I, who preferred a blue one, didn't dare argue with her this time. After all, it was thanks to her that we were here at all.

We entered the Big Top, two girls dressed in faded clothes with a large silvery red balloon, which later disappeared in the skies, with a grumbling stomach that dreamed of a sugar stick and sweet pink cotton candy. And really, no one suspected us. It was lovely, the other half of the circus show.

She went with her sister and their mother to the hospital, and they looked down at Moscu's lifeless body. Around the bed next to their father's, an entire extended family was nursing a patient. One of them, a man of about fifty, walked over to them and told them in a voice full of reproach that throughout the Sabbath, their father hadn't stopped asking for his family.

"How did he ask?" her sister wanted to know. "Did he call out for us?"

"He was waving his arms as if to say, 'Where will salvation come from?' Several times my wife or I went and gave him something to drink. I even fed him some compote. It was the only thing he agreed to eat. Toward the end he really wept, as if begging to say good-bye to you. He suffered, poor man. All through the Sabbath he suffered. May his soul be gathered in eternal life."

"Why didn't you ask one of the nurses to call us?" asked her sister angrily of the only person who had cared for their father in his final hours.

"I asked. The nurse looked at his records and said she couldn't find your telephone number."

"And didn't the nurses go to him?" Her sister was furious at the whole world, but mainly she was furious with herself.

"You know what it's like in hospitals on Shabbat. A dog feels less abandoned than a sick person," said the man who had taken pity on their dad.

"All our lives he lived only for us, and we couldn't even take the trouble to be with him when he needed us," she said to her sister sorrowfully, and her sister told her that she was not to blame. She was, after all, taking care of her daughter. "It's all my fault," said her sister, and fell into a deep melancholy for having abandoned her father.

During the shivah, she asked the rabbi of the Sephardi synagogue that her father had attended on Rosh Hashanah and Yom Kippur what, according to Judaism, the uvula was used for. She knew that, unlike doctors, rabbis have answers to everything.

"The uvula is the covenant forged between the Creator of the Universe and the select few," said the rabbi, when he came to the shivah to console them over the death of their father.

"The uvula is the barrier between the soul and the voice that emanates from a person's mouth. It is like a barrier that says to a person: think very, very carefully before every word you utter, because the moment it has left your mouth, it is no longer yours. It is in the public domain.

"According to Kabbalah, it is through wisdom, or as some call it, the spirit, that God created the world and that there are ten *sefirot*, ten Divine Emanations in the spirit. In the book of creativity that relates to the Patriarch Abraham, it is said: Ten *sefirot* of concealment correspond to the ten fingers: Five against five, they act in unison, as a union between them acts, through the power-word of revelation and the power-word of concealment.

"The covenant that was forged between us and God, as a word of the foreskin—the bris milah—we are all familiar with, but as the word of the tongue, only a very few have received it. You see, my daughter, only a very few, only the selected, the elite, have received the covenant of the tongue between man and God. And it is in this covenant that the uvula is carved. Why are you asking?" asked the rabbi.

"Because my baby daughter's uvula was amputated," she replied.

"You have a very special daughter," he told her, and she said that she just wanted her baby to be healthy and hurried away to the hospital to be beside her sick daughter.

When she was two months old, Noa tasted mother's milk for the first time. Zohara said that she had to learn how to suckle and breathe alternately, and that it was not good to continue feeding her through a tube straight into her intestine. She practiced for hours, and with much love and devotion she managed to get Noa to suck, then breathe, and again to suck, and again to breathe. Most of the time Noa puked up the food through her mouth, or through her cleft palate.

Dr. Mogilner wanted Noa to receive mother's milk and, since she was unable to provide the goods, they were told that religious women considered it a mitzvah, an act of human kindness, to supply mother's milk wherever necessary. They made inquiries in the religious neighborhood of Bnei Brak, but found nothing. Until she remembered baby Rivka, who was born five minutes after Noa. The hospital gave her their telephone number, and she hoped their generosity would be greater than any she could find in her own neighborhood.

She called Rivka's mother, who was happy to hear her and asked after Noa. She told her that she and her husband often wondered how their baby girl was getting on. Yes, thank God, Rivka already weighed over twelve pounds. When she understood that Noa hadn't passed the seven-pound threshold, she asked what could she do to help.

"I need your milk," she said, "not I, I mean, my daughter."

Rivka's mother agreed immediately. Said that she had too much milk anyway, and that her breasts after her fourth baby were loaded with milk and that she'd be happy to express some of it for her.

"Whoever saves one person is considered as if he saved an entire world," she added, and told her that she considered it an honor that they had come to her for help.

"We didn't have anyone else to turn to," she said truthfully.

Every day after work, the man would drive to Bnei Brak to pick up two full bottles of mother's milk, and she, who had been given by Zohara the task of feeding, fed baby Noa, making sure to give her plenty of breaks to allow her to breathe.

Aged three months and weighing seven pounds, Noa was released from hospital to take up residence with her parents, who promised to bring her back three times a week for checkups and therapy.

They decorated her room with colorful wallpaper, to give her something cheerful to look at, instead of all those green gowns and transfusion stands she had seen since the day she was born. She dressed her baby in all the beautiful clothes she'd been sent from Barcelona, the clothes that she looked at every evening with yearning, praying for the day that her daughter would be able to wear them. She hoped that in her own home, with her parents who loved her, Noa would grow strong and flourish, and gain weight.

They bought pacifiers, in which they punched a hole to enable Noa to breathe through her mouth. But their baby didn't want a pacifier and preferred to suck her thumb and choke for lack of air. The complete blockage in her nose became a serious problem now she was at home and it was no longer possible to tube-feed her. Far too many times she witnessed Noa's tiny fists rising, desperate for air, and there was none to be had. She went to open the baby's mouth and Noa would look at her with a grateful expression, as if to say, "Thank you for the air you give me." For hours on end she would stand by the cot, holding her baby's mouth open to enable her to breath. At night they did shifts. Some nights she would wake from a bad dream, in which her daughter was fighting for air, and run to the cot, only to see her husband standing there holding Noa's mouth open, enabling her to breathe. Nothing interested her apart from her daughter. Her husband went out to work and did his best to acclimatize himself to life in a new country and to learn the language and customs, with which he had been familiar as a tourist, but which, now that he was a citizen of the country, were quite alien. She was sorry they had allowed themselves to be persuaded by a friend of his, who had made aliyah two years before and lived with his wife in Rishon le Zion, to buy an apartment nearby. Since the friends had children, they thought they would have fun together. But this was before Noa was born. Once she was born, they never saw those friends again; it was as if those people thought that their home and their sick child might contaminate them.

She had wanted the apartment in Rishon le Zion mainly because of its large balcony that overlooked a rural landscape. But in order to get a telephone from the telephone company, they had to join a long waiting list, and all the documents they brought from the hospital proving that they had a sick daughter made no difference at all; the telephone company had no telephone to supply them, and they continued to be cut off from the world.

She felt sorry for her husband for leaving an easy life in Barcelona, while here in Israel everything was so hard. Compared with his former income, his job in Israel paid very little; he had no friends; his parents were a long way away; his wife was sad and easily irritated, and his daughter was extremely sick. His life had turned upside down, like the Hebrew he spoke, and if he ever wanted to relax in her arms, it was never a good time for her, after she'd been feeding her daughter for hours just to see her vomit it all up afterward.

He would leave her the car—so she could take Noa to the hospital in an emergency—and take three buses in each direction to get to his work in Tel Aviv, and although he finished work at five o'clock, it was seven o'clock before he came home every evening, only to find his wife as pale as his daughter. But he stayed optimistic, even after it was obvious that Noa was suffering from a chronic blood disorder and a weak immune system.

At six months old, Noa was hospitalized again for a period of three months, at the end of which she was released from hospital weighing less than nine pounds. At nine months she weighed the same as a newborn baby. Throughout this entire period, Noa did not digest any food and was constantly hooked up to transfusions so as not to become dehydrated. Again it was hard to find her veins, and she had to be pricked several times a day, and each time tore her parents to pieces.

Every day she would turn up at the hospital at seven in the morning and stay until seven in the evening, when her brother-in-law arrived to take over from her until ten o'clock; that was when the man arrived and stayed the night with Noa. She used to meet her husband for a brief period every evening between eight and nine o'clock, when she would report on the baby's hemoglobin count and if again she'd been given a transfusion after three or four attempts at finding a vein. Only on Saturdays did they spend the day together, nursing their daughter. All week she was on guard, like a lioness defending her daughter against unnecessary germs; there was not the same level of sterility on the children's ward as in the Premature Babies Unit. She was terrified that with her substandard immune system Noa could catch any of the diseases in the vicinity. She had brought Noa's bathtub from home to avoid having to wash her baby in the hospital's facilities, thus offending the nurses, who insisted that they were fastidious about sterilizing the sink between bathing one baby and the next and used the most powerful antiseptics available. But she was adamant that Noa should have her own bathtub and wouldn't allow anyone else come near her. Noticing a nurse about to change Noa's transfusion bags, she was not too shy to ask her to first wash her hands—and made sure that the nurse did so—especially if the nurse had just finished attending a child with an intestinal problem. Above all, she made sure that it was the correct transfusion and that no inadvertent mistakes occurred, God forbid. She was going to allow nothing inadvertent anywhere near her sick daughter. On some days she was on the verge of a nervous breakdown and wouldn't allow any of the medical staff to approach Noa. Her husband told her that she was turning everyone against her, but she said that she would rather they feared her craziness than that "any intern should get the idea that he can experiment on our baby."

During the long hours she spent in the hospital she watched with envy as the nurses changed shifts, handing on instructions from one to the next and returning, after a day's work, to their husbands, their children, their homes. During the night shifts she'd hear the nurse giving instructions to her husband, to bathe their son, to make him an omelet in the shape of a face, because that's the only way he'll eat it, to place two olives instead of eyes and a cucumber for a mouth, so he'll get some vegetables into him. She was crazy with envy of ordinary healthy people, living in regular houses and eating regular homemade food and not a tasteless sandwich from a vending machine, and she prayed for the day that her daughter would be able to eat without vomiting up everything she took in.

One night, when her husband was sick with flu and slept at home, her brother-in-law spent the night at Noa's bedside, and when she arrived at the hospital at six in the morning, he welcomed her with cries of joy; Noa had been weighed an hour ago—life in hospitals begins at dawn—and she had crossed the nine-pound threshold. Her brother-in-law was as happy as if the night he had spent with Noa had finally caused her to gain weight.

"And apart from that, how did the night go?" she asked her brother-in-law.

"Nothing special," he admitted. She'd had to have a blood transfusion, and because they couldn't find a spare vein in her body, but only in her neck, he had been obliged to hold Noa's head on its side with her neck straight and motionless, so the transfusion didn't become disconnected.

"You held her head for four hours?" she asked.

"Yes," he replied, "and then I passed out."

She insisted to the doctors that Noa would never be able to keep any food down and gain weight until she had an operation to unblock her nose. The doctors were adamant, however, that such an operation would help for a short time only; the bone would grow back and continue blocking her airways, and since the baby was weak, there was a serious fear that she wouldn't make it through the operation. The chicken and the egg; what went before what. To their credit, though, the doctors learned in time to consult with her and never changed a treatment or a medication without asking for her opinion. They understood that the instincts of a mother like her are sometimes stronger than medical science, which often finds itself fumbling in the dark. Besides, that damn germ had caused so much damage that there wasn't a department that Noa wasn't treated in: ear, nose, and throat; mouth and jaw; neurology; gastroenterology;

ophthalmology; and, of course, hematology. She was trundled from department to department, from a lung X-ray to draining pus from the baby's ears. She knew all the doctors in the various departments, and she didn't like them. With the exception of the pediatricians, she loathed the doctors' high-handed arrogance. Worst of all in her opinion were the doctors in the ear, nose, and throat department, and they, to her misfortune, were the ones she needed most.

Noa suffered from serious trouble with her ears, which needed constant draining to clear them of the pus that accumulated in them. Since she was young and attractive, the doctor allowed himself to rub his leg against hers when she sat opposite him with Noa on her lap, having her ears drained. Still, she smiled sweetly at the doctor so he'd give her daughter the best care possible, even though all she wanted was to give him a sound kick in the balls. She remembered that time when she was standing at a gas station on the way out of Jerusalem, trying to hitch a ride to Tel Aviv, because she didn't have any money, as usual. She stood on the bend between the exit from the gas station and the spot where cars slowed down before blending into the traffic; she thought this was a good place to catch a ride because cars slowed down there anyway and drivers might not like to lie when asked if they were bound for Tel Aviv.

When she had decided to move to Jerusalem, she tried to get accepted to the Hebrew University and went there to take the psychometric exams, at the end of which she knew she had failed. She knew she had failed because there was no way she could pass exams that test—among other things— a person's ability to fit into an academic framework; after all, where she grew up, she had learned only how to break down frameworks. So she wasn't surprised when a letter came from the university two months later, telling her, "We are sorry to inform you that you were found unsuitable to study at our institute for higher education."

She stood there waiting for a ride, a young woman of twenty-one, straight-backed, her breasts firm, upright, and challenging, incapable of integrating into an academic framework, standing at the bend in the road where the road leading out of the gas station actually does integrate very well into the main road to Tel Aviv, when a car with five macho males, all having the look of being well entrenched in the Israeli crime scene, slowed down nearby. The car almost stopped when the man in the passenger seat stuck his arm out of the window and grabbed her breast with a strength that was humiliating, as if wanting to gain something out of the car slowing down and a girl with upright breasts stand- ing by the wayside. Her Romanian blood rose to her head.

What she wanted was to give him a sharp slap on the face, but he started winding up the window, as if to say, "I've had my jollies, now I'm clearing off."

She wanted to hit him, but a quick calculation told her that she might get her hand caught in the window. In the split second before the window closed and with the instinct of someone who doesn't take lightly to being humiliated, she spat in his eye, a big gob of revenge. Because in Wadi Salib there was no way anyone would ever get the better of her, except for her parents, without her hitting back.

She watched as the spit dribbled down from his eye and his friends laughed at him and clapped their hands for her. They, too, recognized the value of force and the supreme value of "an eye for an eye," or in this case, "a gob of spit for an eye."

Noa was eleven months old and weighed eleven pounds when a new ear, nose, and throat doctor arrived in the department, claiming that he was prepared to risk operating on her. He had only just returned from a five-year term of study in the United States, where he had operated successfully on similar cases. Dr. Marshak agreed to take the risk of operating on a weak baby because he too believed that the baby would be able to gain weight only if she was able to breathe through her nose.

"What's new about your procedure?" they asked Dr. Marshak.

"I plan to make an incision below the palate, bring it down, and saw through the bone from inside. This way there is no danger of the nose getting blocked again. And at the same time, I shall sew up the hole in her palate." He smiled at them.

"And how long with the operation take?" the man asked.

"About four hours. She's a very small baby, which makes

it much more complicated to operate on her," explained the consultant surgeon.

With trembling hands, they signed the consent forms, declaring that they would have no claims if—God forbid—the operation did not succeed.

Noa was taken to the operating theater at eight in the morning. And when she went to the lavatory for a pee, she saw that the bowl was full of blood. From fear, she had peed blood.

Two hours later, Dr. Marshak came out and informed the worried parents that the operation had been a success, and they could go into the recovery room to be with their daughter.

"What about the hole in her palate?" the man asked the doctor, who was well pleased with himself.

"For me this was the aperitif," he answered haughtily.

They watched her breathing on her own, her face relaxed, without the pain of constantly having to fight for every scrap of air. After five days in hospital, they went home with Noa, and within just a month she had gained over two pounds in weight. By the time she was two she had made up all the discrepancies.

Riots in Wadi Salib

My sister stayed at home to reread *Little Women*, and I went upstairs to our Syrian neighbors to play ball with Rocha.

Since we didn't own a ball, we made do with a watermelon. I sat on the edge of one bed, and Rocha sat opposite me on the other bed.

Unlike our own room, which was crammed to overflowing with stuff, the room occupied by the children upstairs contained only beds and nothing else. There was no table, no sewing machine, and no closet; only beds and a floor that was so shiny it could be eaten off of, as my mother used to say.

I didn't dare enter the room occupied by Nissim and Bracha. I was terrified of Nissim, who used to beat his kids with a belt, one after the other.

When my dad explained to Nissim that child beating was a useless way to raise children, Nissim replied that when he was a child in Syria, his father had also beaten him, and in fact it hadn't done him any harm. According to him, if you beat your kids, you are making them resilient and more able to face the harshness of life ahead.

I threw the watermelon to Rocha from the edge of the bed I was sitting on, and she threw it back from the bed opposite. I threw it again, and she threw it back harder. I threw it harder than she did, and she got up on the bed and threw it to me with all the strength of a seven-year-old.

Rocha was a year and a half younger than me, and I got annoyed, wondering where this little kid could have gotten the strength to throw an exceptionally heavy watermelon.

I stood up on the bed and used all my strength to throw the watermelon, and missed. It fell on the clean floor that you could eat off and exploded into tiny red bits all over the room.

Bracha came into the room and saw the bits of burst watermelon all over the floor, and I was sure she'd go out to get her husband's belt and thrash me for ruining the big watermelon they had bought to eat when they got back from the beach on Saturday.

But Bracha called all her children to come up home immediately and told me to go down and call my mother and sister and to come back with them. Mom was in the middle of preparing a pot of *mamaliga*, and I told her to leave everything and come upstairs with me, otherwise Bracha would beat me with Nissim's belt.

My sister agreed to lay down *Little Women* for a few minutes, and we went up together to the second floor.

When we walked into the room, Bracha and her children were sitting on the floor, eating the watermelon that was smeared all over the room. Bracha invited us to join in, as it had been an especially large watermelon, and we sat down with the others and started feasting.

My mother was right. It was perfectly OK to eat off Bracha's clean floor, which she got down on all fours to scrub every single day, even if the end of the world was nigh.

Dad taught Bracha how to play rummy, and she would sometimes join them as a fifth hand in a game. Why only a fifth hand? So she shouldn't, God forbid, spoil the game. Because if Nissim came home suddenly and called down for her to come straight home, she would spring up in fright from the table and leave behind all the rummy cubes. She would run upstairs quickly before he went crazy and shouted at her to stop wasting all her time playing rummy all day with those Romanians. Bracha was always doing things for Nissim, taking off his shoes and smiling at him, as if she even liked him.

The last time they played rummy, Dad persuaded Bracha to tell Nissim that the next time he raised his hand to her, she wouldn't give him any at night. I don't know what Bracha said to Nissim about no longer giving him any at night, but the fact is that it worked. Nissim stopped beating Bracha and only continued beating an education into his children with a belt. I never understood why they too couldn't threaten not to give him any at night so he'd stop whipping them.

By turning our home into a shelter for every battered woman or child who needed it, my dad effectively invented late-1970s feminism on Stanton Street.

Opposite us lived the Abbas family from Morocco, a family of twelve with everyone beating everyone else. The parents beat the children, the older children beat the younger children, and the younger children beat the babies. They all wanted to grow up quickly so they could beat the next-in-line sibling.

And of course, all the older and younger children got whipped by the parents.

My sister used to visit them and warned us not to dare go into their lavatory, even if we were dying to go, because we could fall into the hole. In our building on Stanton, all the lavatories had bowls, but across the road at the Abbas family's apartment the lavatory consisted of a hole in the floor. My sister explained that we were liable to be sucked down into the black hole when were doing our business.

Sima once asked Sefi where she thought the black hole led to, and my sister, who knew everything, told her, "To Auschwitz."

The apartment on the other side of the first-floor staircase—the floor we lived on—was occupied by Yeheskel the Pole. Yeheskel had a savings-and-loan hairstyle. He'd grow his hair long on one side and borrow it to drape over his head and cover his bald patch over to the other side, where it refused to grow. Yeheskel had two albino children, twins who refused to eat. Yeheskel used to take them out to our fancy yard, the private playground that belonged exclusively to 40 Stanton; he sat them on the stone step and let them watch us at play. He would ask us to hold a handstand competition, and as the small, very albino children were watching us in admiration, he would shove a dubious-looking brown porridge into their mouths. No wonder the albinos didn't want to eat. It looked so repulsive, the poor kids spewed it out in disgust as soon at it passed their lips. Yeheskel or his wife would scoop up the now even browner porridge spewed up by the twins and continued feeding them the vomited-up mixture as if nothing had happened. Although I loathed the parents, I would always do the splits for the albino kids whenever they asked me to, because I felt really sorry for them and the way they were being force-fed. When the albino twins had finished eating, we all dispersed, each to his or her own home, because it was time for the sacred afternoon siesta between two and four. My sister and I went to eat our *chorba* soup, whenever the neighboring Mizrahi girls were invited; the Abbas family to their *mufleta*; the albinos had already eaten their vomit; only at Marina's we never knew what was being eaten, because we never got invited.

Marina was a model; I'm not sure if by profession, but certainly by the way she looked. She was blond, tall, and very pretty. She even behaved like a model, and I have no doubt that if Calvin Klein had known her today, he would have

signed her on for life, since Marina was so thin as to be transparent. Because she was obsessed with cleanliness, Marina
never allowed her daughter Nava to play with us. Nava had
inherited her mother's transparency, but where her mother
was serious, the girl smiled a lot and was very cheerful and
impish. As soon as Nava came home from school she'd be
placed straight into the bath, where she was scrubbed clean
as if she were a horse after a wild, sweaty gallop. Her mother
removed every grain of dirt that might have attached itself to
the girl in school, including under her fingernails and behind
her ears. When Marina had finished scouring her daughter,
who was probably transparent from all that scrubbing as
well, she fed her some fruit and sent her to bed. Nava was
never fed hot food at home, only in school, because Marina
didn't want to dirty the stove with cooking. She was sensitive
to gas and to cleanliness. After her afternoon rest, Marina
allowed Nava to sit on the balcony and watch how we
street children played. Of course she was never allowed to
go down to the street to play with us, so as not to get dirty.
Nor was she allowed to invite children home, since children
make a mess. If Marina had been able to avoid sending Nava
to school altogether, she would no doubt have done so, but
she couldn't because of the compulsory education law. In
Wadi Salib, the compulsory education law was sacrosanct;
since most of the wadi's inhabitants had not gone to school
in their countries of origin, it didn't occur to them to send
their own children to school now they were in Israel. But

when school inspectors began appearing at their homes and they discovered that in order to integrate and learn Hebrew it was their duty to provide their children with an education, the parents capitulated. Moreover, in school, their kids were given a free ten o'clock meal of chocolate milk and fruit and a hot dinner, which was definitely worthwhile.

Even we Ashkenazis were considered low-class by Marina; to her it made no difference that we were white and didn't look like those other black barbarians. The fact remained that Nava was never allowed to play with us Romanian girls, either.

I would watch her little face peeping through the bars of her roof apartment, watching us with envy, watching the neighborhood children playing in the street, seeing the promised land but unable to go down to it.

When we asked Dad to do something for that poor girl, he just shrugged and said, "There's nothing I can do, that's the way she came back from the Holocaust."

And the story goes that Marina, who was a girl of about sixteen in the death camp, transparent and very beautiful, was the camp whore, fulfilling the sexual needs of the Gestapo officers. When the war was over, she spent her life scrubbing herself, trying in vain to clean her body—as well as that of her little daughter, who never knew who her father was—of the Nazi filth. I don't know how Marina found her way to our building in the first place, since it had been meant to house police personnel, but she was also the first to move out.

One evening Dad seemed sad and told us that policemen

had shot at someone who was running wild in a café, and that there would probably be trouble.

The next morning we awoke to shouting and rioting in the street. We all went out to the balcony and saw, from the bottom of the street, a mass of people moving upward, bearing black flags and our national blue-and-white flag, stained with blood.

They threw stones at all the houses in which Ashkenazis lived, and Lutzi told us to get inside immediately because they'd be near our house soon and would throw stones at us too.

We all went in, except for my dad, who continued to stand alone on the balcony, watching his neighborhood friends running amok.

Mom shouted to him to get inside immediately, but Dad refused.

"I'd like to see anyone dare throw stones at me," he said. "I'm one of them, after all."

We stood peeping out of the window and saw the masses approaching our building, 40 Stanton.

Suddenly someone shouted: No one touches Franco's house.

"He's one of ours, he's Romanian."

And they all continued to march up the street toward the Hadar neighborhood, throwing stones at anyone they suspected of being Ashkenazi. They skipped our house.

OK, you don't have to be a genius to figure that out—my dad genuinely wasn't Ashkenazi.

"I want to move," she told her husband during one of their quarrels, which had become more frequent over the last year, the fifth of their marriage. "I'm cut off here from the rest of the world. I don't have a phone, and because I want you to get home from work early, I don't even have a car; there are no shops within walking distance or cafés anywhere nearby, not even a decent supermarket, and I'm stuck here in a roof apartment with God, who doesn't give a shit about me."

"But we've only lived here for two and a half years," he replied.

"That's two and a half years too many," she countered. "It was a mistake, and we've paid for it long enough."

"Let's give the place another chance. They'll be developing the area soon," he said with infinite patience.

"I don't want to give the place a chance!" she screamed at

her husband. "I need an apartment that has some connection to life and is close to the hospital. You just can't imagine the fear I live in whenever you're away from here with the car. What's going to happen to Noa? What'll happen if she suddenly doesn't feel well?"

"In Barcelona we moved only once during my entire life," he said, reciting his credo.

"You obviously didn't need any more than that," she said. "I want to move close to my sister; it'll help me with Noa's care. You, all evening you're stuck behind your desk doing those little private jobs of yours. You don't do nearly enough to share the burden of a sick child."

"I have to support the two of you," he said, "and I do all those silly extra jobs so we'll be able to see out the month. You know how important it is for me to get on in my profession, start a business of my own; I don't want to feel I'm a loser."

But she was concerned only with Noa's illness. After the operation, Noa was able to breath through her nose and did indeed gain weight, trying to make up for a whole year of no growth, but she was still in need of heavy medication and frequent outpatient visits to the hospital, where she received intravenous immunoglobulin treatment to stabilize her immune system. They used to return from hospital after a long day of treatments, and she would scrub Noa in the bath, cleaning the hospital off her. Then she would fill the bath for herself and climb in, dead tired.

Over the years that her daughter was receiving treatment

in the oncology/hematology department, she often encountered child cancer patients, who would no longer be there
on her next visit. Whenever she heard that a child had died,
she felt deeply depressed, full of fears. All her frustration,
anger, and helplessness, she turned against their roof apartment and its lack of telephone, and against anyone else who
crossed her path.

The more she talked about moving house in ever-
increasing bouts of hysteria, the more closed and introverted
he became, telling her only that until she stopped being
hysterical, he had nothing to say to her.

They were in the car when one of their quarrels broke out,
on their way to the Davush beach, where they had planned
to meet up with her sister and her family. It was a Saturday
morning.

"I am not hysterical, and I want to move house. Otherwise I'll jump off the roof with Noa in my arms," she
threatened.

"I don't understand how you could have turned into—"
He cut himself short.

"What have I turned into?" she asked in astonishment.

"Your mother. Her whole life, the only things she ever
cared about were her daughters. She didn't care about her
husband, she didn't care about herself, and she cared about
nothing else. Only her daughters."

"Are you trying to say that I don't care about you?" she
asked him.

"You don't have time for me, and you don't care about me," he replied. "You are always, but always, tired at night, and I don't even dare come anywhere near you."

"You are so right. At this point in time, sex is just not at the top of my agenda," she said.

"Your 'at this point in time' has been going on for over two years," he retorted.

"What are you complaining about? I cook you the food you like; you come home to an apartment that is clean and well cared for, even when I've been with Noa at the hospital all day long. Your clothes are always laundered and ironed. You never have to feed or wash your daughter, because I've already done it. What more can I do for you?" she asked. "But when I've been asking you for a whole week already to change a lightbulb in the bedroom, you say there isn't a spare bulb to be found. So damn well go and buy a new one and change the fucking lightbulb that died on us a week ago."

"You're being hysterical again," he said, but she went on shouting.

"And if I tell you even before the beginning of summer that the roof needs seeing to before it gets really hot, it takes you almost two months and only at the end of summer, after Noa and I have almost melted from the heat under the hot tin roof, for you to deign to do it. And even then, it takes two successive Saturdays. Saturdays, the only days on which you can give me some breathing space."

"You see, that's what I'm talking about. You're always whining to me. If I don't do something, then why don't I do it, and when I do eventually do something, why does it take me so long. It's impossible to get out from under you. It's a big roof. It can't be done in just one day."

"Oh, yes," she hissed. "So how come our neighbors managed to get theirs done in three hours?"

"Because they just poured on some paint and smeared it around with a broom," he replied.

"Whereas you painted it on with a paintbrush? The main thing is that it did me out of an entire summer and two Saturdays. And there's no getting back that time."

"I'm sorry I don't meet your expectations. You should have married a man like your brother-in-law. Do you think I don't feel you all the time comparing me to him? What fault is it of mine that he's an Israeli and understands the mentality here, and I have to take home stupid work so we'll make it through the month?" Suddenly he fell silent.

"You don't need to be an Israeli in order to change a light-bulb," she said. "To move house to the center of the country, you don't need to be an Israeli. You just need to want to, and you simply don't want to. Dear God, these quarrels remind me of the quarrels my parents had. And talking of parents, can't your parents give us a little help?"

"I don't want to ask them for any more. It's enough they bought us this apartment," he replied, angry.

"I mean, help us a little with the child."

"What do you want from my parents? They don't live here in Israel," he said, and she thought to herself that if her father were alive and her mother weren't so sick, they wouldn't have thought twice about presenting themselves on her doorstep with an offer to help her with Noa.

They arrived at the beach and he stomped off into the water, disregarding the black flag waving over the waves. And she stayed on the beach with Noa, waiting for her sister to arrive. She watched him from a distance, swimming in the Mediterranean Sea, wondering what was happening to them. But as soon as her sister arrived with her family, they immediately set about building sand castles with the girls.

After a while the man emerged blindly from the water and said that a large wave had pulled his prescription glasses from his eyes. She didn't like to ask him what responsible adult goes into a stormy sea with his prescription glasses on, but only asked if he'd searched for them.

"Of course I searched for them," he replied tetchily, angry over their conversation in the car as well as at the loss of his glasses. "Didn't you notice I was in the water for over an hour?"

"No," she said. "I'm sorry, but I didn't notice. You're not a little kid that I need to keep my eye on." She was as angry as he was over the loss of the new prescription sunglasses he had bought recently for what she considered to be a price beyond their means.

"Whereabouts in the water were you?" she asked. "Why don't you keep an eye on Noa, and I'll go in to look for them?"

"There's no hope of you finding them. Can't you see how high the waves are?"

Now he was annoyed that she wanted to go out searching for the glasses, when he had failed to find them.

"What difference does it make? I wanted to dip in the water anyway," she said, and he pointed at the last place where he'd seen his prescription glasses in the water.

She went into the water and dove close to the sand when she was threatened by a large wave ringed with white foam.

When the wave passed, she dived again with her eyes open and saw something shiny in the water. She grabbed the object and swam up to the surface to take in a gulp of air. She thought all the time about Noa and how she had been able to survive a whole year without the ability to breathe. Just the thought made her stomach shrink. When she opened her hand, she discovered a wide gold wedding ring. With one hand she held on to the ring, and with the other she continued to sift through the water, this time without diving. Soon she was holding on to something. She hoped it wasn't a jellyfish she was holding by mistake, and when she opened her eyes, she saw her husband's glasses. She climbed out of the water, showed her husband the wedding ring, and asked him if he hadn't by any chance lost one.

"I told you it was a waste of time," he gloated.

"So maybe you lost a pair of glasses," she said, pleased, as she opened her other hand to show him his glasses.

She walked over to the lifeguard and gave him the lost ring; afterward she thought to herself that maybe the man or woman who had lost the ring was just one more half of a frustrated couple, and in fact hadn't lost the ring at all but had thrown it into the sea on purpose. When she joined her family in the shade, her sister told her that her husband had said of her that wherever she was thrown—even into stormy waters—she would always come out standing.

"So that's good, isn't it?" she asked her sister.

"I think he was pissed off at you finding his glasses," her sister answered.

That night Noa ran a high fever. They flew to the hospital, fearing that Noa had become dehydrated from her day in the sun. The doctors in the emergency room immediately hooked the child up to an infusion and said they suspected meningitis and wanted to conduct a bone marrow test to determine if it was viral or—heaven forbid—bacterial.

"And what's the treatment going to be?" she asked.

"Usually when it's viral, we don't give antibiotics intravenously, but in Noa's case we will give her antibiotics because of her inferior immune system."

"If you're going to medicate her anyway, what's the point of a bone marrow test?" she insisted on asking, and the Saturday-night-duty doctor in emergency explained impatiently that they needed to know in any case.

"Why in any case?" she continued to insist. "Will it change the treatment?"

"No," said the enthusiastic duty doctor.

"Then I'm not going to sign a consent form for the test," she said.

"It's a procedure we always do in emergency when we suspect meningitis," the duty doctor tried to explain to her.

"So take us out of your regular procedure box. I'm not signing!" she yelled at the doctor, aware of the fact that she was venting on him all the anger left over from the morning's quarrel with her husband.

"I think we need to know." Her husband said his piece.

"We don't need anything!" she screamed at him, and the entire Saturday-night emergency room staff came over to see where all the noise was coming from. On the verge of a complete nervous breakdown, she picked Noa up in her arms, as if holding her hostage, and shouted that no one was coming anywhere near them.

The man tried to get close to her, and she screamed that he was the last person she'd allow anywhere near her. He stopped at a distance from her, hissing at her belligerently to calm down. "I don't want to calm down!" she screamed.

"I want you to call the head of hematology, who's in charge of Noa's treatment," she said to the duty doctor in a split second of sanity.

"She's not on call today, and I'm not going to disturb her at eleven o'clock at night."

"Then I'll disturb her," she said. "What's her phone number?"

The duty doctor refused to give her the number, and she said to the nurse at reception that if they didn't give it to her, she'd take her daughter back home at this very moment, and the responsibility was all theirs.

The doctor nodded, and the nurse handed her the phone number of the head of hematology. She called Professor Zeizov, apologized for the hour, and said she had to hear her opinion, since she didn't believe there was any point in subjecting Noa to a difficult and dangerous test if she was going to receive antibiotics intravenously anyway. The professor listened, asked how the symptoms had begun and when Noa's temperature had started to rise, and then said to her that she thought she was right, and there was no reason to subject the child to the torture of a painful medical procedure.

The professor asked to talk to the duty doctor. She handed over the telephone, and he nodded his head throughout the conversation, writing down the medication the professor prescribed over the phone. After hanging up, he told the nurse that from now on, when a child from oncology/hematology arrived at the emergency room, treatment had to be coordinated with the department doctor in charge. "These are the new directives," he explained.

The test was canceled, and she went aside to break down in silence.

Afterward, and for the rest of the week until Noa was released from the hospital after completing a course of antibiotics, she was beside her daughter's bed day and night and didn't exchange a single word with him. She didn't reply when he spoke to her, and she refused to let him take over from her at the hospital at night. She wanted to punish him.

When they returned home from the hospital, she said that if they didn't start looking for another apartment, she would take Noa and move in with her sister. He told her she could start house hunting.

"Pity it cost me two years' worth of health," she said, and turned her back on him when they went to sleep.

Moving House

This is my substitute, this is my pardon, this is my atonement, this rooster goes to death, and I shall enter a long, happy, and peaceful life.

Together my sister and I held the atonement chicken above our heads, swinging it round and round under the watchful eyes of our mother, who made sure we didn't miss a word of the prayer that accompanied this ritual.

"Any minute this chicken is going to shit on my head," I yelled at my mother.

"You should only be so lucky," she replied. "It's a sign of good fortune."

"But I don't want anyone to shit on my head, not even your stupid chicken," I fumed.

My parents always fasted on Yom Kippur. They never cheated, not even once. Even in the worst *hamsin* heat waves, they didn't let so much as a drop of water past their lips, and they certainly didn't brush their teeth.

Dad went to the Sephardi synagogue, and Mom to the Ashkenazi synagogue.

Dad announced that his prayers this year were going to be a whole lot more meaningful and heartfelt because we were on the verge of turning over a new leaf. After all these years, Dad had been granted permanency at the Autocar factory where he worked as a guard, and he decided that the time had come to get out of Wadi Salib. He was very disappointed with his party and its attempts to quell the race riots and wanted to provide us, his daughters, with a change of scenery, since everyone knows that a change of place brings a change of luck. We moved school too that year, but this was mere coincidence. The authorities, which had no idea how to handle race riots, decided to transfer my sister's class from the Ma'alot Hanevi'im school to the Amami Aleph school. Since no plans were afoot to transfer my class, Mom went to the authorities to explain that it was absolutely out of the question to separate me from my sister, since we spent all our time together, and were actually more or less up each other's backside. The authorities refused, and Mom threw a temper tantrum and made it clear to them that in that case, the older one wasn't going to transfer, either; it was both of them together or neither one of them. In fact, they should put us both in the same class. Only after I explained to Mom that I wasn't such a genius as to justify moving me up a year did she agree to relinquish her demand to have us both in the same class, but she was adamant about our attending the same school. The school gave in and agreed to my mother's deal in order to keep my sister, a straight-A student and a credit to the school.

So we moved house after Yom Kippur. From a one-room apartment on Stanton we moved to an airy three-room rental for which my parents were required to pay an initial key-money deposit; quality of life for the girls.

My dad took out a mortgage, Mum took the rummy, and we moved to Hadekalim Street in downtown Haifa.

Mum opened wide all the windows to let in the air from all directions, and the stench that immediately filled the apartment was absolutely unbearable.

Hadekalim Street, despite its fancy name, was on the edge of the garbage dump belonging to the Turkish market, which was actually located in the courtyard of the building adjacent to ours. In other words, Mom and Dad had bought an apartment right in the middle of downtown Haifa's shit-hole. They told us apologetically that it was the only place they could afford—and even that required a key-money deposit—because it was cheap.

"It's true," my mother recalled, "the windows were always closed whenever we came to examine it thoroughly before deciding on improving our girls' quality of life."

It was the filthiest, most stinky street in Haifa, and we never again went down to play. There was nowhere to play.

The only good thing about Hadekalim Street was, again, our balcony.

The balcony overlooked Jaffa Street, downtown Haifa's main thoroughfare, the street where everything happens. Most of the action took place right opposite our balcony. There was a coffee bar there, although it was more like a saloon, and it was there that all Haifa's lowlife, seamen, and whores congregated to play backgammon all day, drink arak, and have fights. Twice a week they'd break up all the chairs and tables, until the bar discovered plastic furniture.

And every night until late, or until all his stock was sold, the Bulgarian *burekas* man stood at his stall on the sidewalk in front of the café, where, with amazing dexterity, he would slice the *burekas* in two or four sections, peel a brown hard-boiled egg, sprinkle a little salt and pepper on top, and hand it all in a cardboard container to the happy customer.

Right next to the café several stores sold cheap household goods and cleaning materials and stalls piled with duty-free clothing from abroad, smuggled in by seamen and sold cheap on the street until the next police raid. And there was also the delicatessen with the nonkosher salamis and real Bulgarian cheese and all kinds of delicacies that came from abroad and were sold dirt-cheap on Jaffa Street opposite our balcony. From all over Haifa people came to do their shopping downtown, from the Carmel, Hadar, and Ahuza neighborhoods, as well as from the outlying towns, known as the Kiryas.

My sister and I spent hours on end sitting on the balcony at a small table that served as a reserve dining table when we had guests, watching the strangers below and speculating about their lives.

After school we stayed at home, reading books, and my sister continue to educate me in the ways of the world: Keep your mouth closed when you are eating; walk with your head up and your back straight so you don't get a hump; place a book on your head and pull your neck upward as if you can feel someone pulling you up by the top of your head; don't roll your R's, so as not to emphasize that you are Romanian. Swallow them.

Don't swear.

Don't be rude.

Don't spit.

Don't kick.

Smile politely, enigmatically.

Don't look people straight in the eye, even if you are dying to do so; lower your eyes humbly. Stop looking at the world with that judgmental expression on your face.

Say little and learn to listen, because most people in the world have more to say than you have, until you grow up.

These were my sister's ten commandments.

But most important, the most important thing of all, is to be special, to be different from everyone else. No one in my class knows anything about me, no one even knows where I live, and no one knows what my parents do for a living.

I am a complete mystery to them.

"Of course, it's because you're ashamed to say," I said to my sister, and she replied that it's her choice not to say.

In the 1960s, when everyone wanted to be like everyone else and look alike and not be different or stand out, because they wanted Israeli society to be homogeneous, Sefi chose to be different because she understood that different is special.

Sefi attended the prestigious and snobbish Reali High School. When it was her turn to go down to the grocer's store, she made a point of dressing nicely so that if she bumped into someone from her school they would think that she was just passing, same as they were.

Unlike me, my sister never went down in shorts and a T-shirt and flip-flops on her feet; she really made an effort to look as if she was going out on the town. Even Tova and Malka, her childhood friends, were made to swear not to tell anyone in their class where she lived. The whole class, including the teachers, knew that Sefi lived in Hadekalim Street, but they were all certain that Hadekalim Street was a nice street lined with palm trees in the Carmel neighborhood.

And my sister never put them right.

When anyone asked me the way to my home, I used to say, "Just follow the smell, you can't miss." And again my sister said that because I'm pretty I could allow myself to say whatever I like.

"So what?" I said to my big sister, who thought that she was merely wise. "You're pretty, too."

But my mother knew how to take advantage of my natural talents, and when she went to the market, she forced me to go with her. According to my mother, when the greengrocer sees a pretty girl, he gets confused and gives her the best produce and even a discount. The butcher used to give Mom free food for our dog; whereas were it not for my coquettish smile, he would have sent her packing empty-handed. She didn't dare force Sefi to go with her to the market because she didn't think her smile was flirtatious enough. Besides, Sefi would certainly have refused to go because she spent all her time doing homework, so that she could be top of the class in the prestigious Reali High School as well.

The best gift I was given from my life in Wadi Salib was the ability to get along in life.

Sefi was given inspiration.

For six years we lived in the lowest and dirtiest street in Haifa.

When Sefi grew sick and tired of Hadekalim Street, with the Turkish market touching the port, she explained to my dad that if we didn't move house immediately, I would turn into a streetwalker, even though I attended the Leo Beck

High School, since a girl of my age needs company and the only company in the vicinity were those downtown losers. "And she is already that way inclined," she added.

Dad became stressed, persuaded Mom to take an even more enormous mortgage before I turn into a loser, and we moved to Hapo'el Street in the Hadar HaCarmel neighborhood, opposite the Tamar cinema, where that Nazi usher had taunted Dad by refusing to let him in to see *Oklahoma!*

Sefi and I then experienced a rebirth, and were no longer ashamed of our neighborhood and our Romanian heritage. On the other hand, there still wasn't much for us to boast about.

They put their apartment up for sale, and she started doing the rounds of realtors in Ramat Aviv. To exchange a roof apartment in Rishon le Zion for a four-room apartment with no balcony in Ramat Aviv, they would have to add twenty thousand dollars. She told her husband that they could make do with three rooms, but he insisted that he needed a study in which to do the extra work he was obliged to bring home. To her surprise, his parents agreed to the necessary sum, and his mother told her over the phone that she had never understood how they had survived so long in a place that was so cut off from civilization. At long last, after a two-and-a-half-year wait, they finally received a telephone line, which made it possible to respond to potential buyers. After seeing a variety of properties that were above their budget, she walked into an especially neglected four-room apartment and managed to bargain the price down to a sum that would leave them with five thousand dollars to fix it up and another three thousand to cover the mandatory betterment tax.

Her husband agreed that the apartment, with its open vistas on all sides, had loads of potential, but that renovation would cost them much more money than they had.

She persuaded him that they would repair only where absolutely necessary, and they bought the apartment; at the same time they sold their roof apartment to a very nice Argentinean couple. The entire transaction was negotiated and finalized within three months.

When she went to the betterment tax office to check how much they were required to pay on the apartment, the clerk told her that they were entitled to a tax exemption for one apartment, since her husband was a new immigrant. He calculated the price of the new apartment and showed her the total of three thousand dollars they were required to pay.

"And how much betterment tax are we supposed to pay on the Rishon le Zion apartment?" she asked the clerk.

"You don't have to pay," the kindly clerk explained to her patiently. "You're exempt from paying on one apartment."

"Still, how much is the betterment tax on the Rishon le Zion apartment?" she asked again.

The clerk calculated the cost of the apartment they had bought three years before, subtracted, added; raised the interest, multiplied by a third, and arrived at the sum of one thousand dollars.

"Is that the final sum?" she asked him.

"A thousand dollars," he said. "That's the sum, but I must repeat that you are entitled to a tax exemption on one apartment."

"Good," she said to him. "So I shall now pay you one thousand dollars betterment tax on the Rishon le Zion apartment, and I'll take the exemption we're entitled to for the new apartment."

"Suit yourself," said the kindly clerk, and she went home thrilled at having in one instant earned a new kitchen for her new home.

She then called Kushi, who was a Jerusalem building contractor, and asked him for a quote for breaking down walls between the kitchen and living room, between the living room and the extra room, and between the bathroom and the small balcony.

"In Barcelona you quarreled with me because our living room was too big, and here you want to enlarge the living room?" said her husband, who objected to knocking down walls.

"You're right," she said. "I'm inconsistent. Nothing I can do about it, I'm a woman."

"And how much does Kushi want for the renovation?" he asked.

"He told me not to worry," she replied.

"I am extremely worried when I am told not to worry," her husband said, and she agreed with him, except when it concerned Kushi.

Kushi came down from Jerusalem with three workers, who worked on the apartment for a full month while she wandered about freely under their feet, happy that for the first time she was able on most days to leave Noa in a day care center, except for the days they had to spend in the hospital.

Her husband had joined a well-known firm of architects and, to her joy, left the entire renovation project in her hands. Her sister came over and offered architectural advice that she immediately adopted without telling her husband that these were her sister's ideas.

Kushi brought some weed, and between smoking and breaking down walls, they sat back and examined the results, rolling about laughing. She began to feel that she was getting her life back and even agreed to go out a couple of times, galloping over the sand dunes in Kushi's truck, letting the wind dry away her tears. She loved the platonic relationship she shared with Kushi, who brought back to her those feelings she'd had as a girl.

"Why do we lose our minds when we get married?" she asked him as they watched the waves on a wet winter's day.

"I never lost my mind," he replied. "I only ever do what I want to do."

"OK, you have that prerogative," she said, meaning that it was also because he was a man, and because he made a lot of money as a building contractor, and especially because— thank God—he had two healthy daughters and a wife to raise them with unbounded love.

She told Kushi that she had forgotten how she had once been. "Nowadays, everything I do, I have to consider if it'll please my husband or not, and I don't like what I've become. I don't even know what kind of work I want to do. I don't want to go back to the boring drawing board that never suited me in the first place, and I don't know what I should do with myself."

Kushi, who as usual had the knack of explaining things to her about herself that she hadn't known before, told her that she decided to study architecture at the school for architects only because her sister had studied architecture at the Technion. "I've never understood why you thought you were less talented than she is," he said, and added that as a profession architecture suited her sister but not her.

They finished the work after a month, and she loved what she saw. The small apartment had transformed into a single large space. Of the original three bedrooms, only two remained, theirs and Noa's. The bathroom had become a kingdom in its own right once she had joined the small balcony to it, and after the walls had been tiled with local marble, the room took on a Mediterranean look, with clean and simple lines.

"How much do I owe you?" she asked Kushi, and he replied that it was a gift from him to Noa.

When she insisted, he agreed to accept only the cost of labor, which added up to the sum she had budgeted for in the first place, but what they had now was a spacious apartment beautifully designed in the best of taste.

She told her husband about Kushi's gift, and he found it strange that she had agreed to accept something like this from a friend. She told him that anything regarding Kushi could never be construed as strange, and went on to tell him that Kushi had offered—when she was eighteen—to make her a gift of her baby, so she wouldn't have to have an abortion.

"What do you mean, your baby?" he asked suspiciously.

"I told you that I got pregnant by my first boyfriend, Israel. Well, Kushi, who was an officer cadet with the Paratroop Division at the time, offered to marry me so I could keep the baby and then divorce him whenever I wanted. He thought I really wanted that baby, and what he offered was financial backing so I'd be able to raise it. If you ask me, that gift was much more special than this one," she told her husband.

"And why didn't you accept?" her husband asked.

"Because Kushi was wrong. I didn't want Israel's baby. You're the first man I ever knew that I wanted to have a baby with." Her husband hugged her and lifted her in his arms as they entered their new bedroom. Afterward he whispered to her that the renovation had come out extremely well. He said it in Spanish, to avoid making mistakes in Hebrew.

She loved the new apartment even though it didn't have a balcony. She especially loved the fact that there were lots of beautiful parks in the area where she could spend afternoons with Noa; and her sister and mother now lived close by. She felt that now—just maybe—after two and a half years, life was once again smiling on her.

She went for a job interview at the International Bank and was accepted. She wanted to work with people and still be home in the afternoons with Noa, and she had to work only two evenings a week. When she asked her husband to stay with Noa two evenings a week, he explained that he'd only recently started in this new job and he couldn't very well leave at three thirty in the afternoon, so she hired a young student, who fell in love at first sight with Noa, and felt quite safe when she left for work in the afternoon.

The bank manager was aware of Noa's condition and didn't bother her when she had to take her to the hospital for tests or treatment.

She advanced quickly in the bank, and within a year she was already behind a desk in the stocks and bonds department. She decided that Kushi was right; it was quite likely that she, and not only her sister, was successful.

In the bank she had several regular clients who insisted on dealing only with her; and then there were also those who pursued her passionately. She rejected them all, but admitted to herself that she felt once again like a woman. Flattered that she was desirable both in her job and as a woman, she was unable to share her feelings with her husband, whose professional success had fallen short of his expectations when he arrived in Israel. She tried to suggest subtly that he might consider switching to another profession, as she had done, but he insisted sharply that he had spent five years studying the profession he loved and had no intention at this stage of giving it up. A profession, he said, is not an apartment that you can change. Why not? she asked.

One evening she asked him if he regretted that they had immigrated to Israel, while in Barcelona people who had studied with him were advancing at a much greater pace. He replied that he liked living in Israel, and that his time would also come, one day. But he was visibly upset by the fact that her sister was on the verge of success, and her highly impressive presentation had earned her a commission to design the Kodak building; she watched as her six-feet-tall husband shrank in stature before her very eyes. In their married life the cracks began to widen, as if in a badly renovated building.

She enjoyed his parents' annual visits to Israel, when he allowed himself to relax. She was the perfect hostess and often invited his sister and her family to join them in family meals.

On one of his parents' visits, his mother asked her if she wasn't thinking of having another baby. She looked at the older woman in disbelief and told her that Noa needed all the time she could devote to her. His mother tried to tell her gently that in her opinion, she should be open to other things too.

Her own mother used to look at her sadly and then at Noa and sigh, her look saying, "I am here for you, my daughter."

This is the way you raised me, her eyes responded to her mother.

In the mornings she always arose early to cook Noa's lunch, because she wanted her daughter to eat fresh food every day. She did the laundry, hung it out to dry, woke Noa, dressed and fed her, made her a sandwich, took her to her nursery school, and then rushed off to work. At the same time, her husband would wake up reluctant to go to work and spend half an hour in their lovely bathroom. On the few mornings that she wanted him to get up early and get Noa ready for nursery school, it was so difficult to wake him that by the time she arrived at the bank, she was tense and angry. In the evenings, she laid into him for spending all his time in his study, seeing only to his own affairs and not taking into consideration that there might be all kinds of other things to take care of in the house, including a little girl who would benefit from having a story read to her at bedtime, to help her development.

"I don't read Hebrew well enough," he said, knowing that she was actually referring to the fact that her brother-in-law read each of his daughters a whole book every evening, even though the younger one was only six months old.

"All right, then, you do the dishes, and I'll read her a story," she would suggest to him, but when she saw the piles of dishes still in the sink at eleven o'clock at night, while he was still in his study, she attacked them angrily, deliberately making as much noise as she could, so as to disturb him. He would stomp over irately, asking what difference it made to her if he did the dishes at one in the morning, and she'd reply that it would then be altogether impossible to wake him up in the morning.

"What do you want from me? Just ask for whatever you want," he would say feebly in the end.

"I shouldn't have to ask you to do things. You should be able to see for yourself what needs doing and what doesn't," she would say.

"What am I asking of you already? That you tell me what it is you want me to do to help you?" he'd repeat.

"That's just it—you see it as helping me, while I want you to share the work with me and not have to wait for me to issue orders. It's embarrassing," she said in Hebrew, and he asked her what "embarrassing" meant. Noa started crying, and she didn't want the child to think of herself as a burden.

She particularly loathed asking him to take Noa to the hospital in her place, because she too couldn't absent herself from work too frequently. There was a limit, after all, to her boss's patience in the matter. He told her that at his job he had to inform them at least a week in advance, and he really didn't like doing it. She really didn't want Noa growing up with parents who were constantly bickering over who had to do what.

At least her parents' quarrels had always been around her father's squandering and her mother's fear that there would not be enough for the girls' dowry. She had married her husband because she loved him, so why the hell did she have to feel as if she was his sergeant major, delegating chores all day long? Why couldn't he decide for himself what he had to do?

"Maybe we should get divorced," she suggested.

"Why?" He was shocked.

"Because there is something wrong between us," she said.

"It's normal," he said. "They say that all couples go through a crisis after seven years of marriage."

"It didn't happen to my sister," she said quietly, "and with us it only seems to get worse as time goes by."

"I don't understand why you are forever complaining. Lots of people in the office tell me that I am a model husband."

She was completely taken aback by this. "How do they know what kind of a husband you are?" she asked.

"I work with them all day, don't I? They see me calling you at work every day to ask how you are, and in the afternoons when you are at work, I call the babysitter and have a long conversation with her to make sure that Noa is all right. Every Friday I bring you flowers. How many husbands do you know who bring their wives flowers after seven years of marriage? I never forget your birthday or our wedding anniversary."

"Well, thank you very much for that, really," she replied.

"You see. I can't even hold a conversation with you, without you putting me down with your cynicism."

She looked at him and felt like giving him a good slap, but she didn't like to because he really did remember her birthday, whereas she had forgotten his. He even remembered her sister and brother-in-law's birthdays, and those of her nieces, and she herself was really bad at these things.

"I don't know what else to do," she said to her sister, weeping, "he's so hard to live with. I sometimes think that it must be because of the differences in mentality between us. Because of our different upbringing." Her sister said she didn't think that was the reason.

"So what is the reason?" she asked her sister, who replied that she thought it was simply that he couldn't keep up with her. "You are quick to solve problems, and you have initiative, while he is heavy and hesitant and slow to decide, and it drives you crazy. Do you remember that neighbor of ours, Albert, in our house in downtown on Hadekalim Street, how he kept on harassing you?"

"Of course I remember. Why have you suddenly brought him up?"

"You were only twelve, and he was forever lying in wait for you in the staircase and trying to fumble with you, and you were resourceful enough not to go to whining to Dad but to go straight to his wife and threaten her that if her husband didn't stop harassing you, you'd go to the police. And he stopped immediately."

"Sure." She started laughing. "I knew he'd be more afraid of his wife than of Dad."

"And you were only twelve," her sister reminded her. "I'm sure that now, too, you'll find a way to sort out your problems."

"It takes two to tango," she told her sister.

And one day she noticed that he had spent much longer

than half an hour in the bath and emerged perfumed from top to toe and whistling a happy tune.

"I've noticed that you don't like me working at home in the evenings," he told her, "so I've decided to take on another job. I'll be home late."

"Has something good happened?" she asked, and he gave her a peck on the cheek and asked if one had to have a special reason to be in a good mood. For two weeks he whistled and hummed and set off for work even before she had finished dressing and feeding Noa; and when he returned home at ten o'clock in the evening, she asked him if he had a mistress.

"Are you crazy?" He was horrified. "Can't a guy be in a good mood without being suspected of having taken a mistress?" he said and added that from then on he would be returning home every evening at ten o'clock because he had decided to work longer hours at his second job.

The next day she called him at his second office at seven in the evening, and he answered. She was immediately filled with remorse; her husband was working extra hours to increase their income, and she was suspecting him of having an affair.

On Friday he brought her flowers as usual, and she suggested that they take a holiday abroad, since they'd now have some spare cash. "I can leave Noa with my sister," she said, and he replied that he was just about to suggest joining a group of his friends from work, who were organizing a vacation at Club Med in Ahziv.

She agreed, but continued to suspect his good mood,

which seemed to improve from day to day. Now he was even trumpeting to himself in the bath, in which he spent a good hour every morning, emerging eventually squeaky-clean and highly perfumed.

They went to Ahziv with a group of very nice people, including Shula, who was especially charming toward her. She took an immediate liking to Shula, who also happened to be Romanian. But Shula was on her own, without a partner, and when she told her that she was divorced, she immediately suspected her of being her husband's mistress. Especially because he hardly laid a finger on her all week, even though they were alone at last after a very long time. They had sex only twice during that week, and even then she felt that his heart wasn't really with her. She thought she might just be imagining it, but her senses told her that he was dying for the vacation to come to an end.

"You're always complaining that I don't initiate sex, but now when I do, you're not interested?" she asked him, but he was evasive and avoided looking her straight in the eye. He said that maybe he just wasn't in the mood.

They returned from their vacation, and she continued to be suspicious of his good spirits. When she called his second place of work at eight in the evening and someone else answered the phone and told her that he had stepped out a half hour before, she waited for him to arrive, sure that he would be home any minute to sort out the matter of his mistress once and for all.

He turned up at eleven o'clock, and when she asked him furiously where he'd been until then, he understood that she had called him at work and told her immediately that he had indeed left early, but had met a colleague, and they'd been out drinking until a short while before.

"Which friend?" she asked, and he said she didn't know him; it was someone new who had started working in his office that morning.

The following morning when he emerged washed and smiling from the bathroom, she told him to say hello to his girlfriend for her. He yelled at her that there was no girlfriend and that he was sick and tired of her constant suspicions.

"Constant?" she asked innocently. "My suspicions began two months ago."

He slammed the door as he left. Noa looked at her and started to cry.

She put Noa in nursery school and decided that she would visit his office in the afternoon, to make sure that he was indeed going on to his second job.

From four thirty she sat waiting near his office, knowing that he was due to finish at five; but she got cold feet at a quarter to five and drove away. She decided that it wasn't to her credit to be following her husband and that she was only humiliating herself, so she went home to her daughter. When he arrived home at ten in the evening, she said that she really wanted to know if he had someone else, because she would prefer to cope with any truth than live a lie.

He said he wasn't lying and that she was imagining things. During the month that followed she called him only once, at seven in the evening, at his second job, and he answered the phone and returned as usual at eleven. They hardly ever had sex, and he claimed that he was tired from working at two jobs.

On Friday she called his second job at five in the afternoon and the boss told her that he had left at one. He came home at seven, half an hour before her mother was due to join them for dinner. She told him she had called at five and he wasn't at work, and he said he'd had a meeting with an engineer, Zvika, who commissioned him to do a small private planning job for him.

After dinner she asked if he would mind driving her mother back to the retirement home she had been living in for the last two months, but he said he was tired and going to bed. When she returned and opened the door, he was on the phone, and he hung up as soon as he saw her. She pretended not to notice, and the next morning, Saturday, she forced him to take Noa to the fairground without her.

"I need to be alone with myself," she said, and he didn't dare refuse.

She called her friend Gila in Haifa. Gila was a player; when she had fallen in love with a divorced man who had three daughters and became pregnant by him, he left her, refusing to have anything to do with another child, although he loved Gila. In her seventh month, she called him and lied that a scan she'd just had showed that the baby was a boy.

They got married in Cyprus because she was a divorcee and he was a *kohen*, and there is no civil marriage or divorce in Israel, and two months later she gave birth to their first daughter. Two years later their second daughter was born.

She told Gila that she suspected her husband of having an affair, but he was denying it hotly, and it was driving her crazy. Gila asked what he was saying when he got home late. As an example, she told her about the previous night, when he'd said he he'd been at an after-work meeting with Zvika.

"Do you know this Zvika?" Gila asked her.

"Yes, actually," she replied. "When we immigrated to Israel and bought the apartment in Rishon le Zion, I worked for him for a while, until Noa was born."

"So what's your problem? Give him a call and check with him," her friend advised.

"And what, call him up just like that, after not having spoken to him for four years, suddenly I should ask him if he had a meeting yesterday with my husband?" she asked.

"You'll think of some excuse. You do want to know, don't you?" Gila urged her.

"Of course I want to know," she replied, and in the same second she knew exactly what she'd say to Zvika.

She remembered that Zvika had had the hots for Racheli, who worked alongside her in his office, but she was married and quite religious, so Zvika didn't dare make a move. Shortly after she left, Racheli too had moved away, and they'd lost touch with each other. And now—as proof of the small world we live in—just last month she'd been at the hospital with Noa when she ran into Racheli, who told her that she was newly divorced and back living with her parents in Rishon le Zion. They exchanged telephone numbers and promised to keep in touch.

She called Zvika on Saturday morning at eleven. He was quite surprised to hear her voice and asked to what he owed the honor.

"I wanted to pass on best regards from Racheli," she said, and he seemed rather pleased, and took Racheli's telephone number. She told him all about Racheli, and he asked about Noa and then about her, and when she told him that she'd been working for over a year in the stocks and bonds department of a large bank, he said that it was much more like her to work with people.

"And how's your husband?" he asked.

"He's fine," she replied. "Aren't you in contact with him?"

"Do you know how long it's been since I last saw him?" he replied. "It must be at least three years."

Her heart took a nosedive straight into her underpants.

Lies

When Mom prepared her Romanian *chorba* soup, she made a
point of inviting the Syrian girls from upstairs, Sima, Rocha,
and Yaffa, because she knew how much they loved it. Besides,
it's not expensive to make, only vegetables. Sima was a very
pretty girl, but she thought she was ugly because of the large
burn scar on her neck from a Primus stove that had been
thrown on her by mistake when she was crying too much as a
baby. The burning Primus did not calm down the crying baby,
but it did leave her with a large, meaty scar on her neck. Sima
believed that no one would ever want to marry her when she
grew up because of that scar on her neck, and Yosefa used to
reassure her by saying that it's all nonsense, and it's not beauty
that matters, but character. I asked my sister if she really believed that someone would marry Sima, and she said no.

"So why do you lie to her?" I asked, angry. "You know
how Dad hates it when we lie."

"I'm not lying. I just don't want her to be sad," my sister replied.

I went and snitched to my father that Fila was lying to Sima and telling her that someone was certainly going to want to marry her although she knows that it wasn't true, and my dad told me that there are lies that can be told to make people feel good.

That week, our school principal, Dror, who used to beat all the kids, even those who didn't deserve to be beaten, painful, ringing slaps to the face, caught me and two boys and called us to his room to interrogate us as to whether we had been keeping watch by the classroom door when Itzik was peeing into the teacher's desk drawer. One of the boys said he knew nothing about it and straight away got two ringing clouts around the head. The second boy owned up to standing watch and received four ringing clouts, and his parents were called for a hearing. I stood before the cruel principal's florid face, knowing that my dad got very angry at adults who beat little children, even when they are school principals or teachers; besides, that teacher deserved to have Itzik pee in her drawer because she was forever insulting him and telling him that in his house "they're a bunch of primitives who eat with their hands." And when the principal asked me if I had stood watch at the door, I said that I was playing catch outside with Braha, Ahuva, and Adina at the time. I lied so as to do myself good, just as Dad had explained to me, and I knew that Braha, Ahuva, and Adina would never tell on me because they were more afraid of me than of Principal Dror.

"Are you sure?" asked Principal Dror.

"I'm sure," I answered him in a firm voice, and lowered my eyes as I had been taught by my sister, since grown-ups don't like children looking them straight in the eye. It undermines their self-confidence. "The teacher can ask them himself." I was careful to use the right grammar, so as not to be on the receiving end of a slap on the face for not speaking correctly. He didn't hit me. I expect his hand was sore from already having dealt six clouts.

I rushed home and told Dad that I had lied to Principal Dror so as to avoid a beating and he kissed my cheek and said, "Good girl."

On Saturday evening when Yosefa went with Sima to Baruch's falafel stand, she shared her half portion with her friend; one bite for her, one bite for Sima, a bite for her, a bite for Sima, until they came home, when she lied to Mom in Romanian and promised that she had eaten the entire half portion by herself, no sharing.

Since Dad allowed me to lie in order to do people good, I also lied to Shmuel, my sister's friend Shoshi's brother. My sister had a lot of friends, and I had my sister; that was enough for me. Following her friend Chaya's departure to America with all her dolls, and after we had moved to downtown Haifa next to the Turkish market, Yosefa had made friends with Shoshi and visited her at home whenever she wasn't reading, because at Shoshi's place she was allowed to sew purses.

Shoshi's mother sewed bridal gowns, and since they lived in a tiny one-room apartment that housed four people and a table that served as Shoshi's workshop and took up half the room, Shoshi and my sister played under the table. They took the remnants of the white fabric and used them to sew purses. She didn't let me come with her to Shoshi's because there wasn't enough room under the table; but as compensation, she brought me one of the white purses she had made, which I filled with buttons, because I had no money.

But Mom and Dad forced my sister to take me with her to her class evenings, because I was little, and Shoshi's parents forced Shoshi to take Shmuel, her older brother, to her class evenings because he was retarded.

And so Shmuel and I would sit on the fence alone on class evenings that weren't even ours, while my sister and her friends whispered among themselves, each choosing the boy she wanted, and we discussed the meaning of life, which we painted in all sorts of colors.

"Swear you won't tell anyone," Shmuel would say to me.

"I swear." I always swore on my sister, my mother, and my dead grandmother. I refused to swear on my father because I could never be sure I wouldn't break my vow.

"I know you're not going to believe me, but when I grow up I want to get married and have two children, a boy and a girl."

"Why shouldn't I believe you?" I asked.

"Because I'm retarded," Shmuel replied.

"You're not retarded. You're just a bit slow," I told him, because that is what Dad had said about Shmuel, that he was slow. My dad also told me that Shoshi's parents had been in a forced labor camp in Romania and had managed to escape, but the Germans shot at them and hit Shoshi's mother in the leg; she was pregnant with Shmuel and fell down in a pool of blood. Her husband was able to drag her away, and that is why Shmuel was born a little slow. When the time came for Shmuel to go to school—my dad told me, and I always remembered all his stories—the authorities told them he could only be admitted to a religious boarding school. Shmuel's parents loved him very much, but they didn't love God very much, so they sent him to a school for retarded children for half a day, and Shoshi had to watch over him in the afternoons.

"Do you ever want to get married?" Shmuel asked me, and I told him that I had to because I had a dowry.

"What kind of a dowry do you have?" Shmuel asked, and I told him that I didn't know, sheets, maybe, and towels.

"My sister's friend Tova already has a refrigerator," I added.

"And what do you want to be when you grow up?" Shmuel asked me.

"I want to be wise, like my sister," I replied.

"Is being wise a profession?" he asked.

"It's a lot of professions. Wisdom gives you the chance to choose." I told him. "And what do you want to be when you grow up?"

RINA FRANK

"I want to be a gardener," Shmuel told me, and I said that gardening is a lovely job, being responsible for the earth.

"Rina, stop swinging your legs on the fence," my sister shouted at me, "you'll fall off and then they'll have to sew up your bum."

"Is Rina a name from the Bible?" Shmuel asked.

"Sure. In the Bible it means 'joy,' but in Ladino it means 'queen.' That's why my dad called me Rina. Because I'm his queen."

"And I am their prophet," said Shmuel, who may have been slow, but he knew that he was named for the biblical prophet Samuel.

"I am certain you'll get married and have two children," I lied to Shmuel, to do him good. Because he was slow, I wasn't sure he'd be able to get married, but I was certain that he could be a gardener, so I didn't really feel that I was lying to him.

When her husband walked into the apartment, she gave him two sharp slaps to his face. He didn't know what had hit him. "These are for your lies," she told him, and added, "I detest liars. Oh, and best regards from Zvika. He told me that it's been three years since he last saw you."

He was silent.

"So it's high time you told me who you've been swinging around with these last few months. But before you do so, you can feed your daughter and put her to bed. In the meantime, I'm going out to breathe some fresh air. It's suffocating in here, with all those lies filling up every inch of space."

She slammed out of the apartment and returned two hours later.

"Would you like some coffee?" he asked her.

"I want nothing from you except the truth," she replied.

"Well, it's true, I have been having an affair, with some-one from work."

"Is it Tova?" she asked.

"Why would it be Tova?" he replied. "No, it's someone who started working with us six months ago."

"What's her name, this someone?" she asked.

"Adi," he answered her.

"And how long has this affair been going on?"

"Three months." He sat down heavily opposite her, and his hands shook.

"Why are you shaking?" she hissed. "I'm the one who should be shaking." And then she noticed that she was shaking all over, not just in her hands.

"Because I don't want to lose you," he told her.

They sat opposite each other at their dining table that opened to the living room. He was afraid of her, and she was afraid of what she was about to hear.

"So every morning when you left early for work?"

"I picked her up to take her to work."

"And evenings, did you even work in the second office?" She needed to know everything.

"Of course I did," he said.

"Until what time?" she asked.

"Until seven o'clock usually," he replied.

"And every day, every day at seven o'clock you went back with her to her place and stayed until half past ten at night?" she asked.

"Yes," he admitted.

"Every evening?" She insisted on knowing. "You couldn't spend even a couple of evenings a week with us?"

"I loved her," he said. "I wanted to be with her."

"So you loved her." She was inflamed. "So it wasn't just a fleeting fuck for you."

He said nothing.

"Do you love her?"

"Yes," he said, and added immediately that he loved her too.

"I spend my days at the hospital, and every morning off you go to pick up your girlfriend so she shouldn't—God forbid—have to take the bus to work." She desperately needed to prove to him what a bastard he was.

"I always left you the car when you had to go to the hospital." He tried to prove to her that at least in this respect he was considerate of their needs.

"What do you want to do?" he asked.

"First thing I want is for you to get out of my sight. I don't want to see you here anymore."

"Do you want me to leave?" he asked, his voice trembling.

"I can't stand the sight of you," she said and urged him to leave so she could slam the door after him. Shaking all over, she remembered that movie she saw, when the police came to arrest them in that oasis that looked like something out of paradise, and time after time after time after time the girl saw the hotel explode into tiny pieces. That's what she felt like, that her life had exploded into tiny pieces.

Even when she suspected him of having an affair, she had never thought of it in terms of love. The moment he admitted to her that he was in love with that Adi of his, she felt cut to the core, as if her life had fallen apart.

He called two hours later to ask if he could come home, and she said he couldn't.

"Would you like me to come back in the evening?" he asked.

"Don't you want to go to that Adi of yours? That one you're so in love with?"

"I want to come home," he said.

"You can come home only after you tell me that you're through with her," she replied.

"So can I come home now?" he asked.

"Why, are you finished with her?"

"Yes," he replied.

"So come back in the evening," she said to him.

When he came home in the evening, she asked him what he wanted to do, and he said he didn't know. He was too confused to think what was best for him.

"Maybe we should have a trial separation," she said, and he agreed.

"Tomorrow I'll look for somewhere to live," he said.

All night they heard each other twisting, each alone in bed, she with her humiliation and he with his confusion.

She felt all alone in the world, that there was no one there for her, and each time she closed her eyes, she saw the hotel exploding into tiny pieces that can never be put together.

In the afternoon, he called her from work and told her that he'd found a room in an apartment owned by some old woman and that he'd come by later to pick up some of his things.

By the time she'd hung up she was so agitated that she called up his work and asked for Adi. "Just a moment," said the secretary, and someone picked up the phone. "Hello."

"Is this Adi?" she asked.

"Yes," Adi replied.

"Are you the same Adi that's been fucking my husband?" she asked.

There was silence on the other end of the line.

"I'm asking because I want to make sure I'm talking to the right Adi," she said, and added, "Just in case there's more than one Adi in your office."

"There's only one," Adi replied.

"So you just get your filthy hands off my husband, you fucking little whore," she said, and slammed down the receiver.

In the evening when he came to collect his things, she didn't speak to him, and didn't even reply when he asked when he could come to be with Noa.

When she arrived at the bank the following day, she said to Kobi, one of her regular clients who was always sniffing around her, that she didn't feel up to staying at work today.

"So come away with me," he suggested immediately.

"Where to?" she asked.

"I need to fly to Eilat to oversee my workers, who are laying wall-to-wall carpeting on an entire floor of the King Solomon Hotel," he said. "Would you like to come?"

"Why not?" she said, and went to her boss and told him she couldn't face working today because she'd just learned that her husband was having an affair with another woman.

"You've only just found out?" he asked nosily.

"Day before yesterday," she said and went out, with Kobi right behind her. Within two hours they had taken over an entire floor of the King Solomon Hotel, and for the first time in seven years she had sex with another man who knew what women want and made her feel like one.

Only when she returned from Eilat did she phone her sister to tell her that her husband had left home.

"How dare he do this to me?" she asked her sister, who said that maybe he was getting elsewhere what he was missing at home.

"The worst of it all is that he lied to me," she said to her sister. "It's so humiliating to be lied to." Her sister asked if that really was the thing that hurt her the most.

"Yes, what do you mean?"

"I don't know what I mean. I am only saying that you should do some genuine emotional stocktaking with regard to what you want of yourself, of your life."

All night she thought over what her sister had said, and

came to the conclusion that she'd been lying to herself, and her greatest pain was caused by the fact that he had stopped loving her. And then she asked herself if she still loved him at all.

"Let's go for counseling," she suggested two weeks later, when he came to be with Noa. He looked very sad, and her heart ached to see him so. She wanted to ask him if he was eating well, but of course she didn't. He agreed immediately, and they went to a highly recommended marriage guidance counselor, to whom she poured her heart out about his infidelity and the fact that when she was taking her daughter to the hospital, he was spending time with his mistress.

"I can never forgive him for that," she told the counselor.

The counselor told them that since couples usually go for counseling at the very last minute, in most cases she was unable to repair crises that had lasted for years.

The counselor asked him if he was still meeting the other woman, and he said he wasn't.

But she said that even if they were no longer together, they were still meeting every day at work, and it was driving her crazy.

"Can't you give up that job?" the counselor asked him.

"Absolutely not. Not after I've finally managed to find a job that I feel will advance me professionally. I don't want to leave this office."

"So maybe you can tell her to leave?" she hissed. "She's single, isn't she? She doesn't have a family to support. Tell her to leave," she said to her husband.

"I can't do that," he said.

"Why not?" asked the counselor. "It's quite obvious that the fact of your still meeting her every day at work doesn't help the way your wife feels."

"I can see that," he said, "but still, I can't ask her to leave her job because my wife is bothered by her being with me in the same office."

"So you leave, if you are unable to tell her!" she screamed at him in front of the counselor, who told her that she wasn't even trying to see his point of view but was obsessed with proving how wrong he was, compared with her. "You have to understand the underlying problem," she told her, and she replied that the underlying problem was that he was in love with another woman.

"That counselor gets on my nerves," she told him when they went out. "I'm not going back to her." He refused to talk to his Adi about leaving her job, and she called his sister to ask her to try to persuade him to leave his job. She grasped at this as if her entire marriage depended only on whether he met his ex-girlfriend in the office they both worked in. His sister told her that she couldn't dictate to her brother what to do with his life.

When his father told her that as a woman she should be fighting for her man, she felt she had been struck by a bolt of lightning. Did she really want to fight for him at all? After all, she'd used up all the strength she had on her struggle for Noa. She started imagining how her life would look without him, and although she still saw the hotel exploding into tiny pieces like in the movie, she asked herself if it wouldn't be easier to build a new hotel than to try to rehabilitate the ruins of the old one that were spread all over town.

She went through the next three months in a daze, wandering from one friend to another, telling them all about the breakdown of her marriage, hoping they would rebuke him for his behavior. But most of her friends said they'd always seen him as an affectionate, loving husband, and things like that happen all the time and there are always temptations in work situations and you don't get divorced because of an infidelity, and even if she said it wasn't only sex but love, they said they were sure he was in love with her; didn't he bring her flowers every Friday?

She felt as if the whole world was against her, and even her mother, when she tried talking to her, to get some emotional support from her, told her that she was naive if she thought she'd find anything better than him, and with all of Noa's problems, she couldn't afford to even think that she'd ever find a better father for her daughter.

"But he doesn't love me," she tried to tell her mother, who immediately dismissed the whole thing. She knew that the three months she had allocated them to decide what they wanted to do about their marriage were fast running out, and she was still trying to get everyone she knew to agree that he was a shit. But wherever she turned, people were telling her she should forgive him and that you don't throw out a husband after seven years of marriage because of one time he's played away from home.

One day she saw Noa dancing in her room, as if she was putting all her heart and soul in her dance, as if she was floating on air, looking into herself and inventing a whole new world all her own, and her heart ached at the thought that, from the moment of her birth, life had never smiled on Noa, and now that she was four years old, her father had left home—perhaps forever, perhaps for an indefinite time—and her mother was going around like a weapon of mass destruction with anger attacks she couldn't control.

One afternoon they were on their way to the Institute of Child Development when they almost collided with a car coming out of a side street without giving her the right-of-way. She pushed down hard on the brakes, looked at the backseat to make sure that Noa was safely belted into her child seat, stopped the car in the middle of the road, got out, and walked over to the murderous driver who could have killed her daughter and gave her two loud slaps across the face before returning to her car and driving off, so as not to be late for her appointment.

A week later, when her husband came home to be with Noa, she went out to take care of some chores and wanted to park in the Ramat Aviv commercial center parking lot just as some slimy yuppie with the elaborate grammar of a schoolteacher—just her type—shouted at her that she had almost driven into his car. "Why almost?" she asked and backed up, then drove straight into him. This time she managed to knock a dent not only in his fender but in her own monthly salary as well. She thought it could have been worse, and that she and Noa could eat at her sister's for the rest of the month, which would please her sister.

But after the incident in the playground, she knew she had lost it completely.

They went to the playground near their home, and when she wanted to sit Noa on the merry-go-round next to a kid her age, the kid's mother, who herself looked like a Ms. Potato Head, came running up and snatched him off, looking sideways at Noa, whose face was swollen from the steroids she had to take to stabilize her hemoglobin.

"That thing your daughter has, it's not contagious, is it? Can my little boy catch it?" she asked reproachfully.

"Tell me, do you think that stupidity is contagious? And wickedness and ignorance and nastiness?" she asked in return.

Ms. Potato Head said nothing.

"Answer me!" she screamed at the woman suddenly.

"No?" the woman said tentatively.

"Actually, I think it is," she surprised the woman, "which is why I am taking my daughter away from here before she becomes infected by some of your evil."

Ms. Potato Head sat in embarrassed silence, while she was beginning to really enjoy abusing her, asking if she knew the difference between stupidity and genius.

"No," the woman replied, thinking she'd changed the subject.

"No, well, the thing is, genius has its limits. Good-bye and good riddance to you, stupid woman," she said, and carried her daughter off, holding her in her arms as if to protect her against all evil all the way back home.

She filled the bath and put Noa and some plastic ducks into the water and scrubbed away all the nastiness from the playground, and when Noa asked her why she was crying all the time, she said she wasn't crying, it was only the bath making her eyes wet.

Noa looked at her with compassion in her eyes, and she thought to herself that God had given the world ten measures of compassion, and her daughter had taken nine of them for herself. And only one measure remained for all those other billions of people who inhabit the earth's surface. Anyway, who says that life's fair, when Noa had taken all that compassion and left so little for everyone else?

The next day was a Friday, and Friday evening is a time when God is not kind to the lonely. She was alone in her home, all alone with her depression, since her husband had taken Noa with him to spend the weekend with his sister in Jerusalem. She turned on the faucet and filled the bath to its very limit and climbed in, submerging her head in the warm water. And once again, as she had the week Noa was born, she tested her body's ability to survive without air; and she was emotionally prepared to sink down into the waters of salvation, when the phone rang. She ignored the phone at first and tried to reinstate in herself the concentration a person needs in order to die. But the phone continued to ring and ring, aggressively, relentlessly. After counting the twentieth ring, she pulled herself out of the bath, promising the water that she'd be back directly; she wrapped herself in a towel and picked up the phone.

"Where are you?" her sister asked her.

"At home," she replied.

"No, you're not at home," said her sister.

"According to what?" she said impatiently, thinking about the warm water awaiting her.

"According to the fact that all the lights are off in your house," her sister replied. "Eight o'clock on a Friday evening, you're sitting alone in a silent house, not even watching the news." Her sister knew that she liked to watch the Friday evening news, thus making up for a whole week's worth in one go. Who needs to hear all those awful stories every day, anyway? As if life was not hard enough without news items tapping away at your soul every hour, with an added news flash every half hour.

"What's there to see?" she asked her exasperating sister, who was disturbing her plans to die.

"Quite honestly, nothing," her sister replied. "So where are you?"

"In the bathroom," she said. "I'm taking a shower."

"In that case, you are spending too much time in there," her sister said.

"How do you know? Are you watching me?" she asked, turning it into a joke.

"Yes," her sister replied simply.

"How are you watching me?" She was curious to know.

"Through Shlomo's army binoculars," her sister told her.

"Have you been spending all your time watching me through Shlomo's binoculars?" she asked, horrified at this violation of her privacy. Could her sister, who lived right opposite her, across the boulevard, have been using her husband's military binoculars to follow her every movement throughout the nearly two years she had been living there?

"Only since you split up," said her older sister.

"Why are you spying on me?" She was riled.

"I've been worried about you," her sister said. "I've been terribly worried about you. I was afraid that one day you'd lose it completely and suddenly decide to jump out of your eighth-floor window."

"Even if I had wanted to jump, you wouldn't have been able to stop me with your army binoculars," she said to her sister, testing her as usual.

"I would have called you immediately to distract you," said her sister, who was wise and thought of every single thing, with the resourcefulness she had inherited from their mother. "Besides," she added, "what are you taking so many baths for?"

"Maybe my conscience isn't clean?" she replied.

"Your conscience is pristine. Come over to my place," she said, laying down the law. "I'll cook you the things you love best."

"What do I love best?" she asked, still ruminating over whether she wouldn't prefer to return to the warm bath, which had probably gone cold by now.

"Artichoke with butter," her sister replied.

"I don't want it with butter," she bantered, as if they were still little girls and not young mothers. "Make me some mustard and mayo sauce."

"It doesn't taste as good," said her sister.

"I prefer my artichoke with mustard and mayo," she insisted, angry that her sister always tried to decide for her what tasted better, forgetting completely that only seven minutes ago she had contemplated sinking under the water.

"Come on, nuisance," said her sister.

She went back to the bathroom, pulled the plug out of the bath, and watched for a few seconds as the water swirled its way to the sea. She didn't even bother rinsing herself off. She had a clean conscience, and with it, she got dressed and went across to her sister, who would enfold her in her concern.

On Sunday she took Noa to the hospital to have her hearing tested; it appeared that Noa had lost her hearing completely in one ear and would need a hearing aid in her other ear.

She broke down. All the way home she wept like someone demented, and when Noa's caretaker arrived, she called her husband's office and asked for Adi.

"She's not in," the secretary told her.

"Is she no longer working there?" she asked the secretary.

"Of course she is. But today is her day off," she added.

"Can I have her address, please?" she asked politely. "I am calling from the courier service; I have a parcel here that needs to be delivered to her address."

The generous secretary supplied her with Adi's address, and she made her way straight there, taking with her all her pain and frustration from Noa's audio test.

She rang the bell, and a chubby young woman opened the door. She was quite surprised to see the fatso who had ruined her family.

"Adi?" she asked her.

"Adi," Fatso called out, "someone here for you."

Adi emerged from a room and approached her roommate, who remained standing in the doorway.

She stuck her foot in the door. Adi walked toward the door and stood next to Fatso. She was taller than her and appeared quite strong.

"Are you Adi?" she asked, keeping her foot in the door to prevent anyone from trying to slam it in her face.

"I am," she replied.

"Are you the person who fucks around with people you work with?" she asked. She didn't, of course, wish to give her the honor of admitting that it had been a love affair, and before the girl had had a chance to reply, she gave her two powerful slaps, one to the right cheek with her right hand, followed immediately with another to the left cheek with her left hand.

Adi, who knew of course who she was—because people don't usually take the trouble to introduce themselves when they are about to clout someone with six months' worth of accumulated fury—tried to shut the door. She pushed the door wide open and laid into Adi, one vigorous blow after another.

"Hadass," Adi called out, and Fatso tried to hit her from the right.

"Don't you touch me," she said to the chubby roommate. "I have no business with you," and she continued beating Adi with all her strength; she pushed Hadass a little to the side so as to get her out of the way. Hadass continued to wave her little fists in front of her, while Adi, who had managed to recover from the first shock, dealt her several hefty blows to the face, and even scratched her on the shoulder when she turned toward Hadass, who continued to pester her. The sight of Fatso fighting with all her might on behalf of her whore of a friend inflamed her even further—how dare she prevent her from carrying out the job for which she had come here? She grabbed Fatso by the shoulders and pushed her into the depths of the corridor with a strength she had never known she possessed.

"Don't you move away from there or I'll kill you," she told her, and Fatso dug herself deep into the corridor, no longer to be seen. And then she turned her attention back to Adi.

She beat her as she had learned as a girl growing up in Wadi Salib. Whenever her sister felt threatened by some other kids, all she had to do was say that she'd call her little sister, and they would immediately stop picking on her.

Adi of course put up a fierce resistance and hit back, but there is no one alive who can triumph over a woman burning with the fury of a mother who has just learned that her daughter is hard of hearing.

They lashed out at each other with all their might. For a moment it occurred to her that she might after all love her man, and that by beating Adi, she was actually fighting to get him back.

When she decided that she herself had taken enough of a beating, she put a stranglehold on Adi and knocked her to the ground, kicked her a few times in the stomach and legs, followed up with some juicy name-calling—bitch, whore, cunt, and all the text necessary to remind the girl where she had come from—and went back home to her hearing-impaired daughter.

The following morning she got a telephone call from the police to say that a complaint had been lodged against her for grievous bodily harm and she was required to go down to the station.

She arrived at the station, where she was directed to an investigations officer who told her that she was being questioned under caution. She didn't know what this meant, but he proceeded to read out the long list of accusations against her, followed by another list provided by the hospital, where Adi had gone to have her wounds dressed. She listened intently and nodded her head. When he finished reading, she told him that all of it was true, except that he had omitted one important thing.

"What was that?" the officer asked.

"It says nothing about the fact that she was my husband's mistress, and that I had gone to her place to have a conversation with her. I wanted to explain to her my situation with my sick daughter, who has also lost her hearing. All I did was to insist on my right to talk to her logically, to impress on her the need for her to leave the place in which she and my husband are employed, and to stop destroying my family." Of course she wasn't being entirely accurate with the facts she presented to the officer.

"And what happened?" He wanted to know a little more.

"Well, you know, things heated up, and one thing led to another, and I slapped her on the face and she gave me one back and we ended up having a fight. It happens among you men too, doesn't it? What would you have done if you'd been in my place, if your wife had taken a lover? Wouldn't you have gone and tried to have a heart-to-heart conversation with him?" she wondered.

He wanted to know how her daughter was doing, and when she told him the truth about the way they spent days on end in hospital while her husband was fucking his brains out with his whore, the police officer was so sympathetic to her and hated Adi so much that in the end he said he didn't understand how anyone could cheat on a woman like her.

"So what are you going to do with the complaint?" she asked the police officer who so wholeheartedly sympathized with her.

He scrunched up the paper into a tiny ball, which he then tossed at a wastepaper basket a short distance away.

He hit. The paper ball dropped straight into the basket.

"Just let me see her dare show her face in the police station," said the police officer. "I'll have her thrown out on her ear, the nasty little bitch."

Her husband called her that evening.

"You see, it's because of things like this that I no longer love you," he told her.

"What things?" she asked.

"Because you are uncivilized," he said, sounding extremely agitated. "It seems no one ever took the trouble to educate you properly."

"Yes, it does seem so. Do you want a divorce?" she asked him.

"Yes," he told her.

"So do I," she said.

"Let's go for a walk," she said to Noa, and took her to the beach. They stood on the breakwater and watched as the waves exploded against the rocks. The sea was especially stormy. She pulled off her wedding ring, threw it into the sea, and told Noa that she was giving her dowry back to God.

Noa asked her what a dowry was.

"It's a piece of baggage that you carry about with you from childhood," she explained to her four-and-a-half-year-old daughter.

When they arrived back at the apartment, the telephone was ringing stubbornly, and she was afraid that the anonymous caller would hang up before she could get the door opened.

The telephone went on ringing, and she picked up the receiver.

"Hello," she said.

"Rina that in the Bible means joy and in Ladino means a queen?" she heard on the other end of the line.

"Hello, Shmuel," she replied. "How are you?"

"Couldn't be better. My wife has just given birth to a baby boy, and I wanted to invite you to the bris milah."

"Thank you, Prophet Samuel. Congratulations. Mazel tov. I'll be happy to come. Where are you holding the bris?"

"At home. In our garden," Shmuel answered her.